## CRITICAL ACCLAIM FOR MITCH CULLIN

### *TIDELAND*

"The prose is a stage set for Cullin's ventriloquism, which is brilliant and beautiful." —*The New York Times Book Review*
"Beautifully written. Perfectly paced. Sad. Magical. Funny. Excellent woodworking...images kept tumbling off the page and into my eye line–beautifully, clearly, spookily."

—Terry Gilliam

### *WHOMPYJAWED*

"Belongs is a class with *Catcher in the Rye, The Last Picture Show*, and *The Heart is a Lonely Hunter*. It is by far the best book I've read in a while." —John Nichols
"Cullin has created with much skill the loneliness and emptiness of a small West Texas town, with a vivid sense of a place and time that stays with you long after you finish reading his novel." —Horton Foote
"Elicits comparisons to such precursors as Larry McMurty, Erskine Caldwell, or even Sherwood Anderson."

—*Publishers Weekly*

### *BRANCHES*

"A flat out fabulous read." —Max Evans
"A strange and magnificent book." —*The Santa Fe Reporter*
"Cullin is to be congratulated for this hybrid achievement."
—Robert Phillips, *The Houston Chronicle*

### *THE COSMOLOGY OF BING*

"Cullin dexterously blends coming to terms at midlife, coming out, and coming to adult understanding." —*Booklist*
"Cheerfully chaotic...a relaxed, confident comic novel with just enough of an edge to keep it poking away at your memory." —*The New York Times Book Review*

# FROM THE PLACE IN THE VALLEY DEEP IN THE FOREST

Mitch Cullin was born in 1968 in New Mexico. He is the author of four novels: *Whompyjawed* (1999), *Branches* (2000), *Tideland* (2000), and *The Cosmology of Bing* (2001). Besides being a featured writer at The Texas Book Festival, he has been the recipient of many awards and honors, including a Dodge Jones Foundation grant; writing sponsorship from Recursos de Santa Fe; and a poetry fellowship from The Arizona Commission of the Arts. He resides in Tucson, Arizona, where he is currently collaborating with Peter I. Chang on the illustrated novel *Undersurface*.

# FROM THE PLACE IN THE VALLEY
# DEEP IN THE FOREST

stories by
## Mitch Cullin

Dufour Editions

First published in the United States of America, 2001
by Dufour Editions Inc., Chester Springs, Pennsylvania 19425

Both art pieces (...From East and ...To West)
are courtesy of Peter I. Chang

ISBN 0-8023-1336-1

Library of Congress Cataloging-in-Publication Data

Cullin, Mitch, 1968-
    From the place in the valley deep in the forest / Mitch Cullin.
      p. cm.
    Contents: Voice of the sun -- From the place in the valley deep
    in the forest -- History is dead -- Wormwood -- Five women in
    no particular order -- Viv's biding -- Sifting through -- Totem.
    ISBN 0-8023-1336-1
      I. Title.

PS3553.U319 F76 2001
813'.54--dc21                         2001023824

Printed and bound in the United States of America

For Amon Haruta,
and
for A. Chad Piper

# Acknowledgements

The author is grateful to the Dodge Jones Foundation, and to Recursos de Santa Fe for assistance during the writing and editing of this book.

Portions of "Voice of the Sun" first appeared in different form and title in both *The Bayou Review* (1995) and *Texas Writers Newsletter* (1997). "Five Women In No Particular Order" first appeared in *Austin Flux* (1995). "Sifting Through" also first appeared in *Austin Flux* (1996), and was reprinted in *Best American Gay Fiction 2* (Little, Brown). "Wormwood" was a finalist in *Santa Barbara Review's* Phenomena of Place contest (1997). "Totem" first appeared in *Harrington's Gay Men's Quarterly* (1999).

With gratitude to the following for support, advice, friendship, and inspiration:

Ai, Bill Bishop, Brian Bouldrey, Richard Bradford, Maralyn Budke, Kevin Burleson, Joe Canon, The Christians, Barbara Cooper, Robert Drake, Demetrios Efstratiou, Max Evans, William Finnegan, Horton Foote, Mary Gaitskill, Howe Gelb, Jemma Gomez, Akihiko Haruta, Bill Hicks, Ha Jin, Ike Kalangis, Burt Kennedy, Jesiah King, Steve King, Tom Lavoie, John Nichols, Bill Oberdick, Kenzaburo Oe, The Parras, Robert Phillips, Dith Pran, Colleen Rae, Charlotte & Michael Richardson, Charlotte Roybal, Renee Severin, Martin & Judith Shepard, Clay Smith, Marah Stets, Joe Strummer, Carol Todd, Cole Thompson, Jeff Tweedy, Kurt Wagner–and, of course, my father Charles Cullin, Brad Thompson, and Peter I. Chang.

# Contents

The iris blooming in this pond is crazy and belongs to a crazy age!

—Masuji Ibuse, *The Crazy Iris*

I.

# Voice of the Sun

## 1.

With an ear pressed against Saiichi's bedroom door, Ichiro suspected his younger brother wasn't sleeping and that he was probably standing before the window (robe tied loosely at his waist, head cocked to the heavens). For four days he had routinely ventured upstairs, pausing beside the door and listening, becoming familiar with Saiichi's movements by the faint creaking of the floorboards–such slight and ghostly steps, coming and going from the window during the nights, letting Ichiro know his brother was still alive.

But although he wanted badly to slide the door open, to go to Saiichi and comfort him, Ichiro remained in the hallway. "Better let him alone when you visit," Keiko had suggested. "Best if you tend his house, bring him meals–he needs time." So Ichiro intended to follow her advice, no matter how conflicting it felt; after all, she was a widow and certainly more knowledgeable than he about Saiichi's kind of grief: "Trust your aunt Keiko, just having you around is appreciated–he'll be grateful you took off work a few days, I'm sure." Even so, he wondered if his brother really didn't like him staying there, or if the soups, pots of tea, rice crackers, and pickled plums he left on a tray outside the bedroom door were welcomed. "Nonsense," Keiko assured him over the phone. "Stop worrying."

Still, Ichiro feared that his being at the house only kept Saiichi from leaving his room. Indeed, his brother rarely enjoyed company, preferring instead the solitude of his beachside residence (a once dilapidated traditional-style dwelling far removed from Tokyo's bustle, meticulously renovated over the years by Saiichi and his late wife, Masako). How organized the place was usually kept, everything ordered and clean in the main downstairs room: the many books on Saiichi's built-in desk arranged by subject and author's name; the open-hearth fireplace devoid of ash; the latticed, paper-covered doors lacking any tears or smudges. Most likely, Ichiro suspected, his brother would frown at the sight of him lounging about the main room, occupying himself with chess, sleeping there on an unmade futon.

But Ichiro could easily understand why Saiichi favored an uncluttered home overlooking the ocean. Each morning he sat outside on the long porch, glad to be away from the tight cluster of houses and busy streets, breathing contentedly while savoring the sea air. Before dusk he jogged along the desolate beach, stopping occasionally to watch the waves falling below a bright first quarter moon (just yesterday, when the moon had finally grown full, he removed his clothing and ran naked into the surf, his body tensing in the chilly water). Then every evening, after preparing his brother's dinner, he took a seat at the built-in desk and began practicing calligraphy, all the while listening for Saiichi's faint footsteps above.

Of course, the evening hours were too early for Saiichi, and Ichiro rarely heard any movements until later; often he would awake on the futon, stirred by his brother's bedroom door sliding open and then slamming shut. Though when going upstairs to investigate, he always saw the same things– the tray sitting in the hallway (teapot and bowls empty), a dim light glowing behind the bedroom door. And now standing before the door, Ichiro hoped Saiichi could sense his presence in the hallway—and how he wished for him to speak his name, inviting him to enter. Then he imagined his brother at the window, studying the nighttime sky with a rapt expression—lips parted, eyes wide and transfixed, as if he were glimpsing the face of God; it was an expression Ichiro knew well, having observed it many times during and since childhood.

"Look, brother," he recalled Saiichi whispering years ago, pointing at the box kite their father Kiichi sailed over the beach near Kamakura. His brother had recently turned seven, though already he was gazing skyward with an otherworldly stare, engrossed by anything which floated between the earth and heavens. "Look—"

What an enduring memory it was—a warm afternoon in 1941 and just days after President Roosevelt had frozen all Japanese assets in the United States, placing an embargo on the oil supply. But, being ten then, Ichiro hadn't yet embraced the nationalistic fervor shaping the country, had little interest for the military invasion of China. In fact, on that warm summer afternoon, he cared only about the box kite as it faltered high above the sand, watching as his father—the man's shirt sleeves rolled to his elbows, sweat glistening across his brow—gave one desperate yank on the spool of string and muttered, "Shit," while the grand white kite careened toward the beach, dully hitting the sand.

"You almost saved it," Ichiro told his father. "It almost stayed up."

Kiichi nodded somberly, his eyes following the uneven, billowing trail of slackened string from where the kite had crashed to his hand.

"It almost stayed up," Saiichi echoed absently, his attention suddenly focused on a shiny ball bearing he'd found among the shells and tide-washed stones. "You almost saved it." The ball glinted in the sunlight, momentarily stunning his right eye.

"Let's try again," suggested Ichiro.

"Go get her," said Kiichi, patting his son's neck.

So Ichiro–his school pants pushed to his knees, his father's necktie tied around his forehead–ran barefoot and shirtless along the beach, pausing briefly to shout back: "How do you know it's a her?"

"She told me," Kiichi yelled, reeling in some of the string, making the line taut.

"It's a her?" Saiichi asked with surprise, glancing from the ball and cocking his head at Kiichi.

Kiichi bent forward, bringing his eyes level to Saiichi's face, saying, "Her name is Hiroko." He gave Saiichi a wink.

Standing there in undershorts and wearing his father's jacket (a black dress coat which enveloped him like a long cape), Saiichi began smiling. "Father says it's her because she's Hiroko," he shouted after Ichiro, who–now holding the kite aloft–chose to ignore him. Saiichi shrugged, then he dropped the ball bearing into a coat pocket, adding it to his collection of shells and stones.

Taking several steps backwards, Kiichi wound in more string. "Let's see how fast I can run," he said. "Let's hope she'll fly for us."

"Can I try?" Saiichi said.

"Are you fast enough?"

Saiichi nodded, earnestly drawing his thin lips into a narrow line.

"Faster than wind?"

Saiichi nodded again. He pointed beyond his father, aiming a finger at the distant buildings of Kamakura. "I can run there. I can go all the way to Kencho-ji."

"That's very far," said Kiichi, envisioning Saiichi tearing through the streets and into the mountains, the dress coat flapping and shells spilling as he raced toward the ancient Zen temple.

"I'll show you."

"Perhaps you should help get the kite up first," Kiichi said, offering Saiichi the spool.

"Then I'll run there," Saiichi said eagerly.

"Of course," Kiichi said, gently wrapping the boy's fingers around the spool, faintly aware of Ichiro's protests carried in the afternoon breeze ("Father, don't let him, please—you do it!"). When Saiichi began running, the kite lifting from Ichiro's hands, Kiichi sat down in the sand, seemingly uninterested in the kite's fate, and looked out toward the ocean.

Those same eyes, Ichiro remembered now. That same faraway stare shared by both his father and brother, as if they were searching outward and inward all at the same time. Perhaps too his father had recognized Saiichi's eyes, had seen himself in his youngest child's face. For Saiichi was the favorite, Ichiro believed. The man was always quick to spoil him, to let him have his way. Whenever their mother left, when she disappeared weeks at a time—then months, then years—Kiichi would pull Saiichi close to him as they walked down the street; he would hold the boy's hand tightly while Ichiro strolled behind them. Often he would whisper promises into Saiichi's ear before bedtime, mentioning leisurely train trips through the countryside or pilgrimages to distant shrines or afternoons flying a kite at the beach. Some promises he kept, most he didn't. In any case, little Saiichi usually got what he wanted—a bag of sweets, a new pair of binoculars, a chance to run with the kite even as Ichiro felt certain it was a bad idea.

But that day at Kamakura, Saiichi had run fast and far enough—and at last the kite remained sailing in the sky. "Very good," said Ichiro, joining his brother. Then the two found a bulky, knotted chunk of driftwood, where they tied the string, allowing the kite to hold its own for a while. Afterwards, Ichiro dropped to his knees near his father; he pushed his hands into the sand and began digging. And soon Kiichi and Saiichi were at his side helping him build a castle with a moat, their hands mixing in the loam and turning an orangish-brown. Eventually, they moved down the beach, leaving the kite behind, and dug an elaborate Sun God, fashioning the face with seashells and stones. "We need nose holes," Ichiro said. "Get some black rocks for the nose," he told Saiichi, who immediately wandered away in search of nostrils.

So while waiting for Saiichi, Kiichi and Ichiro sat cross-legged beside their creation, the wind ruffling warm around them. "We're okay," Kiichi said quietly. "Ichiro, don't you think?"

Ichiro looked at his sandy feet, avoiding his father's stare, then glanced up and spotted Saiichi standing in the ocean (his brother faced the waves, holding his palms outward in an attempt to stop the tide's advance). "Saiichi's in the water again," he said. And when Kiichi sprang to his feet, calling out Saiichi's name, Ichiro was relieved to see his father go.

"The man bores me, you know," his mother had once confessed. "School teachers think they know everything. He gets drunk and bores me. Talks too much, always teaching—just bores me. Not like you, Ichiro. You're not like him—you're smarter, right? I enjoy hearing you."

She had come to Ichiro's bed late at night, waking him. Earlier in the night there had been another argument—something about his mother's comings and goings, about the money she spent at the pleasure district bars—and Ichiro heard his father yelling: "I'll kill you! Or I'll kill myself, you think I care?" Then he heard Kiichi crying—and during the entire fight his mother's voice never rose above her normally soft tone. "Do what you want," she had calmly said. "I don't care. In fact, do me a favor—kill us both."

Later, she woke Ichiro with a kiss on his forehead. She stroked his hair. Then how beautiful she looked sitting there, her round face partially concealed in shadow, her pale skin smooth and still youthful. "My smart boy," she said. "Not like your father—not like him—"

Ichiro knew she was leaving again. He understood that by morning she would be gone—and for nights afterwards his father would drink sake before bed and mumble to himself and drunkenly embrace Saiichi. "I'm no good," he would tell them. "I don't deserve this life—I'm better off dead, I'm sorry."

Yes, Ichiro thought at the time, we'd be better off if you died. But it was for Saiichi and his mother, mostly, that he wished Kiichi dead. So he had prayed for it to end somehow (the continual fights, his mother's need to escape within the pleasure district, the frowns from neighbors as Kiichi stumbled outside on his way to purchase more sake); his father, he knew, had too. Yet there came moments of relative peace—those rare occasions when Kiichi didn't drink a drop after returning home from his teaching position, when he behaved like a father and laughed with his sons and seemed mindful of his children's well being.

"Please, you must take care," Kiichi told Saiichi that afternoon at the beach, warning him about the currents, about the undertow. "It runs underneath the surface," his father explained. "It runs seaward, see?"

And while Saiichi sat upon his father's lap, Ichiro studied some low hanging clouds that moved slowly in from over the ocean. Then he saw shapes unfold in the clouds, one right after the other, changing in the wind, swirling into nothing. "Look in that cloud," he said, "it's a boat—with sails."

Saiichi jumped from Kiichi's lap and went to Ichiro. "Where? I don't see."

"You know what?" Kiichi said. "There's a whale up there."

"Yeah," Ichiro said. "That one. It's a whale."

Saiichi squinted. "A cat too."

"I don't see a cat," said Ichiro.

"A cat and a tree," Saiichi said. "And there's Mother."

"You're making that up. I don't see Mother."

Soon all three were on their backs, side by side in the sand, their eyes exploring the shifting clouds.

"I see something," said Saiichi, excitedly. "I see birds."

"Seagulls," Ichiro told him. "They're not clouds."

"Not them birds. In the cloud there's birds."

"Saiichi, stop making stuff up. It's not fair."

Kiichi smiled and said: "Of course, I've told you boys about Pan-san, the old ghost who haunts Yotsugawa Station."

"Not that," Ichiro sighed.

"See, these two monks were debating over this very cloud you see now," said Kiichi, his voice becoming playful. "One monk said, 'The cloud is moving.' The other monk said, 'The wind is moving.' Then Pan-san appeared and said, 'It's not the wind moving. It's not the cloud moving. It's the mind moving.'"

Saiichi laughed and Ichiro sighed again. "I hate Pan-san," Ichiro said.

"I do too," Kiichi said. "He's a spook."

"A spook," Saiichi repeated.

They fell silent for a while, saying nothing as the waves tumbled and seagulls cawed. Then Kiichi, his whisper carrying in the breeze, faintly said, "I'm lying–" Ichiro glanced sideways at his father, who was still gazing at the clouds with Saiichi and mumbling to himself, "This is false–the next thing I say is false–the last thing I said is true–"

Suddenly Ichiro's body felt unbearably hot, so he climbed to his feet and began running toward the ocean. Gaining speed, he jumped over shells and rocks on the beach until he was knee-high in the water. Reaching a standstill in the surf– his hands slapping at the waves, his pants growing heavy with wetness–he squatted down, allowing the water to lap across his chest for a time. Eventually he removed his pants, and his legs, freed from the bulk of clothing, seemed weightless. Then he tried floating off. He stretched out in the water, shutting his eyes. At one point he thought he might have drifted far into the ocean, buoyed gently on the surface–but opening his eyes he realized that he had only floated a few feet away. "Oh well–," he said, sitting up. "Oh well–," he said, when reaching for his pants.

"Come back," Ichiro heard Saiichi yelling. "Brother– come here–!"

Wandering from the water, returning to where his father and brother sat on the beach, Ichiro arrived as his father finished drawing in the sand with a stick. 1+1=1 his father had just written, and Ichiro, his pants hanging across his shoulders, said, "But one and one can't make one."

Kiichi regarded Ichiro's comment with a sigh. "This is what I'm talking about, Saiichi. There's always someone saying it's not so, saying that's not how it is. Always someone out to defeat someone's ideas. What else does someone defeat when he defeats someone else's ideas?"

Saiichi was leaning tiredly against Kiichi, his skin bright red. "I'm hungry," he said. "I want to go in the water."

Kiichi tossed the stick at Ichiro's feet. Then he wrapped an arm around Saiichi and cradled him. With his other hand he took a handful of sand, slamming it onto the beach. "There," he said, fixing a hard stare on Ichiro. "Two lumps of sand coming together merge as one. Does one plus one make one then?"

"That's dumb," Ichiro said.

"That's dumb," Kiichi mocked.

"Isn't fun," Saiichi yawned.

"Those two clouds above you–look, see–they're coming together," Kiichi said. "Does one plus one–"

"Stop it!"

Kiichi rubbed cheeks with Saiichi, then said: "See how the waves move, Saiichi? See how the kite goes like that? All those clouds up there? But you and I, even Ichiro and your ma, we're messier things, aren't we?"

"Messy things," Saiichi said, wearily.

"Why do you always do that?" Ichiro asked his father.

But Kiichi only shrugged. Then he looked at the sky, his lips jutting as he frowned like a child. Of course, Ichiro was familiar with the mercurial nature of his father's moods. He had grown used to them. "When he acts up," his mother had advised him, "simply ignore him. Go somewhere else. He'll get over it."

"Come on, Saiichi," Ichiro finally said, reaching for Saiichi and taking his hand. And when leaving his father, he understood that the ease of the afternoon was bound to be too much, that it was a matter of time before everything turned sour. He briefly glanced back at Kiichi, who had picked up the stick and was drawing in the sand.

"See," Saiichi said, tugging on Ichiro's hand. "See," he said, pointing at a gap in the clouds where a single bright white star glowed. "See it–?"

"Yes," Ichiro said.

"It's beautiful, I think."

"Yes."

But it wasn't the star that held Ichiro's attention, nor the clouds moving over the gap–it was the amazement on his younger brother's face, that mesmerized expression which would grow more and more awestricken as Saiichi became older. Then how envious Ichiro would be of his brother's passion for the stars, because, he believed, any real connection with the heavens was lost on him; indeed, as a teenager and then young man, he felt hopelessly earthbound–forever doomed to follow his brother's gaze, never quite seeing the same things. For Saiichi had a safe escape, a richer world to explore when their parents were fighting, when their mother at last stopped coming home. And Ichiro–keeping himself busy in school, stealing sips of Kiichi's sake at night–had nowhere to go; he was grounded.

Still, Ichiro spent many late nights with Saiichi, both sitting outside, knees drawn to their chests while studying the sky. A lantern illuminated the star charts they diligently maintained day after day, year after year. Occasionally Ichiro would wonder aloud about what time it was or where they were in the season. Then Saiichi would note the positions of the stars, the locations of the planets, the phases of the moon; when Orion was high in the east before sunrise he knew that cooler weather was around the corner. In the fall, when noticing longer shadows on the sidewalk–the sun's southward shift, the way light no longer passed directly through the east-facing windows–Saiichi would move the indoor plants accordingly. "It's all rather logical," he often told Ichiro, his eyes drifting upward to the familiar pattern of bluish-white stars. "The universe is fairly consistent, you know."

So perhaps Ichiro didn't know the stars by name, but he did know they were always there; he knew they would remain there long after he had passed away. And on those nights outside with Saiichi, Ichiro loved his brother more than anyone, sometimes studying him from the corners of his eyes and trying to imagine himself inside Saiichi's body; how badly he wished for access, how much he wanted to scan the skies with those keen eyes that somehow saw all that Ichiro couldn't. Such a humorless boy, he thought now. Never smiling much, so serious a young man.

And standing there in the hallway, listening for signs of his brother, Ichiro stared at the pictures hanging on the shadowy wall: three wedding photographs of Saiichi and his dead wife Masako–the groom beaming proudly in each shot as he stood with his bride (Masako's head-dress tilted to one side, a diminutive grin on her face), his mouth curved in a manner that was far from his normally stoic demeanor. Yet it wasn't the marriage celebration that Ichiro found himself recalling–not the cups of sake shared between families, or the exchange of betrothal gifts–but rather a day years earlier, when their mother had taken him and Saiichi to the center of Tokyo.

That morning, he and Saiichi had stirred to find her preparing them breakfast, whistling while she broke eggs over bowls of rice. "Today we'll have fun," she said, after greeting them with kisses. "Your mother is very glad her sons are awake–so we'll go have fun until Father returns home. So no school today for you, I've decided." Neither boy knew what to say; they hadn't seen her in nearly six months, and suddenly there she was fixing their meal, behaving as if she hadn't ever left. "Eat up," she told them. Then following breakfast, they all wandered leisurely past the wooden shops and houses in Miyamoto-cho, saying very little, eventually stepping aboard a streetcar for the journey into Tokyo's heart.

"Mother, where are we going?" Ichiro asked.

She glanced surreptitiously at a handsome young soldier riding nearby, then smiled at Ichiro: "Let's pretend I'm your aunt Keiko today–don't I look like your aunty? She's much more fun, I think."

Saiichi frowned, glaring in the soldier's direction.

"But where are we going?" Ichiro said.

"Wait," she said, touching his chin. "Just wait."

Soon enough their destination became known: a park in the city center, above which loomed the Imperial Palace. It was a place frequented by an elderly man who took photographs of visitors, who stood beside his tripod wearing an elegant white summer jacket, telling passersbys, "Please, it would be my privilege to make your picture–only a few yen."

"I'd like three pictures of my sons together," their mother told the man, handing him some yen and an address where the photographs were to be sent.

"Of course," the man said, bowing and nodding. Then he went about positioning the boys so that the palace would be visible in the photographs (seating Ichiro upon a foldout chair, asking Saiichi to stand behind his brother with a hand resting on Ichiro's shoulder). Finally looking through his camera, he said, "Good, thank you, please smile."

Ichiro forced a grin. But Saiichi wouldn't smile; his hand tensed on Ichiro's shoulder, digging nails into his brother's shirt while squinting at their mother. "Just this once," she urged. "You've got such a lovely smile, Saiichi. You're so handsome. Look happy for Mother." And when the first shot was snapped, Ichiro grimaced as his brother's nails broke skin.

## 2.

Last week Keiko told Ichiro, "He needs family–he needs you with him." Masako had, after a prolonged struggle with leukemia, died almost a month previously ("Poor Saiichi understood the risk," Keiko said at the time, shaking her head sadly. "Marrying someone from Nagasaki–what else can be expected?"), so Keiko phoned Ichiro at home one evening, asking if he'd go visit his brother. "Stay a few days," she said. "Until I can get away to come down myself."

"I was thinking of going anyway," Ichiro explained.

"That's nice of you," she said. "Please be careful driving– or will you take a train?"

"Drive, I think."

"Then please be careful. I'm sure he will welcome you happily."

Indeed, Saiichi did welcome Ichiro upon his arrival, but not happily. He greeted his brother on the porch–robe unlaced, face drawn and ashen, ribs poking from his chest– and thanked Ichiro for coming before inviting him into the house. "Make yourself comfortable," he said moments later, then retired upstairs to his bedroom, remaining there ever since.

How desolate Saiichi appeared, how different from the composed man who had overseen his wife's funeral–helping prepare the body with Masako's sisters and dressing her in a white garment, passing out small packets of salt to purify visitors from death's pollution, dutifully keeping record of who attended and how much money had been given. Then the night before the funeral, while Masako's coffin sat downstairs in the main room, Ichiro shared Saiichi's bed; the two lay awake for hours talking about their Miyamoto-cho childhood during the war (Ichiro stealing candy from a neighborhood shop, the drunken arguments between their parents, the nights spent outside with their lantern and star charts). When at last Saiichi fell asleep, Ichiro slipped an arm across his brother's chest and had to stop himself from holding him too tightly: he had never held his brother so close, though in their younger days he had often wanted to–especially as they stargazed, legs touching while they reclined on the roof of their house. "If the galaxy were made a bit different," he recalled Saiichi saying the first evening they ventured onto the roof, "we wouldn't exist now."

"Really–?"

"Yes, just a slight shift, one minor upset–the sun, let's say, a little nearer or further–then no Ichiro and Saiichi–no Mother and Father–no Japan, nothing here."

Even as a teenager, Ichiro could tell Saiichi preferred the nighttime world; he observed in the way Saiichi perched contentedly on the dark roof–sometimes mumbling something to himself–that his thirteen-year-old brother was already grappling with lofty considerations. The big binoculars around his neck had turned him into an apparently more inquisitive boy than most, and Ichiro had to ask him what it was exactly they were looking for that night.

"Our own star," Saiichi told him, pointing at the vastness above.

"Oh," Ichiro said, following his brother's gaze. You've been searching for it a long time, he thought. I know you have.

"All gone," Saiichi said that afternoon at the beach, no longer able to find the bright star he had spotted moments earlier. Already the clouds had moved inland from the ocean–and as the day approached evening, the brothers rested with their backs against the large trunk of driftwood. Overhead the box kite swam wildly in the wind, alternately plunging and rising abruptly. "Brother," Saiichi said, bringing his eyes to Ichiro's face, "is Father mad again?"

"I don't know," Ichiro said, opening the lunch box Kiichi had brought for the trip (nothing much inside–three biscuits and two pieces of chocolate). He glanced over a shoulder at his father, who was stretched in the sand several yards away, hands folded across his stomach, seemingly napping. "He's probably tired."

"Me too," Saiichi said, before squinting his eyes and yawning.

"This is yours," Ichiro said, handing Saiichi a biscuit, hoarding the chocolate for himself. Then they ate quietly there in the shade of the driftwood, backs to the sea and their stares fixed on the swaying scrub which dotted the nearby dunes. Soon Saiichi's half-eaten biscuit slipped from his hands, plopping into the sand between his legs, and Ichiro realized that his brother had dozed off. "Saiichi," he whispered, "you didn't finish your lunch." But Saiichi didn't respond; his head slumped forward, his body sagged some.

So Ichiro continued eating, glancing skyward to watch the kite soar and swoop, pleased by how deftly it moved. Still, it had not been the kite he wanted, even though his father had said, "Pick what you want, Ichiro, go on," when they stopped by a toy shop earlier that morning. "You don't want just any kite, do you?"

The front counter was lined with photographs of all the kites for sale—some quite beautiful, others rather plain—and, because there were so many to chose from, Ichiro couldn't make up his mind. "I'm not sure," he said.

Saiichi stood on his toes, doing his best to view the photographs. "They're different," he said, his fingers gripping the edge of the counter.

"What grabs you?" Kiichi asked Ichiro.

Ichiro shrugged; he was torn between the kite with the red flaming dragon and the one that looked like a black kimono. By the time the fat clerk behind the counter came to assist them, Saiichi had grown bored and wandered off into an aisle of dolls, wooden swords, and slingshots.

"Tough decision," the clerk said, his acne-scarred face hovering in close.

But right as Ichiro was about to mention which kite he liked, his father asked the clerk, "What costs the most? What's the best one here?"

"Up there," the clerk replied, aiming a finger past their heads, nodding.

Ichiro and his father turned, spotting the box kite suspended by fishing wire from the ceiling. Without hesitation Kiichi said, "We'll take it," his voice booming.

"It's ugly," Ichiro protested, causing the clerk to laugh. "It's not like a real kite."

"Oh," Kiichi said, his expression softening. "We don't have to get it. We don't have to get anything. You decide." He put his hands in his pockets.

Ichiro frowned. He was embarrassed to look at the clerk. He knew his father was disappointed, though wasn't exactly sure why. This is how it always is, he thought. "Father, it might be okay," he finally told him, the lie twisting in his stomach. "I don't mind it."

"Great," Kiichi said, clapping his hands together. "Good choice."

Dumb kite, he thought while finishing his biscuit on the beach. For a moment he studied Saiichi–how peaceful his brother appeared, resting against the driftwood, snug inside their father's coat. Then he inhaled deeply, his belly feeling satisfied. Lying down in the sand, he gazed once more at the kite. "No," he heard Saiichi mutter in his sleep, followed by a faint snore, a soft release of air escaping past his brother's lips. And soon, without quite discerning it, Ichiro shut his eyes.

As Ichiro remembered it now, he awoke sometime later, stirred at dusk by an increasing wind. The tide had pushed further inshore, reaching the driftwood, and he sat up while hearing the imminent rush of water. Just then he realized his backside was wet and muddy, the warm sand where he had slept was dampened with foam. When casting his eyes toward the dark-blue sky, he noticed that the kite no longer sailed overhead. "Saiichi," he said, looking around. But Saiichi too was gone–so was the lunch box and the biscuit his brother had dropped. "Saiichi–?"

Bracing a hand on the driftwood, Ichiro climbed to his feet, and, peering down the dim beach, spotted the figures of

his brother and father standing together in the sand. Then he
saw the kite floating out over the waves. He watched as his
father's arm raised, throwing the spool of string to the water—
suddenly, like a bird shot during flight, the kite wavered
before plunging into the sea. At that moment Ichiro felt inex-
plicably miserable. Stupid kite, he thought. "Stupid–" he said,
and began crying.

Or perhaps Ichiro's memory wasn't as reliable as he initially believed; perhaps, he wondered while standing outside
his brother's room, it had been Saiichi who had wept after the
kite's final dive. Maybe, overall, the trip to Kamakura was an
enjoyable one–a pleasant outing between a father and his
sons (an opportunity to gather some much needed comfort
from each other, to forget for a while their mother and wife's
most recent leaving). Even so, it would be the last real trip the
three ever took together. For within a year of the excursion,
Kiichi's drinking increased considerably, eventually to the
point where he was dismissed from his teaching position—
then the man found sporadic employment (several months
doing part-time delivery for Watanabes' noodle shop, almost
two years spraying the entire neighborhood with pesticides
for the public health and sanitation division, finally–as fewer
jobs became available–volunteering to aid the war effort by
working in an armaments factory).

Though by the time the war drew to an end, Kiichi had
ceased working altogether and Ichiro's mother had long since
disappeared for good. Of course, during the American air
offensive–when those B29s dropped incendiaries with devas-
tating results, burning out nearly sixteen square miles of the
city in a single night–thousands of Tokyo's residents simply
vanished without a trace. Still, Ichiro never believed that his
mother had somehow died in the bombings, nor did he think
she might not return home again. So while peddling his bike
around the residential streets of Miyamoto-cho, sometimes
rummaging with his classmate Mitsuharu through the heavily
bombed ruins surrounding their neighborhood, Ichiro
glanced at the women walking along the sidewalk, hoping to

glimpse his mother's face. And once he caught Saiichi doing the same (Ichiro couldn't forget: it was the day the Emperor spoke on the airwaves, urging the people to lay down their swords); his brother stopped his bicycle abruptly, gazing almost longingly in the direction of some woman coming toward them. "Let's go," Ichiro told him. "It isn't her."

"Are you sure?"

"Yes, absolutely."

Ichiro knew perfectly well what his mother looked like. It was more difficult for Saiichi; he was only eight when she left, Ichiro had been eleven. Then, in the hours of Japan's surrender, Saiichi was eleven and Ichiro fourteen—yet the boys had very different images of her: to Saiichi she was somewhat ghostly, an apparition who preferred soft light and shadows and the night; for Ichiro she was a beautiful woman, someone so youthful and unpredictable, who had constantly told him how much they were alike, how much they resembled one another (at fourteen, she was as vivid in his mind as anything—all he had to do was stare into a mirror).

But if Ichiro had questioned the exactness of his Kamakura memories, he at least trusted his recollections about that August day in 1945—when Saiichi thought he spotted their mother, when later they rode their bicycles beside the railroad tracks that ran near Tenso Jinja, the local Shinto shrine; both boys peddling past Saiichi's elementary school and the volunteer fire brigade hut, then clusters of homes and Jizo pavilion—until they reached the burnt-out building of Yamanote station, around which wild grass grew tall and thick in the abandoned train yard.

Cicadas rattled as they slowed—spokes clacking, wheels rolling to a stop. For a while they straddled their bikes in the train yard, brushing away sweat, squinting at the gutted building (such an eerie place, Ichiro remembered now, all sooty inside and hollow). Then they walked the bikes onto the loading platform, leaning them against a blackened wall. Soon Ichiro rested on his back, shutting his eyes in the shade while listening to the cicadas. So Saiichi found his own spot, sitting where his legs could dangle off the platform, eventually asking, "What are we doing–?"

"Waiting," Ichiro said.

"For what?"

"Mitsuharu, of course."

"Oh, okay," Saiichi said, sounding somewhat glum and just like Kiichi: "Oh, okay," their father had said earlier, after Ichiro announced he and Saiichi were going for a ride. Then as his sons rode away, Kiichi stood in front of the house calling to them, asking if they would be gone long.

"Maybe," Ichiro had said, refusing to look back. But Saiichi looked back, no doubt saddened by the sight of the man standing there with a lost expression on his face. And Ichiro knew that if Saiichi hadn't done so much crying that morning, his brother would have wept again when their father lifted a hand to wave. "Don't stare at him," Ichiro said, pedaling ahead. "He wants you to feel sorry for him."

Indeed, whenever Kiichi behaved badly or carried any guilt for things he had done, it seemed he required Ichiro and Saiichi's pity–sometimes tripping over his own feet and falling to the floor, other times displaying a downcast, almost child-like pout (a sorrowful affectation which rarely failed to bring sympathy from his sons). Yet on that morning, Ichiro had nothing but contempt for the man–especially since Kiichi had again sold two of his mother's finest kimonos and some of her expensive fabric in order to pay off loan sharks. Still, if Saiichi hadn't woken him, if he had just let Ichiro sleep a few more minutes, then possibly he wouldn't have ever known about the kimonos and fabric. But Saiichi had woken him, had pushed his fingers against Ichiro's shoulder, saying, "Get up!"

When Ichiro stirred, finding Saiichi leaning over him, he slapped at his brother's hand, telling him, "Leave me alone–"

"Get up," Saiichi whispered. "Brother, those men are here–they're talking to Father."

Ichiro, realizing his brother was crying, propped himself on an elbow: "Saiichi–what is it?"

A low sobbing came from Saiichi's throat, making the words difficult: "They're taking Mother's clothes."

Ichiro's stomach tightened. "Not again," he said, climbing out of bed.

"I'm scared."

"Stay here," Ichiro said, crossing the room. "Stop crying."

Going into the hallway, Ichiro heard his father frantically opening drawers in the master bedroom, searching through his mother's possessions (grabbing at items she had left there for safekeeping, taking expensive gifts once passed to her from relatives). Coming to stand in the main room's doorway, he observed the two men there–both wearing black ties and white shirts, dark slacks and dress shoes, their black jackets hung on pegs beside the front door; the two sat on the floor drinking tea, and, because one was much older than the other, Ichiro thought they might be father and son. Suddenly he felt self-conscious to be half naked before such well-dressed strangers–but he fixed them with a bitter stare anyway, remaining unnoticed for a while. Finally, the older man glanced around the room and saw him. "Hello," the man said, nodding.

"What do you want?" Ichiro asked.

The older man sighed, saying nothing. Then he took a sip of tea. Then he shook his head at the younger man, who appeared a bit nervous and wouldn't look at Ichiro.

"Bastards!" Ichiro cursed.

"Ichiro!" his father shouted from the master bedroom.

The younger man gazed uncomfortably into his cup, but the older man frowned and shook his head again. In that moment, Ichiro wanted to kill them both: "Bastards!"

"Ichiro!" Kiichi yelled.

How curious it was now–all those years since–for Ichiro to have discovered an entry in his brother's journals about that day; although Saiichi made no mention of the loan sharks or of much else that transpired (simply a scant paragraph regarding August 15, 1945, written in hindsight and describing what phases the constellations were in at the moment the Emperor addressed the people, concluding with: *Spent time with Brother, rode our bicycles around the old neighborhood, the shopping street bustled with grim faces while shop owners polished their swords in preparation for the Honorable Death of the Hundred Million that never came).* Within the main room of Saiichi's house, Ichiro had flipped through four hefty binders containing his brother's most recent star charts and writings. It was here that Saiichi did his work, where he would go from his desk to the telescope that was aimed at the southern hemisphere above the ocean horizon, where Masako would find him when she awoke in the mornings.

So Ichiro spent hours reading each of the binders left on his brother's desk, engrossed by the diary-like text which Saiichi had revised from time to time. In a brief passage, his brother pointed out that during the hour of their father's death the Quadrantid Meteor shower was in peak, visible near dawn in the northern quadrant of the sky. Elsewhere, Saiichi noted that on his wedding night the planets Saturn and Venus almost merged in the western evening sky. Sometimes his brother's entries detailed his past, revealing information Ichiro had not known before (when reading that Saiichi had lost his virginity at fifteen while the moon was at perigee 370,142 km, Ichiro was stunned). And in an entry written on Ichiro's thirty-eighth birthday, Saiichi wrote: *Used telescope to spy the softened, misty Beehive star cluster in Cancer. Wonderful view from the porch.* Scrawled in the margin, *Happy Birthday, Big Brother,* as if he knew someday Ichiro would be snooping inside his journals.

# 3.

On the second day of Ichiro's visit at Saiichi's house, Keiko had phoned him from her noodle shop, asking with a distracted and ragged morning voice, "Does your brother need a doctor?"

"Don't think so," said Ichiro, the receiver cradled on his shoulder. Then he answered Keiko's questions about Saiichi's weight ("Very thin, but not sickly"), about the food Ichiro was serving him ("Soup mostly—some vegetables and rice—whatever I can find here—I'll get by the market tomorrow").

Keiko suggested getting Saiichi outside, perhaps for a walk or a drive somewhere. "Is a cinema anywhere remotely close? A picture might do him good."

"I'll check," Ichiro told her, though he knew Saiichi would never agree to go.

"Please do," she said. "Oh, Ichiro, must hang up—a customer. I'll be there this weekend—so let me know what he needs." Grief, she then told him, was healthy. "Life is loss," she concluded—but Ichiro wasn't exactly sure what she meant.

Every morning she called to check on Saiichi, finishing their conversations with some odd phrase Ichiro couldn't quite grasp ("Misery can be a welcome friend," or, "Pain is a companion, you know, not a master"). Still, he always admired her manner of taking bad fortune head-on, the diligence in which she cared for Kiichi as he grew sicker from liver cirrhosis, the calm way she delivered the expected news during his fourth year at Tokyo University: "Your father died last night," she told him over the phone. "I wish you could've been there, but didn't want your schedule disrupted. It was quite peaceful, actually. I tried phoning your brother, but he won't return my calls. Please inform him, will you?" Then years later, when Saiichi's wife was too ill to leave her bed, Keiko arrived unannounced at the beach house to assume duties—cooking meals, bringing Masako fresh cut flowers and magazines everyday.

"It's just life," Keiko stated yesterday, before hanging up the phone. "The complicated business of life." But she wasn't speaking of Saiichi's mourning, or anything associated with death; she had been discussing her own need for romance, telling Ichiro she had started seeing someone, a younger man who frequented her noodle shop. Of course, she didn't want Saiichi knowing, not yet anyway. Even so, she delighted in telling Ichiro that the man had taken her out for dinner. "He squeezed my hand underneath the table," she said. How thrilled she felt, a bit frightened as well: "I couldn't shut my mouth–talked to him like a virgin in love, hardly ate a bite."

"I'm happy for you," Ichiro said–except something about Keiko's romance with a younger man, for surely it would prove to be another fling, depressed him. That evening he opened a bottle of sake, drinking from it as he wandered the beach, stepping on broken shells which shimmered beneath the full moon. When he returned to the house, Ichiro added a sloppy note inside one of his brother's journals, writing, *Got drunk with the moon at perigee 361,845 km.* Then he found himself flipping again through the pages, searching for the entry concerning the Emperor's historic radio broadcast; because, Ichiro believed, he apparently remembered much more than Saiichi did and felt inclined to add his own words to his brother's text. There's things you've forgotten, he thought. Saiichi, there's things you should know.

"Listen to me," Kiichi said, his hands gripping Ichiro's shoulders. "It's not what you think, okay?"

They were in the hallway, and Ichiro, his fists clenched, could see the loan sharks from where he stood–the two men still sipping tea, paying little attention to him and his father.

"They want Mother's clothes," Ichiro said. "You said it wouldn't happen again."

"No, they don't want them–it's different this time." A cigarette wiggled precariously between Kiichi's lips. "Otsuji-san is a friend–he'll pay them for me and keep the clothes at his shop–until I can pay him back." Smoke curled and spiraled, floating away in rings. "These men are going with me to see Otsuji-san. They don't want the clothes, understand?"

"But you said—"

"It'll be fine, I told you."

Ichiro nodded, uncurling his fingers: "Saiichi's upset."

"I'll talk to him when I get back." Kiichi's hands slid from Ichiro as he stepped away. "I've got to go now. Everything's okay. Otsuji-san will work it out for me."

When Kiichi and the men left, Saiichi joined Ichiro in the main room—then both peered through a window, watching their father shuffle forward (head down, arms hugging his wife's kimonos and fabric) with the two loan sharks beside him. "If he had a job this wouldn't happen," Ichiro said, turning from the window.

"It's not his fault," Saiichi said, continuing to gaze after Kiichi.

"He hasn't even tried," Ichiro complained, placing himself across a tatami by the open front door, lounging there while sunlight warmed his chest.

"He has."

"No, he hasn't."

But just as Saiichi was about to tell Ichiro he was being unfair, he noticed a sparrow picking at crumbs on the street. "I'm hungry," he said instead. "Do you think Takenishi-san or Oda-san will use a ration coupon and get us rice today?"

"Saiichi, our neighbors have their own families to feed." Ichiro slipped three fingers into his underpants, lifting the band. He studied the tan line around his waist. "I wish Mother would come back," he said, with an air of nonchalance.

"Me too," Saiichi said. "I'm hungry."

"Me too," Ichiro said, dreading another meal inside the crowded government food hall, where weak zosui was served from large metal pots and tasted watery.

And later, while resting on the platform at Yamanote station and waiting for Mitsuharu's arrival, Ichiro tilted his head to spy Saiichi positioning himself before a wall. Then his

brother undid his pants, saying, "Don't look," and began uri-
nating. So Ichiro shut his eyes, listening as piss splattered
against the station, imagining the stuff puddling around
Saiichi's shoes. "Zosui," said Saiichi. "My pee smells like
zosui."

"Be quiet," Ichiro told him. Because he was sick of zosui
stew, the smell alone could make his stomach churn—and
how he missed their mother's cooking, all those many rice
balls and buns and soups—the memories of which, unfurling
in the warmth of a summer's afternoon, caused his mouth to
hunger: for sometimes his mother had poured green tea over
rice for breakfast, a particular favorite of his; on occasion she
prepared a school lunch of seaweed-wrapped rice balls with
pickled plums or fried mashed potatoes blended with peas
and carrots and ground pork. In fact, Ichiro loved her food so
much that, when she was no longer home, he too became
skilled at creating rice balls (mixing in sesame seasoning and
shredded seaweed, meticulously rolling rice lumps into
round, almost triangular palm-sized shapes).

Then once, on a night not long after his mother had
finally gone, he carried ten rice balls within one of her
scarves, holding the bundle tightly in a hand as he awakened
Saiichi. "I don't know when I'll see you again," he whispered,
"but when I find Mother I'll bring her home, okay?"

"Can I go?" Saiichi asked, wearily.

"Not now," Ichiro said. "I better go on my own."

"Tell Mother to come home."

"I will."

Soon Ichiro was on his way, leaving the house and walking down the middle of deserted back streets, heading uphill
toward the railroad tracks—where he moved past closed
shops, dark alley apartments, and a late-night bar which
offered homestyle cooking (a place eventually put out of business due to rationing). When crossing the quiet shopping
street, he grew aware of electricity humming through overhead power lines—a faint buzz that persisted until he passed
the gateway of Tenso Jinja shrine. Here the neighborhood

was darker, so Ichiro–proceeding uneasily, turning his jacket collar up–began whistling to bolster his courage. But while approaching the tracks, a train suddenly blew its horn, startling him. Then as the train rumbled by, Ichiro found himself running in the opposite direction, hurrying downhill–unaware that his mother's scarf was coming loose, or that rice balls had started dropping; the last of them falling a few yards from Tenso Jinja's gateway. Only after reaching the shopping street did he stop, taking a moment to catch his breath–and realizing the scarf was empty, he threw it on the ground, saying, "I don't care–it doesn't matter!"

Afterwards, he wandered home, pausing en route, inhaling the night air, scanning the nighttime sky. And when entering the house near dawn, Ichiro immediately saw the end of a cigarette glowing in the dimness of the main room. "Where were you?" he heard Kiichi ask.

"Nowhere," Ichiro replied, sliding the screen shut.

"Nowhere, really?" Kiichi said, going to him. "Let me see your eyes."

"I haven't been drinking."

Kiichi nodded: "You're okay then?"

"Yes." Even with his father standing in front of him, he could barely see the man's face.

"Just wanted to get out, huh?"

"Yes."

Kiichi grabbed hold of Ichiro's arm and pulled him close. "You're not very happy," he said, exhaling smoke while gently patting his son's neck.

"No."

"Listen, I know things are difficult now."

"I know."

"But it'll be better."

"I know."

"It'll change."

"I know." Ichiro felt his father's heart beating.

"Don't you know it? Things are changing."

"Yes."

His father stepped away, placing his hands on Ichiro's shoulders. He asked, "Want something to eat?"

"That's okay—I'm just tired."

"Get some sleep then. Sleep in today—how's that? I'll get Saiichi to school. You can go with me later to check on some work. You want to do that?"

"Yes," said Ichiro, moving around his father. But when stirring that afternoon, he found Kiichi unconscious in the main room, a newspaper spread across his chest and an empty sake bottle beside him. You don't even try, he thought. "I hate you."

Still, Ichiro now wondered if perhaps he wasn't too hard on his father in those days, a little too forgiving of his absent mother—particularly considering what he came to understand about her. After all, Kiichi had never abandoned him or Saiichi; he had, before the worst of the rationing, kept plenty of food in the house and urged them to do well in their studies. His mother, however, seemed unconcerned with their welfare. Of course, as Keiko once mentioned, their mother had jumped into marriage at an early age: "Very selfish, I think—very young—but your father belonged to a good family, so it was ideal—though no one on his side approved, you know—they thought, how dare this young thing from poor folks attach herself to such a smart and educated man. He was foolish as well, I suppose—couldn't help his feelings, loved to buy expensive clothes for his bride, asked nothing in return but her loyalty. A mistake for him, I think—almost drove him crazy, as we know—except, Ichiro, if it could be done all over again today, believe me, it wouldn't turn out the same. Sometimes girls don't figure what they want until they've gained some experience. Some girls shouldn't rush into marriage and have children until they've lived for a while. It's called growing up, I suppose. At least I am fortunate enough to redeem myself somewhat in the eyes of the people I've neglected—at least I've tried—others aren't as lucky."

This coming from Keiko, who, having found the pursuit of accepted family life unbearably dull, worked as a respected hostess in a nightclub and eventually opened a small noodle shop. How Saiichi couldn't stand the woman, refusing her an invitation to his wedding–rarely speaking her name or acknowledging her presence, even as she tended Kiichi and, later, Masako. Yet Ichiro had made peace with her, although it wasn't easy: for he had encountered her quite by accident during his first year of college, after stumbling drunk into her place of employment with two friends–and, to his astonishment, there was Keiko serving drinks to salarymen, walking gracefully while holding a tray; she hadn't changed much, still looked girlish from a distance. But when approaching her, saying, "Mama-san," Ichiro noticed the wrinkles near her eyes, the flesh hanging underneath her chin.

"Ichiro," she said, taken aback, "is it you?"

"Mama-san–?"

"Is it really you? My, you've grown–"

Then he didn't know what to say. And if she hadn't laughed nervously, smiling so sweetly, he might have slapped her face; he might have told her she was worthless, a terrible mother. Instead he laughed too, nodding and waving for his friends to join him. "Meet Keiko," he told them, slurring the words. "Meet my long-lost aunt–my father thought she was killed in the bombings–my brother believed she was dead! It's amazing!"

Yes, Keiko agreed, it was amazing. A miracle. So there would be many drinks on the house, there would be a celebration of sorts–with Keiko entertaining Ichiro and his friends. "This is my nephew," she delighted in telling her regular clientele, introducing Ichiro to the salarymen who stopped by their table.

"Looks just like you," one said. "Could be your kid brother!"

"Thank you," she replied, bowing her head. "He is a handsome young man, I agree."

Nevertheless, bumping into Keiko offered little significance to anything now–especially as Ichiro had been recalling events of that August day, remembering when Mitsuharu hauled his bike up to the platform at Yamanote station, grinning slyly: "Brought us a present—snuck it right under my old man's nose—dumb ol' Michihiko—"

But Mitsuharu's father was far from dumb, and Ichiro couldn't help envying how the man provided for his family in those meager times, buying and selling goods through the black market. In fact, Michihiko had done so well, his own children grew plump while classmates like Ichiro remained skinny and malnourished. As for Mitsuharu, his clothes were always clean, his face washed—a pretty boy, some joked, because of his round eyes and curved brows, his chubby soft hands and the fresh soapy smell his skin exuded.

"So what'd you steal off ol' Michihiko today?" Ichiro asked, running across the platform toward Mitsuharu. "More candy I hope."

Saiichi, jogging alongside his brother, gazed at Mitsuharu with anxious eyes. "What kind of candy?" he said, when coming to a stop with Ichiro.

"Not candy," Mitsuharu told them, leaning his bike against the building. Then, as if using both hands to scratch at his lower spine, he tugged something out from a rear pocket and kept it hidden behind his back. "You'll never guess."

"Hardtack?"

"No—why would you care about hardtack?"

"Cigarettes?"

"No—but it smokes."

Ichiro frowned, wrinkling his brow. "What is it?" he said, becoming impatient. "Hurry—unless you want us to knock you on your ass and take it from you."

"I'm sure you've never seen one," Mitsuharu said, still grinning. "You wait, it'll fetch a high price—a fortune." Teasingly, he brought his left hand from behind his back, showing them it held nothing, and wiggled the fingers: "Worth more than cigarettes and rice." But before Ichiro could protest any further, Mitsuharu suddenly produced his right hand, extending his arm and pointing a Russian service revolver at Saiichi's forehead. "How's this?"

Ichiro's eyes widened. "It's great," he said, patting Mitsuharu proudly on a shoulder. "It's incredible."

"Is it real?" Saiichi asked, ducking the barrel.

"It is." Mitsuharu lowered the gun, holding it on his palm so the brothers could get a closer look. "The bullets are real too."

"Better than your slingshot," Ichiro said.

"Yes," Mitsuharu said. "I'll show you, Ichiro—set the bottles up."

"Then it's my turn!"

"I don't think we should," Saiichi said, but Ichiro was already jumping, sailing from the platform to the gravel below.

Mitsuharu nudged Saiichi in the stomach with the barrel. "It's like holding a firecracker—it'll shake your hand until it hurts."

"You've used it?" Saiichi said.

"What a stupid question—just last night I shot four birds, killed them in the dark," Mitsuharu bragged, although a slight uncertainty in his voice suggested the truth was otherwise. "Anyway, I've shot lots of things."

When going down into the train yard, standing several yards from where Ichiro had set four discarded bottles upright on a track rail, Mitsuharu brandished the revolver over his head, waving it around as Ichiro and Saiichi stood behind him near the platform—then he leveled the barrel, taking aim. "Cover your ears," he shouted, squeezing the trigger, wincing: a popping noise, like a firecracker exploding, filled the air, followed almost instantaneously by the tinging of the rail getting struck; the bullet ricocheted, whining within inches of him and right above Ichiro and Saiichi, thwacking the station wall. "Shit!" he said, continuing to gaze along the length of his arm while setting his aim higher. "I was off a little." Immediately the second shot rang out, and once again the bullet ricocheted, singing past Ichiro as he ran to join Mitsuharu.

"It keeps doing that," Saiichi yelled, glancing at the building, searching for signs of the bullets' damage. "I think we should stop."

But Ichiro wasn't interested in his brother's concern—for his belly tickled with anticipation, his body shook wildly with adrenaline. "Heard it go by," he told Mitsuharu, who was busy probing an ear with a finger. "It came close."

"Can't hear a thing," Mitsuharu said, offering Ichiro the gun. "Give it a try."

"How many bullets left?"

"Bullets—?"

Ichiro nodded.

"Oh, four, I think."

Ichiro accepted the revolver eagerly, feeling its weight in his hand, studying the barrel.

"Just point and pull," Mitsuharu said, stepping backwards.

Of course, it was conceivable that Ichiro's recollection of firing the gun had been embellished by memory, that possibly what transpired wasn't exactly as he imagined it years later. Still, he recalled without question the strange sense of purpose that arose in him when aiming the gun deliberately beneath the bottles—then, pulling the trigger, how his arm jerked from the recoil and a bullet sparked against the rail before shooting back in his direction. Goodbye, he thought—shutting his eyes while discharging another bullet. Goodbye. And he wondered if the reverberation stunning his ears might actually be a scream, a deafening outcry escaping his throat. Or perhaps he already understood that the roar existed somewhere inside his head—a gaping mouth in his mind, shouting down men with loan shark debts and sake breath, women who go out one evening and disappear, all the unrealized promises and pitiful words about everything being different someday; so he allowed the roar to erupt between his lips, bellowing even after the remaining bullets were spent and the emptied gun went click click click—never once hearing the muffled yells of the others, unaware of the ricochets that had almost hit Saiichi's chin and whizzed by Mitsuharu's right ear and shattered a station window.

"Stop it!" Mitsuharu said, shoving Ichiro.

"You could've killed us!" Saiichi tackled his brother, throwing his arms around Ichiro's waist. "Could've killed me–!"

But Ichiro didn't resist Saiichi's efforts to wrestle him to the ground, nor did he fight when Mitsuharu yanked the gun from his hand or Saiichi sat upon his chest slapping at him. Instead, Ichiro's body went limp; he began weeping loudly, saying, "I'm sorry–I don't know what to do–I'm sorry–" The pain in his voice, the wretchedness apparent on his face, so confused Saiichi that he scrambled off Ichiro and ran sobbing toward the platform.

"It was a dumb idea," Mitsuharu said, squatting beside Ichiro. "If my father finds out–"

"I'm sorry," Ichiro said, embarrassed by his crying. Then he exhaled deeply, sighing. Mitsuharu smiled, touching Ichiro's cheek, brushing away a tear–with his other hand, in a single unbroken movement, he passed a comforting palm across Ichiro's stomach; at that moment Ichiro stopped crying altogether–and he would have smiled too had it not been for Saiichi speeding past them on his bike, the wheels stirring up dirt as his brother peddled home.

"Don't worry," Mitsuharu said. "Saiichi's a baby."

"I could've hurt him," Ichiro said, wiping his eyes and sitting up.

Mitsuharu shrugged: "Could've hurt me as well–won't catch me bawling."

Yet soon afterwards Mitsuharu would indeed be bawling, though not from unhappiness–so would Ichiro, both boys weeping with those who were also huddled around a radio in front of a government food hall; for they had happened on the crowd while silently walking their bikes along the shopping street. Then it seemed like every person in the neighborhood stood at the food hall–some craning their necks, others bowing their heads, no one saying a word as a single voice spoke to them from the radio: "What is it?" asked Mitsuharu, tugging on an elderly woman's sleeve.

"Quiet," she told him, "the Emperor is speaking."

"The Emperor–?" Mitsuharu said, incredulously.

"Really–?" questioned Ichiro, because it was such an average voice, so human and uncommanding (surely not the voice of an Emperor, not the tongue of a living god who had frequented his dreams and soared through the sky). "What's he saying?" he asked the elderly woman.

"It's over," she said, bursting into tears. "The war ended!"

"The war ended!" another echoed–and within seconds most everyone else there was crying, including Ichiro and Mitsuharu; the bittersweet sobs and chatter of the crowd drowning the radio broadcast.

"Must tell my father," Mitsuharu said, climbing aboard his bike. "I'm going home, Ichiro."

"Yes, me too," Ichiro said, waving as Mitsuharu turned his bike in the opposite direction (the revolver bulging in his friend's back pocket, the barrel sticking out).

"It's a great day," Mitsuharu yelled.

"Yes, it is!" Ichiro said, straddling his bike. "It's tremendous!" With that he started home, passing people bustling about cheerfully as if the imperial proclamation had blown away a terrible storm, peddling so fast that the wind dried his tears. And when he arrived, Ichiro rushed into the house, exclaiming, "The war is over!" But neither Kiichi or Saiichi was in the main room to hear the good news. So he went down the hallway looking for them, eventually finding both asleep on Kiichi's futon. "The war is over," he whispered, stepping into his father's room: Saiichi napped on his right side, one arm tucked underneath himself, the other placed across Kiichi's neck. As Ichiro moved closer, he saw his father's chest rise and drop and rise again, in steady rhythm. "It's over–"

Kiichi's hands twitched briefly, Saiichi's dirty toes fidgeted, and Ichiro could hear them–two faint snores, two different breaths escaping. Then he realized his own weariness, sensing that the eventful morning had at last drained him wholly. Outside, smaller boys were laughing in the street–

how brazenly they cackled, no doubt delighted by one boy's boisterous impersonation of the Emperor's human voice; their laughter soon dissipating into the afternoon's stillness. Presently Ichiro lowered himself to the futon, sliding in against his father and bringing an arm over the man's stomach, placing a palm on Saiichi's shoulder. Moments later his body settled, his breathing slowed—and for a while he rested as the sunlight coming through the screens gradually shifted, pushing patterns up the walls, casting shadows where they slept.

Shortly before dawn, Saiichi spoke from inside his bedroom, letting Ichiro know that he was aware of his presence in the hallway, quietly saying, "Brother—it's beautiful." Ichiro, sliding the door open, believed his brother must be referring to the blue-black and orange-red hues now bleeding together at the ocean's horizon. "How are you?" Saiichi asked, staring from the unclosed window—his robe in a pile near his feet, his pale and emaciated body in stark contrast to the dimness of the room.

"I'm fine," Ichiro said, coming toward him, stepping around the futon on the floor. "How are you?"

But Saiichi didn't answer; he continued looking through the window, even as Ichiro moved in next to him and studied his profile: a cool breeze smoothed his thick hair, goose pimples had appeared on his chest and arms. Then pointing a shaky finger, indicating an area in the sky, Saiichi asked, "Did you see Jupiter earlier?"

"I'm sorry, no."

"I see," he said, sounding disappointed. "You didn't see Alpha Librae poised between the moon and Jupiter?"

"Missed it, I'm afraid."

"That's a shame—"

For some time they remained standing there, feeling the wind, gazing at the ocean. Finally Saiichi turned from the window, going to the futon—where he lay down on his stomach, spreading his arms. So Ichiro crossed to him, bringing his hands to Saiichi's frigid skin, massaging along the spine, rubbing the cold from his brother's back and gliding his palms over a body as familiar as his own. And soon Saiichi started talking, mumbling at first, the words slowly becoming clearer: "–our fates are tied inextricably with the fate of the sun–brother?"

"I'm right here."

"I was trying to tell you–"

"Yes–?" Ichiro said, stretching out beside him. Because with the night concluding, all he wanted to do was hold his brother close, listening intently while Saiichi began speaking of the sun–that unexceptional dwarf star burning amidst a remote galaxy, warming a tiny sphere in a solar system surrounded by nothingness–which, as Ichiro gently pulled Saiichi against him, was just beginning to show itself on the horizon.

# From the Place in the
# Valley Deep in the Forest

## 1.

The past didn't really find me until I had escaped the exhaust fumes of Ho Chi Minh City. And when bicycling into the countryside on Route One—passing increasingly smaller villages, inhaling the humid tropical air while seeing rice paddies and water buffalos alongside the road—what I had hoped would be somehow different was unchanged. Then it seemed like the thirty years since I last saw this country could easily have been just a few months. Except the fear was gone, along with the American flags that at times had reminded many of us about why we were serving here.

"Marie, I'm so proud," my husband Al said yesterday while lighting our incense sticks, "and I'm so ashamed." Once the sticks were smoking, we stuck them in the ground and then gazed quietly at the grassy fields of the My Lai memorial, listening as cicadas buzzed somewhere within bamboo stalks. My stepson Kenny strolled around with his camera, moving between tombstones, photographing whatever caught his attention in the ghost village—several sculptures, empty spots where straw homes had stood, the trench in which villagers were murdered by Company C soldiers.

"It's okay to feel proud," I told Al, taking his hand in mine. "You can feel ashamed too. It's the same for me."

But while neither of us had anything to do with the My Lai killings (Al having arrived in Vietnam nearly two years afterwards, ending up with the 101st Airborne Division at Camp Evans; my arrival being almost a year following the massacre, working as a nurse in the 91st Evac. Hospital at Chu Lai), it was impossible to not carry a sense of culpability when visiting the memorial. As for Kenny, his curious grin and roving camera made me realize that this place was, to him, pure history–a bad chapter from a distant war, something awful that had occurred before his birth. Even so, his long brown legs took him cautiously through the tall grass, betraying his desire to be respectful of the people and homes no longer existing there; at nineteen, I suspect, he already understands what it is to walk upon old soil which hasn't yet become firm.

"Weird bringing my son here," Al said, scratching an ant bite on his elbow. "Ever imagined you'd see Kenny in 'Nam?"

"Not really," I said. "Never imagined seeing myself here again."

"Me either," he replied, and his expression–so thoughtful, somewhat sad–suggested that the enthusiasm which had propelled him forward throughout the morning, which had kept his mountain bike well ahead of mine and Kenny's in the afternoon, was beginning to fade as evening approached. "Weird," he whispered to himself. "Just too weird–"

I suppose the worst for Al came and went before we met– those confusing years after Vietnam, the hard drinking and the nightmares and the depression, the first wife who vanished from his life for good and left him with their only child; it is something he talks about freely now, almost boastfully, as if he's overcome some great burden which many others have failed to subdue. But I'm different; I don't discuss the war very often, even though Al wishes I would. And he doesn't believe me when I insist nightmares never really plagued me, when I tell him that my periods of relative calm and serenity aren't masking darker feelings. There is nothing I haven't already confronted, I've told him. There is nothing else lurking beneath the surface. I'm not a character in a TV movie, or a textbook case of delayed stress syndrome. The war doesn't govern me. "Sounds like you're convincing yourself," he had said.

"No," I replied, "I'm completely resolved. Anyway, you're the one compelled to dig it up over and over."

All the same, Al wasn't in the mood to delve into the war yesterday, to talk it out once more. Over the last few days he had grown increasingly reflective, inward—though at times his humor emerged, and he appeared delighted by the villagers waving at us while we rode by. Earlier, four or five barefoot children followed us while we walked our bikes down the dirt path leading to My Lai. "You America?" we were continually asked. "Americas?"

"Yep," Al repeated, smiling, "I'm America." He would point at me. "She's America." He would point at Kenny. "He's America."

"You America?"

"Yep, I'm America."

Surely how odd America must have looked on that wide path: such a stout black man with a gray beard and a prosthetic right leg, walking beside his short Asian wife and his lanky son; the three wearing helmets and tight yellow shirts and blue spandex shorts. Still, our being Americans was only a mild curiosity to the children; their real interest was in Al's prosthetic, that metallic and otherworldly appendage below his kneecap, a state-of-the-art replacement for what had been blown away by a VC toe popper in 1971. So before entering the memorial, he allowed the children to touch it, chuckling as their tiny hands took turns exploring the prosthetic limb: "It's The Terminator," he told them. "I call it The Terminator."

"What happen you?" a little girl asked, glancing up at him.

"Blew up," he said. "Long time ago—" Then he made an exploding noise.

"Oh," she said, flatly. "Don't worry, be happy."

"I will," he said, laughing. "You too."

I was relieved Al didn't try explaining to her that he considered his missing leg a memento of the war. "A painful momento," he had told others back home, strangers we encountered while riding our bikes or working out at the gym. "Then there's Marie—she's another momento, but a sweet one, got her stateside—my sweet Mariko."

"So you're Vietnamese," these strangers often said.

"No," was my usual curt reply, "I'm Japanese, born here in Houston." Although sometimes, depending on the person, I also explained that I too had served in Vietnam. But rarely have I offered little else, as I'm generally less gregarious than my husband. Of course, I probably should talk more—except strangers bother me, even when they're trying to be polite. And the assumption that I'm Vietnamese, the notion of all Asians looking the same, always recalled those angry young soldiers I had tended, those few boys refusing my aid because, to them, I was just another slant-eye, a gook. How could I have explained that to a stranger? It would be easier, I think, to mention that I fell in love with Al at the VA Hospital, that I was charmed by this black vet who knew I was either Japanese or Korean and could pretty much discern one slant-eye from another.

"You America?" the little girl asked me, sounding surprised by her own question.

"I'm afraid I am," I told her, heading into My Lai.

"Don't worry," she said, watching me go, "be happy."

"Okay," I said, "thank you."

Yet the happiness, I suppose, remained outside the memorial with the children. As our incense burned, Al and I held one another in the stillness of the evening, waiting for Kenny to finish taking photographs so we could leave. "I'm beat," Al said. "My muscles are murdering me—"

"You need rest," I said. "We've pushed it pretty hard, we need a break."

"Yeah, that–or at least painkillers."

So today we are near Da Nang, having biked clear of my base at Chu Lai (a place I have no tangible desire to revisit). And I'm sunning myself on China Beach, relaxing before tomorrow's arduous trek up the Hai Van Pass. Aside from several locals selling baseball caps and Chicago Bulls T-shirts, the stretch of sand is mostly deserted. Down the beach a fisherman and his two grown sons are sitting beneath a tree, each meticulously repairing frayed sections on a large net. What I didn't know–until Kenny told me and Al a few minutes ago– is that the fisherman has no feet: "Just two stumps–I think his sons help him get around, like human crutches."

"Do they speak English?"

"One son does a bit–not well though. Didn't mind me taking their pictures–didn't ask for money either. I'm pretty sure the dad's a vet."

"Probably."

And now, while I shut my eyes and let the sun warm my aching legs, Al and Kenny are wandering together toward the fisherman. No doubt Al intends showing off The Terminator again, urging the fisherman and his sons to run their hands all over his painful momento as Kenny lifts his camera for a shot. Later, the three of us will gather sand, pouring it into empty plastic Tylenol bottles.

## 2.

This afternoon it rained, showering on us on the downhill side of Hai Van Pass. We had started the climb early and in good spirits; except the steep incline—with its endless switch-backs and the constant flow of vehicles speeding dangerously by—finally began testing Al's stamina. "Fuck," he'd grunt loudly, doing his best to maintain his lead on me and Kenny. "Goddamn!"

"Dad, let's stop," Kenny yelled at one point. "Let's pull over a while!"

But Al either didn't hear him or chose to ignore him, because he continued upward: "Fuck!" He had to reach the summit before us—and once there he would waste little time aiming his bike toward the valleys below, sailing downhill while we followed somewhere behind. I'm sure that in two days, when we reach the former DMZ, he will be first cross-ing the bridge; his symbolic taking of the north, like a general leading his command across the enemy's front line.

"I'm pulling over," Kenny told me, slowing his bike.

The two of us stopped on the shoulder, where we paused long enough to sip water and catch our breaths. Then before starting again, Kenny dug out his camera, taking three or four quick shots of the scenery. "Wouldn't know this is Vietnam," he said, focusing the lens at the dense forest growing beyond the pavement, those far from tropical trees which lined the pass and recalled, to my mind, the lush hill country in central Texas.

"Hurry," I said, "we're losing Al—he's gone around a hair-pin."

"One more," said Kenny, adjusting the aperture.

Soon we were back on the road, gradually making our way along the incline. With every turn I expected Al to appear—his body hunched, his legs cycling methodically—but he eluded us, had somehow kept going onward without stopping for water. Or, I found myself worrying, had a car accidentally pushed him past the edge, sending him plummeting through the deep forest and into a valley basin. So I looked for skid marks, some sign of tragedy, imagining a vehicle knocking Al from the road. In a sense, it was all remotely amusing–this conception of my husband perishing in a place he had once been lucky enough to survive. But if he were to die here, I believed the Pass of Ocean Clouds was a better departure point than the rice fields we had passed days ago.

"Yep, the mountains are nice, much nicer," Al said last night, after turning out the light in our room at The China Beach Hotel. "Can't see a damn rice paddy and not think of dipping my helmet in that awful water 'cause it's the only water around–drinking filth all nasty with animal waste, human waste, you name it–knowing that a VC is probably nearby just hoping to get you in his sights–give me the mountains, that's for sure."

While I too was glad to be pedaling away from the long fields, I began missing the flat valley roads when climbing Hai Van Pass. Even Kenny–who had been so eager for this morning's difficult trek, who had already dressed before Al and I stirred–occasionally glanced back at me with an anguished expression. "This sucks," I heard him say, shifting gears. "Bad idea," he uttered minutes later, as if regretting the entire trip–an adventure which had been his idea from the very start; although it was a hard sell, taking several days to convince Al and me to go with him. "Don't you want a good memory of the place?" he had argued, unfolding a travel brochure on the dining room table. "Don't you want something positive from it, instead of remembering it like a terrible part of your past?"

"Whether I make the trip or don't," Al told him, "it'll still be a terrible part of my past–nothing changes that."

But we heard Kenny out anyway, listening patiently while he explained his proposed itinerary: bicycles would be bought in Ho Chi Minh City, and from there we would take a bus to Qui Nhon–then bike north along Route One until passing what had been the Demilitarized Zone; afterwards, our bicycles would get sold at Dong Hoi and we'd head on toward Hanoi by train. "I mean, what a memorable cycling opportunity for us," Kenny concluded, "and an awesome visual essay for my photo journalism class—me and my vet parents doing our family vacation in 'Nam! Ten times cooler than homeless families, right? Or crack houses in the Fifth Ward."

"We'll consider it," Al said. "Don't get your hopes up, okay? It's a bit like inviting Jackie Kennedy to a picnic on the grassy knoll."

Except, to my surprise, Al was hardly reluctant about doing the trip. Still, he and I discussed the pros and cons involved in such a journey, both emotionally and financially. "Not sure it's worth it," I told him one night in bed. "In a way it'd be interesting—in another—I'm completely unsure—"

"Know what though?" he said, putting an arm around me. "I've dreamed of crossing the DMZ, literally. I've actually had those dreams. Something I've always wanted to do too, Marie—just move across it into the north and keep going for Hanoi without looking behind me—or getting shot at or anything. Didn't think I'd get the chance, you know? Seemed sort of silly and pointless, I guess—but if ever there's a dream that haunts me in my old age—it's certainly that one."

"You're being dramatic," I told him. "Anyway, you're not old."

"Sometimes," he said, kissing my neck, "I feel almost a hundred years old."

Near the summit, Kenny and I encountered an uphill traffic jam—a line of vehicles stretching to the top, a standstill disrupted by drivers periodically hitting horns and shouting incomprehensibly from rolled down windows. But whatever had stopped traffic wasn't at first apparent—so we cycled forward along the narrow shoulder, effortlessly passing cars and trucks. Then—when seeing a large group of people standing in the road up ahead, gazing at where a passenger bus sat idle and blocked both lanes—my stomach sank. It's Al, I thought.

The bus hit Al. I suppose Kenny must have had the same concern, because suddenly the two of us were pedaling as fast as possible, our bicycles inches apart. Fortunately, by this point the incline was becoming level, and reaching the bus meant expending only a minimal amount of energy. Nevertheless, we arrived at the scene short-winded and barely able to speak.

"Suitcases," Kenny wheezed, wiping his brow.

Indeed, the road was strewn with suitcases—and sacks and boxes and bikes, all having slipped off the roof of the bus. Several passengers were angrily confronting the young bus driver, others ran about rescuing their fallen luggage. Catching my breath, I couldn't help laughing a little to myself—partly from relief, but mostly on account of the poor bus driver's oddly resigned manner; the lazy way he scratched his chin as those around him raised their arms and yelled in his face.

"Al doesn't know what he's missing," I told Kenny. "I bet he's already reached the bottom. We should keep chasing him, I guess."

"Why don't you head on," Kenny said, going for his camera. "I'll be coming soon, don't worry." Maybe he mistook my desire to find Al for impatience. Or perhaps he resented our bikes traveling so close together. Regardless, I left him and went on, but not before letting him know that I'd wait once I reached the summit.

"Take your time," I said, pushing off. "No hurry."

As it happened, the peak was closer than I suspected—about a quarter mile, possibly less—and, while I imagined he would do otherwise, Al had taken a break at the pullout. He huddled beneath a sugar cane juicer's umbrella, seemingly taking shelter from the storm clouds overhead (clouds that I hadn't paid much attention to until reaching the peak). The juicer, an elderly man wearing a Dodgers baseball cap, was nodding emphatically, telling him, "Mua, mua," as I joined them.

"He says it'll rain, Marie," Al said, grinning.

"Smells like it," I said.

"Mua," the juicer told me, "mua."

No sooner had he spoken when thunder erupted, a massive boom which was followed by the juicer's delighted cackle. "Very good," Al said, shaking the juicer's hand. "You're a weather man."

"Me too," the juicer said, uncomprehending Al's words. "Good, okay? Yes, I think so."

By the time Kenny found us, the rain had begun falling–a light shower shrouding the valleys below in a soft-white haze. "Should we quit a while?" he asked. "Give it a chance to clear?"

"Can if you want, but I'm not," Al replied. "Perfect for biking, rain cools everything, keeps heat exhaustion away."

So now Kenny and I are coasting through the mist, breezing into the valley behind Al. But Al isn't riding anymore; at the moment he is standing on the shoulder a few yards downhill, staring at something in the forest. And as we stop alongside him, I can tell his mood has changed–his face appears stern, somewhat reflective and unbothered by the drizzle that continues dampening him. "Look over there," he says, pointing toward the glistening trees, jabbing the air with a finger.

"Where?"

At first I see nothing–other than this dark green forest made wet and obscure by rainfall, branches crisscrossing and dripping. Then I notice the concrete bunker hidden beneath a maze of vines. Then I observe a doorway, and small openings designed for rifle barrels.

"Jesus christ," Al says, brushing water from his cheeks.

"Dad–?"

Kenny rests a hand on Al's shoulder, but he hasn't spotted the bunker yet. He is studying the forest, scanning the trees, frowning.

"Forget it," Al says, patting Kenny's hand while climbing back on his bike. "Let's hit the road–let's go."

Except I'm not quite ready. I'm breathing deeply, inhaling the earthy scents of the mountains we are leaving. And–as Al rides away and Kenny quietly searches for what he can't seem to find–I'm aware of the silences that sometimes inhabit these places, how everything becomes enveloped by a sudden stillness; then one might exhale and, just briefly, believe it is a distant voice she is hearing.

# 3.

Something claims my mind today as I begin cycling, as I progress north in the valleys and between fields: I have held a young man's brains in my hands, a boy around the age of Kenny. I'm not suggesting the memory of it upsets me often, but its unwelcome emergence causes my stomach to drop; then everything surrounding me—the clouds hanging low, the deep forest, the road—appears stark, incredibly pointless even while the air smells clean and birds fly overhead. When such feelings overtake me, I summon my friend Julie Yamamoto, who died in Chu Lai after a mortar shell exploded beside her. I envision her chubby round face, her gentle smile, and her telling me years ago, "If everything is really meaningless—then we should create the meaning for ourselves." For some reason that does the trick; my mind settles and I can proceed. It is like my prayer, my mantra, a way of connecting with someone vanished. And sometimes, like the boy's brains, she presents herself to me—taking a coffee break or waiting for the helicopters to bring incoming patients, writing poems while others talked and smoked.

Back home, tucked away inside a cardboard box, are two legal pads containing her handwritten poetry. To be honest, my original intention had been to send the legal pads on to her parents, but because her poems were written mostly in Vietnam (chronicling our time together as nurses, our rotations from ward to ward), I couldn't bear parting with them—although I probably have no right possessing their only daughter's words. Still, I believe her poems are my poems. And while not brilliant by any means, they recall that period almost better than I can: training at Fort Sam Houston, being fitted in uniforms and ponchos and combat boots, learning how to march and hold M-16s we would never fire. Through it all, until her death, I was always somewhere nearby—a supporting player within verse, wandering with Julie through the orthopedic ward at Fort Devons in Massachusetts, where our patients were Vietnam casualties shipped from Japanese hospitals. Those dozen or so early poems, before we went overseas, are less bothersome reading than the lines that would soon follow in Chu Lai.

*What do I know of these boys in these beds.*
*Some can't get assembled again, yet breathe*
*without legs and without arms, no genitals,*
*no faces—not a thing there from ear to ear.*
*What do I know of these boys around me,*
*except that their choices were taken away*
*and what is left resides here for my watch.*

In a sense, as nurses and medics, we were alienated from the rest, from the men getting shot at everyday. Our role was more complicated. They risked death in the fields, we bartered death in the operating rooms—arguing over who we could try saving, who was better left for dead. At times the selection was based solely on a pair of open eyes, maybe a faint expression on a soldier's face; small signs could hasten a boy's chances. Then there were the lifeless ones needing just a moment of our attention, requiring only an extra morphine dose to finish them off. It was never easy, I suppose, but it became easier: the poor kids I helped with departure, the pulses going going gone. Occasionally—when holding a boy's limp hand, when comforting him in his very last seconds—I felt wonderfully peaceful, impossibly sacred; because I understood that death itself, like birth, was a brief and mostly effortless ordeal: *The getting out of one car,* Julie wrote. *The climbing into of another.*

So inside that cardboard box, hidden behind shoes on a closet shelf, are two legal pads that function as a part of my memory. I know all that is mentioned, the exact order of the untitled poems, the narrow shape of Julie's stanzas. I know the poems to think about, I know the ones to ignore and pretend weren't ever written (those stillborn POW babies, that twelve-year-old VC who killed five GIs, the alcoholic MP bleeding from a bullet he fired into his own skull). It isn't as difficult as one might imagine: I simply pick the poems I find useful and keep them with me; the rest stay forever inside that box, like snapshots that are too ugly to look at.

"You must understand, it's important remembering," Julie once told me. "It's important I don't forget any of this–otherwise I can't find the meaning." She was answering my question about why she wrote. Perhaps–if I hadn't continued being a nurse following the war, if I hadn't returned intact and used my experience in Houston emergency rooms–it would be important for me as well. But I've glimpsed many more terrible things stateside–countless gunshot wounds, ice picks in throats, poorly executed suicide attempts, beer bottles shoved up rectums, grieving parents and family members and lovers. I've seen so much violence inflicted that I am somewhat impervious–and the wards at Chu Lai are just a short chapter in what has become a long life of aiding the suffering, the hopeless, the dying; in this I create my meaning.

Now the day has started shifting gears, heading in reverse. The sun is arching for the distant hills. I remove my helmet and speed along without gripping the handlebars. It is a stupid thing to do, but I enjoy it–especially going downhill here near the coast, where the breeze is warm, vaguely tropical, and the trees on either side of the road are lush and tall. I hold my arms out and make believe I'm flying–an oversized bird lacking feathers, holding a biking helmet in one claw. But a curious sensation bubbles around my gut, as if a tiny voice is telling me that I should be careful–so I put my helmet on, then bring my hands to the handlebars.

"You're nuts!" I hear Kenny yell. He is behind me–and Al, confident in his lead, is within reach. Suddenly I can't help myself: I wait until I'm close enough–then I accelerate, hunching down, and sail swiftly past my husband.

"Where you going?" Al shouts.

"The DMZ," I tell him, shaking a middle finger in the air. "I'm taking it before you do!"

I don't turn my head to look. I don't have to—I'm sure Al is on my tail, pedaling like a madman, doing his best to recapture his lead. Soon I'll let him have it—but not without some effort. And not before I can enjoy this road as my own—no one ahead of me, everything somewhere behind. Because I'm working off my regret about avoiding Chu Lai altogether, about steering clear of that once sprawling military base—a place where poetry was written, where sea grass now sprouts upon the old runways.

## 4.

An accident occurred: Kenny has fallen badly. I'm not sure how it happened, or if his injuries are serious. All I know is that seconds ago he was chasing his father, calling Al's name; now he is stretched facedown across the road with his bike twisted upon him, the lower part of his left leg entangled awkwardly in the frame. At first, while jumping from my bike and running toward him, I expect him to move, to rise up–but he remains motionless there on the asphalt. And I'm waving my arms overhead, hoping that Al will glance back and see me; except Al is already on his way, far beyond the sound of my voice. So–aware of the DMZ's proximity, of my husband's need to reach it by midday–I drop my arms, saying, "Goddamn you! Goddammit–!"

I'm too tired to yell anymore, too weary to make such a pointless racket; my fatigue being the result of spending the night beside a river, where evening light glittered in the water and long boats floated. On the other side, women washed clothing and children swam. Of course, we hadn't planned on sleeping outdoors, but Al insisted we get as close to the DMZ as possible before stopping. At last exhausted, unable to go any further, we found ourselves at the river, hungry and sweaty and irritable. "Guess we're roughing it tonight," Al said. "Just like army days. You'll be amazed at how good the earth can feel, you'll see."

The earth, following eight hours of cycling, did indeed feel pleasant–although our initial camp was in the path of huge roving red ants. But once we'd found another clearing–sheltered amongst trees, between the roadway and the river–I was able to relax, using my fanny pack as a pillow, my helmet as a prop for my feet. Still, the mosquitoes were fierce, completely unfazed by the Off we repeatedly sprayed on ourselves. Moreover, dinner was meager (water, three candy bars, some gum Kenny had purchased from a roadside vendor). Fortunately, we had had a large meal earlier, something substantial in Dong Ha: rice, fish, and greens.

"You know, there's probably tigers nearby," Al told us, chewing his candy bar. He mentioned the ground attacks in Dac Glei, a small town southwest of us: "Some of the worst fighting ever–tigers roamed the battle zone tearing bodies apart. True story."

Later, when Kenny had settled into sleep, I helped Al remove The Terminator and leaned it carefully against his bike. Afterwards, the two of us lay side-by-side, arms touching, our ears attuned to the rushing of the river. We looked for stars, gazing past the branches high above us, and talked about the foolish idealism of our youth, the firm notion of war as a deterrent against greater evils, the belief in a freedom which could ease the guilt of those responsible for the fatalities of others. At some point I mentioned something I had read recently–that the deliberate killing of women, children, and elderly people was permissible if enough could be gained from it.

"You think so?" Al asked.

"No," I said, "I don't think certain acts can be justified no matter what the consequences."

Al went silent. Finally he said, "Haven't worked that one out yet. Not sure I ever will."

Eventually we gave up on ethical and moral musings, preferring instead to listen to the river for a while. We continued staring at the stars, remaining quiet even while a bluish-green meteor streaked through the sky and disappeared from view. Then when Al yawned, I yawned. But, as opposed to him and Kenny, sleep wouldn't come easy for me. In the darkness I heard Al begin breathing lowly–and the river burbling, and leaves rustling deep within the forest from an approaching breeze. Suddenly the air smelled strangely sweet, like honeysuckle nectar.

"Big day tomorrow," Al said, surprising me. "Let's get an early start, out of here by dawn."

The very idea filled me with dread–all that relentless biking, the maintaining of Al's compulsive pace. Maybe we could take it slower, I suggested. Maybe we could cross the DMZ together, the three of us doing it as a leisurely ride for a change, a less exerting effort on the big day.

"Can if you want," Al said, "but not me—I'm gone by first light. Do whatever pleases you—"

He didn't mean to stir my anger. Yet something in his worn-out voice, his flagging and dull tone, enraged me. "This isn't your trip," I told him, trying my best not to wake Kenny. "This is our trip. It isn't Al's show, okay? So stop acting like it is—stop acting like you're here on some singular mission that only you can accomplish. It's unfair. If it's so incredibly important to do everything on your own, you should've come by yourself. To be honest, I don't even know why you're so determined to zoom across the DMZ—it's bullshit the way you're always riding ahead of us, you know?"

"You're tired, Marie," he replied evenly. "We're both tired."

That was the end of it; he had nothing else to say and neither did I. Minutes later I caught his snoring, a soft hum vibrating from his throat. Just then I felt alone, completely isolated amongst the trees. The harder I tried falling asleep, the more difficult it became; so as I lay there I imagined the hotel awaiting me at the conclusion of the next day, and saw myself washing away everything I had accumulated during the trip, and the three of us gladly selling our bikes in Dong Hoi before nightfall. I imagined other things as well, each increasingly vague and dream-like while I drifted further inside myself.

It's impossible remembering when I slipped into sleep—but I do know that it consumed me thoroughly, for I hardly shifted an inch and never once woke. I didn't see the darkness lighten, or grow aware of Al sitting up and reaching past me for The Terminator; nor did I sense his leaving, wheels clicking as he walked his bike toward the road. And if it weren't for Kenny shaking my shoulder, saying, "Come on, Dad's going without us," I could have surely slept hours more. I could have slept until sunlight cut through the trees and blazed down on my face.

"My camera," Kenny says.

"It's fine," I tell him, although I don't know if that's true. His camera bag is beneath the rear spokes, bunched near his right foot.

When I attempted lifting the bike off him earlier, carefully trying to extract his left calve from where it's wedged in the frame, he screamed out and pounded his hands on the asphalt: "Don't! Something's wrong! It hurts–!"

"Okay," I told him, "I won't–not yet anyway."

So now I'm inspecting his left calve, touching it lightly with my fingers, applying pressure. "Feel that?"

"Yes."

"That?"

"Yes."

I reach under the rear tire, bringing a hand to his right leg. "How about that?"

"It hurts," he says, sobbing miserably. "It hurts–"

"It's all right," I say, bothered by the blood coming from a gash on his chin. "Don't worry," I tell him, taking his water bottle. And I should be ready for this, I know. I should know exactly how to help him. But all I do is give him water and hold his hand and wait. Because soon a car will appear, or Al will regret leaving us behind and turn around. Either way, I offer what I can: I squeeze Kenny's hand, I smile, I whisper softly like a mother. I say, "Don't worry, you're all right," and for some reason that calms him. Then I understand again the easing of my own voice, the comfort of my touch–and I feel Kenny's pain lessening, and I'm conscious of this mastery in me, this hard-earned talent gained in wartime and carried with me thereafter; nevertheless, it is not something I am necessarily proud of.

# History is Dead

## 1.

Comrade Sleepy Eyes referred to Ratha as "Melt Ear," a taunt in honor of her missing left earlobe. During high school she was called Miss Nibbled (not that her lobe had actually been nibbled away by someone, or even melted for that matter). In truth, Ratha's deformity began in the womb, but, considering she only lacked a small fleshy pendent, most people never noticed or cared—except for a few annoying high school boys, and now, years later, Sleepy Eyes. A fine one to tease, thought Ratha; he was, after all, Sleepy Eyes—a fat soldier whose thick eyelids gave him a perpetually dreary, half-awake appearance. Anyway, she rarely encountered him, sometimes went months without hearing his insults, because he supervised the irrigation builders and she worked in the rice fields—cultivating, transplanting, and husking rice alongside the other women of Red Flag village.

For almost two years it had been the same, Ratha and her aunt Navy stood in the puddled fields. Using either a hoe or a sickle or blistered hands, they toiled to meet the day's work quota—laboring from early morning until dusk, breaking twice for water and thirty minutes of sitting—but often the mix of humidity and fatigue and hunger became so severe that Ratha wanted to stretch her malnourished body in the muddy soil, pull her krama over her eyes, and nap while sinking slowly into the earth. Yet she could never act on such a wish, otherwise there would be serious trouble with comrade Vong, the young soldier who supervised the women as they worked. So Ratha pressed on, rhythmically lifting and dropping her hoe, pausing only to wipe the sweat from her face—or, as was regularly the case, to ask Vong's permission to relieve herself in the paddy: "If you must," he usually answered in his brusque manner of speaking, then watched as she untied her belt and squatted among the rice.

"Smiley," Navy called Vong behind his back (Smiley because the man's expression was always so stern—so humorless and unforgiving, perhaps feigned in its hardness—that Ratha's aunt couldn't help making fun of him). Still, compared to most of the younger Khmer soldiers, he had his generous moments—like when he occasionally allowed the women the privilege of listening to his portable radio during the daily breaks, or granted a few extra minutes of sitting in order for frayed kramas to be mended. Then, when the clouds swelled and heavy rains suddenly poured down, he waved the women from the fields with his rifle, ordering them to wait out the storm beneath palm trees rather than continue working—a courtesy that was rarely offered in other labor camps.

And everyday before the first and second breaks, Vong sent Ratha off through the jungle to a nearby river, where she filled two buckets and then returned carefully as not to spill a drop (one slip, one sloshed bucket, and there wouldn't be enough fresh water for each woman to wet her face and rinse her hands). But Ratha had become efficient at the chore; so good, in fact, that she took her time wandering along the overgrown trail toward the river. In seconds she filled both buckets, and made the trip back as leisurely as possible. Truth be known, she could have fetched the water in less than ten minutes—Vong had calculated twenty—though why hurry when the dense jungle provided such welcome shade and the iridescent tropical birds swooped about and the tiresome paddies needed her continual tending?

Naturally, some of the other women resented Ratha's visits to the river. But it wasn't worth her bother; anyway, she figured those who were envious were already full of resentment, glaring at her with eyes that were at once angry and dispirited while forever mourning lost husbands and children and relatives. These were the same women who tested comrade Vong's patience by weeping in the fields, the ones that raised his ire, causing him to shout, "You, stop it now or else!" The worst of them ended up with the butt of his AK-47 rammed against their shoulders, his high-pitched boyish voice spewing a familiar warning: "Keeping you is not profitable for us, discarding you is no loss!" It was a popular Khmer motto, echoed routinely at Red Flag educational sessions, an admonition regarding the consequences of suspect behavior and emotional outbursts no longer tolerated in the new society.

As for Ratha, she had lost the urge to cry months ago. So had Navy, who had last shed a tear while embarking on the slow march from Phnom Penh. Though Ratha's aunt soon made the best of an intolerable situation, maintaining good humor even as she grew rawboned in the fields or her palms bled from hours of tilling. If it weren't for Navy's lively resolve and influence, Ratha felt certain she'd be no different than the other women—angry and scared and aching quietly with misery. Still, survival in the labor village was never easy, but Ratha accepted Navy's reminders about being lucky to live there; her uncle Moly shared the belief, often saying, "It could be worse. We might be in the northwest, and then we'd be dead already." So Ratha considered herself fortunate. She had heard the rumors of what frequently occurred in the northwest region, had once spotted three bloated and naked bodies floating down the river from someplace else, bobbing within the currents like large dolls that had been cast away.

The recent arrivals, women brought to Red Flag to help maintain the production quota, whispered similar stories of widespread disease in distant villages and the roaming packs of ravenous wolves that attacked small children. Then there were the arrivals who couldn't or wouldn't speak—suffering with malaria, hunched over from the weight of their swollen bellies—whose eyelids barely slid open; pitiful replacements for those who had died or who had left Red Flag under mysterious circumstances. The life expectancy of such enfeebled laborers was normally a month—some collapsed in the fields, some went noiselessly in their sleep, some just disappeared in the middle of the night. Or if a replacement was young, attractive, reasonably healthy, she might be selected as a bride and become the wife of a soldier (presumably forced marriages meant better living conditions—more food for the bride, less work—yet no one knew for sure). So a bride would go and a replacement would arrive: "Ghost people," Navy called them. "Never stay too long, all look alike—she leaves and another appears, one face with a hundred different bodies."

Ghost women, Ratha imagined, each of them lacking her aunt's humor and pleasant nature (only once had Ratha seen her aunt become violent—except that was years ago in a Phnom Penh market, where a drunkard had said something cruel about her niece's ear, and Navy dealt with the man by slapping his face with both hands and shoving him to the ground; even then she carried a smile, refusing to let such rudeness dampen her spirits). If it wasn't for Navy and her uncle Moly, Ratha could have easily turned into a ghost woman too. Or, she wondered, perhaps they were all ghosts at Red Flag. It was hard to tell otherwise, especially considering the sameness of the villagers—the black pajama uniforms, the kramas, the sandals fashioned from old tires that every man and woman now wore.

Yet if she and Navy were ghosts, then they were enlivened ghosts, showing their amusement in the fields by trading cautious smirks and surreptitious glances. But as the work day closed, as evening dimmed the paddies, Navy let herself be heard; she sang for those nearby, letting her gentle voice drift about the rice like a soft breeze. And as long as she didn't sing too loud, as long as the words were from revolutionary songs, comrade Vong allowed her to continue. Then how odd it was seeing the grim soldier mouth the words in the remaining light, his lips parting silently while Navy sang:

*As the summer wind blows,*
*The sun shines on the rice fields,*
*Where workers and peasants move together.*
*Some have sickles in their hands,*
*And some carry pots of water on their heads.*

*Look at the ripe rice,*
*As the wind moves across it in waves.*
*The workers are happy in their hearts,*
*Working nights and mornings,*
*With no fear of getting tired.*

*We are overjoyed to be increasing the output of village and district.*
*Our economy has made great steps forward.*
*We have surpluses now,*
*To put in the granaries,*
*To supply the revolution.*

Though Ratha never mentioned it, she believed Vong was secretly infatuated with her aunt. And if Moly wasn't around, she felt positive the young man would claim Navy for himself. Why wouldn't he? Compared to the other ghost women, her aunt was so alive, possessing a wily vitality that kept her scrawny body moving, her gaunt face bright. It would be better to drown in the river, thought Ratha, than exist with no Navy—better for Uncle Moly to hang himself than go on without her. When Moly returned to Red Flag each night, after working on new irrigation systems intended for doubling rice production, he always sighed with relief at the sight of Navy (she had his bawbaw soup ready and a damp krama so he could clean his face). Then later, while sleeping on the mat in their hut, Moly held his wife from behind, keeping a palm pressed against her stomach until it was time to stir.

But the nights were not only for sleep, and Ratha, sharing the same mat as her aunt and uncle, frequently awoke to the sounds of their lovemaking; she smelled the sweat from their bodies, could almost make out their fervent whispers. Or sometimes before drifting off, Ratha asked Navy about the past, knowing the same story would get told: there had been a place along the Mekong River where rambutan and mangoes thrived, where the fish were plentiful and could easily be caught by hand; in the dry seasons of Navy's childhood, she and her mother and father and brothers and sisters left their clothing on the sandy beach and swam within the cool inlets— a city family vacationing in an abundant paradise, leaving Phnom Penh's rabble for a few days of jungle camping. For breakfast it was sliced mangoes, for lunch and dinner it was coal-fried fish with rambutan sauce. While the boys played soccer all afternoon, the girls fashioned intricate necklaces and bracelets from slender green twigs. "Till I met Moly and bought pretty cloth and perfumes," explained Navy, "those were my most treasured things, that silly jewelry." So Ratha often fell asleep hoarding her aunt's memories, as if the recollections were scarce candies in a sweet shop tin—and how badly she wanted to savor each piece before they were all gone.

## 2.

In Phnom Penh, Navy and Moly's home was Ratha's favorite place to spend an evening. The three of them would often dance in the living room, practicing the tango or the jitterbug while Moly's turntable went through a stack of 45s (her uncle's music collection containing his most valued possessions—four Frank Sinatra imports, two Elvis singles from the Sun era, and a variety of big band and pop music; all of which he purchased from a French expatriate who had once lived down the street). Sometimes, just for a laugh, Moly played the flip side of The Beatles' "Hello Goodbye" single, cracking a grin as "I Am the Walrus" came from the speakers—a song that sounded alien and spooky to Ratha, especially after Moly sped it up on the turntable. And even though none of them really liked the distorted music or understood the lyrics, Navy eventually memorized the chorus, singing in Pidgin English, "I eggman, you eggman, I the wal-us, goo goo goo joob, goo goo goo joob," as Moly tap danced in the middle of the room and laughed. Then, later in the fields at Red Flag, Navy would occasionally hum that flip side for Ratha, whispering at times so her niece could hear, "Goo goo goo joob goo, goo goo joob goo."

But usually on those evenings when Ratha stayed with her aunt and uncle, they would all stay up late and play poker as the government radio station broadcast popular music. Because Moly had been a card dealer in Prince Sihanouk's gambling casino, Ratha found herself learning foreign games (the names of which became known as Moly deftly shuffled the cards: "We'll try Skinball, then I'll show you Trente et quarante, then Slippery Sam"). Or the times Moly was gone all night planting sugar palm trees, Ratha helped Navy prepare the prahoc, a fermented fish paste that her aunt sold every morning from a pushcart. Afterwards, the two would take an evening walk through the crowded markets, where French champagne sold for a much cheaper price than in

Paris and young mothers begged for coins while cradling infants. Then how like sisters they appeared—some seven years apart in age, childless and attractive, both the spitting image of Navy's mother—going arm-in-arm past the bins of produce.

Strolling around the market, inhaling the strange mix of pineapples and fresh fish, it was difficult for Ratha to comprehend her country at war with itself (the rockets and artillery shells hadn't begun to fall on the capital), impossible for her to know that the city would eventually be surrounded by rebel soldiers (Marshal Lon Nol, the chief of state, hadn't flown into exile). "If the Red Khmers get control," her uncle had warned, "we're done for." Yet moving between the food stands, wandering among the elderly and half-naked children and students and married couples, life in Phnom Penh seemed more ceaseless than ever, incapable of any significant change for the better or for the worse. Red Khmers aren't as hardened as this city, Ratha imagined telling Moly. So how can they win?

Still, aside from the capital, the Khmers soon occupied the entire country and the revolution was about to begin, arriving with a swiftness few could fathom. Then one April morning—as Moly hung banners on the front gate proclaiming the Buddhist New Year, and Ratha and Navy were busy cooking a large celebratory meal for the entire family—the government radio station went dead; at noon, a Red Khmer's voice briefly claimed the airwaves, repeating again and again, "We did not come here to talk. We enter Phnom Penh not for negotiation, but as conquerors." After that, all stations fell silent. By nightfall, Ratha and her aunt and uncle were swallowed in the sea of people being herded from the city—the entire population of Phnom Penh, over two million inhabitants, barely going forward and filling the roads that led into the dark countryside. Within forty-eight hours, the capital city was mostly deserted. Stray dogs roamed the barren streets and markets. The front doors of ransacked houses and looted shops remained ajar. Hospitals were empty.

On the afternoon of the Red Khmers entry into Phnom Penh, soldiers had traveled around the boulevards in trucks, saying through loudspeakers that every man, woman, and child was expected to leave the city immediately: "American planes are coming to bomb the city!" For three days only, the revolutionaries had promised, then everyone could return–but Moly, having once served as a captain in the Cambodian army, didn't trust the communists. While walking from the city, his stare fixed on an armed revolutionary who strolled among the packed crowd, he told Navy and Ratha, "They're up to something–this isn't good."

"There's no point in being frightened," said Navy. "The war is over."

All the same, Moly sensed it was safer being a farmer than a city dweller. If asked, it was better to avoid any mention of former military service. So a smart man would make himself a simple farmer, someone visiting the capital in order to shake hands with the victorious Red Khmers. How hard it was convincing his wife and niece that they too had never been residents of Phnom Penh. They had not assembled on the sidewalk, curiously watching the young Khmers move down their street (such bewildered-looking teenagers, thought Ratha, all dressed in black and wearing Ho Chi Minh sandals and Chinese caps–boys and girls draped in grenades and antitank explosives, brandishing AK-47s while remaining oblivious to the people's cheers). No, Moly and Navy and Ratha weren't the ones standing by when the soldiers ordered them out of the house, the ones who said nothing when the New Year's banners were torn from the gate. "We're just farmers," explained Moly. "We've always been farmers. From now on, we support the revolution."

Then how clear it was that they might never return home, how apparent that the capital city was now forsaken (except, as hushed rumors suggested, for the death squads prowling the streets on bicycles and Vespas, seeking out individuals in hiding). So Ratha began pondering the fate of her parents and brothers, half expecting to bump into them somewhere along the road. They mustn't be too far off, she figured, either ahead or behind—because all four were due at Navy and Moly's house for the New Year's feast. Yet while searching the thousands of faces around her, scanning the confused and downcast expressions, she saw no one familiar: no one from her school, no one from her neighborhood, no one from her family.

Though once—before getting placed in the workers' unit destined for Red Flag—Ratha encountered a boy who greatly resembled her younger brother Chath. She had paused a moment to shake pebbles from her sandals when the boy brushed past (same yellow shirt, same short black hair, same oval birthmark on his right calve). So Ratha called his name. "Chath," she said, waving a sandal, "Chath! It's your sister! It's Ratha!" But the boy continued onward without looking back, his small hand held by an older boy she didn't recognize. "It's sister, it's Ratha!" In haste she put on her sandals—"Chath!"—and then ran after him, zigzagging between those stragglers obstructing her way. Catching up with the boy, she touched his shoulder lightly and spoke her brother's name again—only to find herself gazing at a stranger's tired little face, the child's puzzled eyes making it known that a mistake had occurred. Then all she could do was watch him walk away, his plodding body tugged forward by the older boy. When Moly found her, Ratha was weeping at the side of the road. "They're dead," she told him. "Mother and father and Satya and Chath—"

"Don't think like that," he said. "You don't know."

Except Ratha's father was a physician, her mother a high school teacher. Satya, her older brother, was an engineer. She had paid attention as evacuees were questioned at gunpoint, how sometimes a teacher or a technician or a student would get asked their occupation—"An architect? Very good. Your kind is most useful"—and then, without much fuss, the man or woman would leave with a few soldiers, heading into the jungle to help gather fruit (people escorted off in this manner, Ratha observed, rarely returned).

And along the march, while elderly people and children collapsed from exhaustion, impassioned declarations blared continually through bullhorns, stating, "Two thousand years of Cambodian history have ended! The old society is corrupt, this is the new society! No more exploiters and no exploited, no masters and no servants, no rich and no poor! Today your lives are starting at zero! The revolutionary organization will be obeyed! History is dead!" But Ratha wanted to cover her ears as those declarations were announced. Furthermore, the revolutionary songs chanted by the Red Khmers–songs meant to encourage and arouse the weary throng–merely deepened her fears:

*Glittering red blood blankets the earth–*
*Blood given up to liberate the people:*
*The blood of workers, peasants, and intellectuals;*
*The blood of young men, Buddhist monks, and girls.*
*The blood swirls away, and flows upward, gently,*
*Into the sky, turning into a red, revolutionary flag.*

"They'll kill father," she told Navy, "and everyone else and little Chath–"

"Don't worry, Ratha," Navy assured her. "I know they're okay. They're smart like us, they'll keep themselves safe."

So on those first nights at Red Flag, when despair and anxiety wouldn't let Ratha rest, Navy lulled her to sleep with visions of Ratha's parents and brothers (even as Moly nudged his wife, nervously whispering, "Be quiet, you'll get us in trouble, someone might hear"). She would mention exactly what her niece's family was doing at that very minute ("Everyone is eating rice and sipping tea and laughing"), what her parents now looked like ("Boran has flowers in her hair, Kunth is growing a gray beard"), and how well-fed and happy her brothers were ("Satya has Chath in his lap, and Chath keeps poking Satya's belly because he's getting fat").

Then Navy would take Ratha into the future, describing a joyous bus trip back to the city–where everything would be found just as it was left: the table set, the banners on the gate, the New Year's feast ready for grumbling stomachs. Shortly thereafter, one by one, they'd come walking past the front door. Boran followed by Kunth. Satya and his new girlfriend. Little Chath with his gapped-tooth smile and favorite yellow shirt. And soon Ratha sank into sleep with thoughts of that future, halfheartedly believing it was simply a matter of time before they would all eat together and at last celebrate the New Year.

# 3.

Two rainy seasons and two dry seasons passed at Red Flag; in between came two fleeting cool seasons where the temperatures dropped into the lower sixties at night, and the days were clear and breezy for the rice harvest. This reaping weather, while considered chilly by the other workers, felt pleasant to Ratha (her sweat didn't run as much in the fields, the hut was less muggy, sticky, and uncomfortable during sleep). But the evening that Moly vanished, when he failed to return from the irrigation sites, she found herself shivering on the mat and rubbing her arms for warmth as Navy lay nearby. There in the darkness, Ratha couldn't understand how no one had seen her uncle go missing; although someone did remember him sipping water during a break, another vaguely recalled him stacking rocks that afternoon. Yet, until her aunt went hut-to-hut questioning the men, Moly's disappearance was seemingly unheard of by his fellow builders.

"I don't get it," said Navy. "He can't be beside them and then not be beside them without anyone knowing why—just doesn't make sense."

Now it was Ratha's turn to become the assuror, to reach for her aunt with cold fingers and say, "Don't worry. He's okay."

And though her voice sounded uncertain, Navy said, "I know he is. Moly's fine."

"Of course he is. So let's sleep. Tomorrow he'll come home."

"Yes, of course—"

But it was to be a sleepless night for Ratha. Navy shifted fitfully—her body sometimes writhing, her voice gasping out her husband's name—as if, imagined Ratha, she were struggling against an invisible attacker. By morning, everything had changed.

"Moly—?" Navy arose suddenly, glancing around the hut. Then before dressing she stared from the window, watching the irrigation builders leave for work (the men shuffling through Red Flag silently, shovels propped against shoulders). "Comrade, where's my husband?" she asked Old Ouk, who shook his head, refusing to meet her gaze as he walked past the hut. After that, Navy said nothing. She didn't roll up the mat or smile at Ratha, offering her customary, "Good morning." Instead she drew inward, absently buttoning up her shirt, finding her sandals with the same lost eyes Ratha had glimpsed on the ghost women.

"Please, don't lose hope," Ratha begged her. "If no one knows where Moly is, then that's good. He might've fallen asleep by the ditches. Or he could be hiding in the jungle."

Except Ratha knew Moly would never leave the village without them. Nor would he sleep somewhere else (such a transgression, the master Khmers had cautioned, meant summary execution). And while Ratha, for her aunt's sake, attempted a calm surface, she worried that Moly had been found out. Perhaps his onetime service in the Cambodian army became known. Perhaps he revealed this fact to someone he worked alongside with and was turned in: No, she concluded, he was too smart, too careful. Anyway, if it were the case, she and Navy would have gone missing as well. They wouldn't be getting ready for work, or breathing in the crisp morning air. They would be dead. Still, as they headed toward the paddies, Ratha stopped talking too—not because she could no longer comfort her aunt, but because her words, striving so hard to ring positive, came out sounding hopeless.

Then how unbearable it was to be standing in the fields, how disheartening to lift a sickle while stepping amongst fallen rice straw. Navy—her movements uncommonly sluggish, her hand frequently losing its grip on the sickle—offered no grinning side-glances at Ratha, no gleeful whistles when harvesting near her niece; instead she worked in an apparent stupor which eventually caught comrade Vong's attention: for a long while he studied Navy with a furrowed brow—until, finally, he shouldered his rifle and went over to her.

"Are you ill?" asked Vong.

Navy shook her head.

"Would you rather sit and winnow?"

She shook her head again and continued past him, languidly hacking at the rice stalks. Though soon she let the sickle drop. Then she turned, wiping sweat from her neck, and gazed around at the hundred or so women harvesting within the single hectare (each woman toiling on the two meter wide section she was expected to clear before nightfall). If Navy had been anyone else, Vong would have bullied her with warnings of starvation–"You don't work, so you don't eat!"–or he would have taken his rifle butt and nudged her in the spine: "You think you're better than the rest? Get busy!" But as Navy sank down into the mud, sitting so that only her face was visible above the rice, he simply wrinkled his brow once more and frowned.

"That one needs a lesson," said comrade Sleepy Eyes, who had just come from the village with three younger Khmers. He now stood beside Vong at the edge of the paddy, his AK-47 aimed casually in Navy's direction. "She's taking advantage of your kindness, Vong."

The Khmers laughed, and Vong blushed as they all patted him on the back. "No," he told Sleepy Eyes, "it's not like that. She's not well today."

Sleepy Eyes lowered his rifle. "I'm sure," he said, smiling to himself.

Then the group moved closer together while Vong passed out cigarettes. A moment later, they were consumed by a gray haze which streamed from their mouths and nostrils, the smoke dissolving in the breeze along with their hushed conversation.

Important business, thought Ratha. She could see her aunt staring at the men without expression, just penetrating eyes and narrowed lips. But Ratha wanted to tell her that Vong was okay–she had seen him give Sleepy Eyes and the young Khmers cigarettes after they questioned Navy's idleness, had even struck the match himself, gently placing a hand on each man's shoulder when bringing the flame near their chins.

"Ratha," Vong suddenly yelled, "go fetch the water! Be fast!" He pointed toward the ground with his cigarette, indicating the two buckets by his feet. And for some reason Sleepy Eyes began chuckling, his lazy stare following Ratha as she trudged from the paddy. Setting her sickle aside, she bent and reached for the buckets, only to feel ash sprinkle across the top of her head.

"Sorry," said Sleepy Eyes, brushing the ash from her hair. "I didn't see you there, Melt Ear."

Then everyone burst out laughing, including comrade Vong.

But Ratha simply grinned as she stood upright. She nodded respectfully at the men, about-faced and headed for the jungle. Within seconds she was on the slender path, engulfed in the shade of the palm trees, where already Sleepy Eyes and his joke seemed like a faraway memory. Then how she tried to forget everything—Moly's disappearance, her aunt's melancholy, the fields of rice that needed harvesting.

Better yet, Ratha could pretend the jungle was her own garden, the expansive back yard of her estate home—and now she hurried to meet Vannah, a handsome boy she had privately admired in high school. Today they would rendezvous at the river and fall into each other's arms, eventually removing their clothing on the warm sand. So there upon the shore, she reclined and thought of Vannah (he had never made fun of her ear, had never joined in on the teasing; he was, imagined Ratha, the finest of all boys). And even though Vong had told her to be quick with the buckets, she knew he was just showing off in front of Sleepy Eyes. Anyway, she never stayed gone long—she always had enough time to enjoy Vannah and the rush of the river and the stillness of the jungle.

"A bullet then—?"

"Not worth a bullet."

"No, not worth wasting a shot—"

"I agree, of course."

It was Sleepy Eyes and his men, talking as they ambled down the path, their loud voices preceding them and disrupting Ratha's tranquil garden. Fearing what they might do or say when finding her alone, she scrambled from the bank with the empty buckets. Then concealing herself behind tall bamboos, she saw the men file past, their sandals clomping while they spoke (someone was saying that Vong had promised a feast of meatballs and fried rice and corn liquor on his wedding day, another joked about their comrade's future bride still having a husband). "Poor man," said Sleepy Eyes, "his wife ends up with tiny Vong—poor woman too, she'll be sleeping with him—"

All the men laughed, and as the foursome reached the river and began walking southward along the bank, one of them said, "She isn't so great anyway. I think we're doing Moly a favor—"

Only later did Ratha wish she hadn't heard her uncle's name mentioned; she wished her ears had been covered, because then she wouldn't have followed. Pushing through the thick overgrowth, spying on them from the jungle, she watched the men stoop to take a large stone off the shore—a methodical process in which a chosen stone would often get cast aside for one that fit more snugly in a fist. Then they proceeded onward, traveling several yards to where the river veered west and the bank stretched further outward and a solitary palm tree grew upon the beach.

For a moment it appeared that the men had spotted Ratha; they gathered on one side of the big tree, stones in hand, and seemingly gazed toward the jungle. Though from Ratha's vantage point—crouched nearby amidst the thick foliage, the tree standing between herself and the men—she realized it was something else that now held their attention, something right in front of them. Rubbing the nape of his neck, Sleepy Eyes shook his head, saying, "Let's get this over with." How grave their faces suddenly looked, how sullen; so without saying a word, each man stepped forward and hurled his stone at the trunk—then, after all four had pitched their stones, they spread out across the bank, silently heading downstream with Sleepy Eyes leading the way.

When they had receded from sight, Ratha left her hiding place and ventured across the beach. At first she noticed the rope tied twice about the wide trunk, the four stones dotting the sand—next, as she came around the tree, the dangling left arm, the curled fingers and bleeding forearm; finally, the inert and naked body sagging against the trunk, a dead man kept upright by the rope crisscrossing his bruised chest. Someone had crammed a banana deep into his throat, and his head was so badly crushed and swollen and bloodied that Ratha couldn't discern his features. But perhaps it was Moly, though Ratha told herself otherwise. "No," she said under her breath, "no, no—" Turning and walking swiftly away, she didn't look back. Nor did she go fetch the buckets. Instead she ran toward Red Flag, taking a shortcut through the dark jungle—bamboo whapping her arms and chest, vines scratching her ankles—thinking all the while that nothing had been seen at the lone palm tree, nothing save a few dirty stones. Yet her hands were trembling, her stomach felt uneasy. And although she had trouble inhaling, she wouldn't allow herself to stop moving—not until reaching the rice paddy, not until she could see her aunt and the clear sky.

But when Ratha returned to the fields, Vong was waiting for her with clenched fists: "Where have you been? Where's the water?" Just then Ratha remembered leaving the buckets in the bamboo, except she was too winded to explain anything. Scanning the paddy, her eyes darting from woman to woman, she couldn't find Navy. "What's wrong with you?" he said, slapping her forehead. "You're useless today! You both are!" Then—because she hadn't flinched while being struck, because she ignored him and continued searching the paddy—he looked puzzled. "Ratha, go home," he said, his tone lessening a bit. "Go take care of Navy."

Go take care of Navy.

Those words made her breathe easier. She nodded at Vong, relieved to know her aunt hadn't vanished like Moly.

Leaving the paddy, she sensed the women glaring at her with envy, their sickles pausing as she wandered by (little bitch Melt Ear, she imagined them thinking, always getting favors from comrade Vong). Then slowly she moved through the fields east of Red Flag, trying her best to forget the big tree and the body and the sting of Vong's hand. Anyway, the weather was perfect, very breezy and mild. So she would be glad that her day was finished, happy that she was going home early. She would tell Navy that she had rested at the river and daydreamed of Vannah again. "He kissed me in my garden," she would say. "It was almost real."

But all ruminations about Vannah faded within the hut. Navy lay motionless on the mat, her eyes open and staring up at the roof that Moly had made from banana tree strips. When Ratha said her name, Navy didn't respond. Furthermore, her aunt was still dressed for the fields, her clothes and sandals muddy. So Ratha wet a krama, then she wiped Navy's face and hands and ankles and feet. Afterwards, she sat beside the mat, studying her aunt's vacant face, hoping to catch some glimpse of the old Navy, that smiling woman who just yesterday had sung during the harvest.

Sometime later Vong arrived with a large covered bowl of steaming rice: "You can have some, Ratha, if you give me and your aunt a few minutes." He held his cap in one hand, the bowl in the other; his hair was combed and his face washed. Then how much younger he appeared, how handsome–the hardness he mustered in the fields was now replaced by an apparent softness, a slight tremble in his voice as he spoke. "I won't be long," he told Ratha, "then you can eat." Saying nothing, she went outside and sat in front of the hut.

Already the sun was setting. A dusty haze hung over the fields and village, and an orange sky spread above the jungle. The air smelled like compost. On the far end of the street, plodding along with their tools, came the irrigation builders (the same men, observed Ratha, minus one). Just then a pang seized her stomach, making her think: Hopefully Navy won't eat it all, hopefully Vong will bring dinner every night. But no sooner had Ratha thought this when her aunt yelled, "Never! I will never–!"

A long silence followed, broken by the sounds of Vong's sandals thudding from the hut. He stopped next to Ratha without looking at her. Finally, he sighed and put his cap on, shaking his head regretfully as he went forward into the evening. If her stomach hadn't been hurting, if she wasn't in such a hurry to go inside and lift the cover from the bowl, Ratha might have called after him, saying, "I know what happened, comrade. I understand everything." Of course, as Moly had always warned her, some things were best left unsaid. Some things were best packed away and forgotten.

"Bastard," Ratha heard Navy mutter when entering the hut. "The bastard–"

Her aunt was hunched over on the mat, legs crossed, and wept while staring at Vong's offering. The cover had been removed, sending steam up into Navy's tear-streaked face. Immediately Ratha took the bowl and, using her fingers, began shoveling rice into her mouth. She ate until her stomach felt satiated, grateful for a dinner that wasn't bawbaw soup. Then she set the bowl near Navy's feet, saying, "There's plenty, go on. You must eat." But her aunt wouldn't take it; she kicked the bowl across the floor and continued crying.

"Bastard–"

Ratha scrambled about on her hands and knees, collecting the scattered clumps, blowing dirt from the rice as she put it back into the bowl. Eventually, she went to Navy, easing her aunt to the mat. Then she stroked Navy's hair past nightfall, combing it with her fingertips. When the crying ceased, when it seemed her aunt had calmed, Ratha asked her for a story: "Please, tell me of the Mekong, about Grandpa and Mother and your twig bracelets." But Navy didn't speak, nor did she move; her breathing had become deeper, and Ratha suspected she had fallen asleep.

So there in the quiet of the hut, Ratha began whispering in her aunt's ear. "Soon," she said, before mentioning the joyous bus ride back to the capital, where victory banners would be hung over the boulevards and firecrackers would spin in the air. "Soon," she repeated, then described the feast that would be eaten (Uncle Moly would tell his jokes at the table, afterwards Navy would sing her favorite songs). How thankful everyone would be for having survived—Boran and Kunth, Satya and his new girlfriend, little Chath. Soon everything would be as it had once been. "Soon—"

Then Ratha yawned. She couldn't think of anything else to say. Holding Navy, pressing a hand against her aunt's belly, she saw the full moon through a crack in the roof, brightening the darkness inside the hut; light spilled down across a wall and engulfed a white T-shirt on the floor. It was Moly's nightshirt, and touched by the radiance of the moon, every fiber gleamed, vibrant and luminous.

Ratha closed her eyes. Beyond the village, she imagined, the fields were glowing, and the fallen rice straw shimmered in the mud; it would be like that throughout the night. But tomorrow the harvest would continue—there was always work to get done. Tomorrow she would carry the buckets again. In the morning, Vong would arise with Navy on his mind. Perhaps he would bring more rice in the evening. And if it weren't for her ear, Ratha thought while drifting off, Vong would have wanted her as a bride instead of Navy—and then Moly's nightshirt wouldn't be crumpled on the floor. "Yes," she mumbled, "Yes—" Then, at last, she sank into the carelessness of sleep.

# 4.

At dawn Ratha awoke to find herself alone in the hut. Climbing from the mat, she said her aunt's name while glancing about, and quickly noticed two things: Moly's nightshirt had been folded neatly; the last of Vong's rice had been eaten and the bowl sat empty near Navy's side of the mat. Then Ratha had a terrible thought: perhaps her aunt had run off, perhaps she had left Red Flag in the middle of the night and went searching for Moly. So Ratha didn't bother to wash her face or don her krama. She paused only to slip on her sandals, button her shirt, and then ran from the hut toward the fields.

If she hadn't spotted the solitary figure working in a paddy, hadn't heard the distant humming of Navy's voice (something vaguely familiar, something Moly had once played on his stereo–that strange recording that made everyone laugh), Ratha would have kept running. She would have continued onward, going deep into the jungle to look for her aunt. But there was Navy, hacking with her sickle in the early morning light, hard at work before the others had arrived–behind her lay a vast amount of cut rice, at least a one meter wide section. When Ratha began wading through the mud, Navy looked up and smiled, her lips pursed and humming as Ratha asked, "What are you doing? I was scared–"

"No time for talk," said Navy, playfully winking an eye. "Make yourself busy." She aimed her sickle, pointing it past her niece and in the direction of the Red Flag road. "You don't want to anger Smiley."

Ratha turned and saw Vong leading the women down to the fields. Then soon it became obvious to all: while the village slept, Navy was doing the harvesting of three women. What funny faces, thought Ratha. What surprise. As the others started fanning out into the paddies, she wanted to laugh at Vong's cocked eyebrow, at Old Gen's scornful head shaking, at Old Chanrithy's distraught huffing and sighing.

"Get working!" Vong shouted the inevitable order, adding, "Let this hard work be an example to you all! No break until the rest of you finish one meter!"

At that moment Ratha realized she had forgotten her sickle inside the hut. Casting her eyes downward, she went over to Vong and said, "I'm sorry, I've left my sickle."

"Where—?" he asked, his stare still fixed on the large section that had been cleared by dawn.

"At home."

And Vong—somewhat oblivious to Ratha's words, listening instead to her aunt's faint humming—now studied Navy as she stood nearby wiping sweat from her chin. "Is she okay today?" he said. "Is she better?"

"Yes, much better," said Ratha. "Thank you for the rice—it helped, I'm sure."

Vong nodded, reaching into a pocket for a cigarette. "So— you lost your sickle?"

"I know where it is. I just left it. I can get it and be right back—"

"Comrade," said Navy, "she can use mine for a while. I deserve a rest." She had trudged from the paddy and was approaching them with her sickle held out in offering.

"Yes, of course," said Vong, lighting his cigarette and puffing smoke. "You've done an amazing job this morning, Navy—" He returned Navy's smile even as she suddenly lurched at him and swung the sickle into his neck, the blade severing his jugular, slicing to his throat. The cigarette fell, and blood began spurting across the blade. But, with the color leaving his face, Vong didn't look frightened. He didn't reach for his rifle or attempt to dislodge the sickle. He simply staggered a step, blinking his eyes dumbly, and continued smiling—seemingly unaware of the mess that gushed from his neck, drenching his entire shirt, spreading into the front of his pants. Then it was like large invisible hands were pushing him down, bringing him to his knees, making it easy for Navy to finish the job; she kicked at his forehead, sending him backwards—where he shuddered on the ground, twitching his feet, opening his mouth while struggling to speak (his voice silenced behind a thick red bubble that oozed from his mouth and popped without a sound).

But Ratha, unable to look away, couldn't bring herself to help him. Like a fish trying to breathe, she thought. And in the seconds following his death she felt very little, other than some sadness for the rice dinner she wouldn't get that night. "We'll starve for this," she told Navy.

"No," said Navy, who had crouched beside the body. She tugged Vong's rifle off his shoulder and held it in both hands. Then she frowned, as if the consequences of her actions were beginning to settle in. "Go home," she eventually said. "Get out of here." She picked Vong's cigarette from the ground, placed it between her lips, inhaling.

"Navy–?"

"Go home, please."

The women had started walking slowly from the paddies, wandering toward the palm trees at the edge of the jungle; for they had witnessed everything, had done nothing to save Vong, and now were escaping the crime's immediate proximity. Like the women, Ratha didn't head for Red Flag, nor did she stay by her aunt's side. Instead she joined the others, going forward to stand among them in the shade of the trees. But no one spoke or showed any concern for what had happened; there was no questioning in their eyes when staring back, watching Navy cradle Vong's rifle and flick ash to mud mixed with rice straw and blood. Then how discordant Navy's voice sounded as she began singing, uttering such incomprehensible words: "I eggman, you eggman, I the walrus, goo goo goo joob, goo goo goo joob–"

Just then, believed Ratha, her aunt's strange language summoned the wind, causing a sharp gust to ripple through the rice. Soon Navy's song became lost in the breeze, her voice no longer reaching the women. Still, Ratha could see her aunt's mouth moving, could imagine the words slipping over her tongue–goo goo goo joob goo–and she knew without a doubt that the earth would eventually shake with thunder and take

Navy's breath away; a tempest would finally rain upon the fields, consuming the mud and her aunt and possibly everyone else. But, like the others, all she could do was remain sheltered and wait—even though the storm had yet to commence and Navy sang below a clear blue sky and comrade Vong's inert eyes gazed upward at the heavens—*I the wal-us, you eggman, goo goo*—as if he too were somehow entranced by what was surely a blessed and liberating incantation.

# Wormwood

## 1.

To hear my mother tell the story years later–everything happened as if in a strange fable. I was there, of course, but, being six at the time, recall almost nothing of that Friday evening when the sky suddenly glowed. She has told the tale so many times, though, I can imagine it quite well: beyond the street where we lived, catherine wheels of fire, like eruptions from a massive Roman candle, exploded in the distance with a dull roar.

It was my father who called us to view the spectacle. He was smoking in the backyard, talking with our elderly neighbor Mr. Ozhegov, and noticed a brilliant flash reflected in Ozhegov's glasses, an instantaneous expression of wonder on the man's face.

"Oh my," Mr. Ozhegov uttered.

When my father turned, lifting his chin upward, he found himself smiling at the red and orange streaks bursting against twilight. Then, in his nervous and customarily polite manner, he shouted for us, saying, "Nina, Valentin, please come quick, it's fantastic!" And my mother, still a young woman with a soft, haughty face, grabbed my hand in the kitchen and dragged me outside in tow.

In the backyard, my father hoisted me to his bent shoulders, exclaiming, "Amazing," as another pinwheel of flames appeared. "So amazing!"

My mother, her fingers wet from washing dinner plates, covered her mouth in astonishment. Mr. Ozhegov applauded with delight.

For my parents and Mr. Ozhegov, perhaps for me too, something verging on the supernatural occurred in the sky that evening. No natural explanation presented itself, other than the idea that elaborate fireworks were being tested for the upcoming May Day festival. But soon the mystifying stars faded, leaving only thick trails of vapor, which every so often ignited with flames.

Eventually, my mother and I returned inside, and she undressed me for bed. "If we're lucky, Valentin," she said, "maybe the lights will visit tomorrow evening." And when she and my father went to bed that night, she told him the same thing.

The following day brought clear skies. Spring came disguised as summer, far from mild, hot. It was Saturday, and the families in the neighborhood left their homes to enjoy the weather. My father, a cigarette fixed between his lips, busied himself in his garden, where he tended blue crocus petals and pushed away withered leaves. My mother swept dust from the front porch, stopping for a while to chat with Mrs. Ozhegov, a frail woman who had slept through the previous evening's excitement. Though everyone on the street went about their weekend routines like nothing in the world had happened, the subject of the mysterious light show was mentioned by each neighbor that wandered past our house. Yet it seemed no one, including my parents, considered the nuclear power plant. And that evening, most of the people in Chernobyl went outside to gaze at the sky. But, aside from a few dim flare ups on the horizon, the phenomenon wasn't repeated.

Then on Sunday morning, Mr. Ozhegov—wearing slippers and a yellow bathrobe—knocked on our front door. When my father answered, he noticed the old man's blanched face, his freckled hands in fists at his sides, his crooked fingers methodically rubbing the palms.

"Is Mrs. Ozhegov okay?" my father asked.

"Yes," said Mr. Ozhegov, "she's fine. May I come in?"

"Of course."

Sitting in the living room, Mr. Ozhegov told my parents he had just heard from his nephew, a technician who lived in Prypiat, the village where workers assigned to the power plant lived with their families.

"There's been a crack at the reactor," he explained, "but my nephew thinks it's not serious. He says they're fixing it, but he wanted me to know. And I want you to know."

"Thank you," my father said.

"Would you like breakfast?" my mother calmly asked Mr. Ozhegov. But in her mind she was thinking of the wondrous fire display on Friday. She sat with her hands folded, wringing her apron, and glanced at Mr. Ozhegov's brown slippers, which had large holes in them, exposing the big toe on each foot.

"No," said Mr. Ozhegov. "I should be going, I think."

"Don't worry," my father said. "The size of the crack must be limited, otherwise we would've heard."

"Yes," said Mr. Ozhegov, "I suspect so. I'm sure you're right."

In my mother's story, she remembered couples getting married in Chernobyl that Sunday. Classical music played from a radio placed under an open window. Friends got drunk together. A woman on our block gave birth to a baby girl. But it was a Sunday warmed by a relentless sun, veiled in something without taste and texture, like an invisible rime covering the city.

On Monday, buses carrying inhabitants from Prypiat moved through Chernobyl at dawn. The evacuations had begun. But in our neighborhood, the signs of disaster were unapparent. Men and women headed to work in their usual slowness. As a child, I was no different: being a scraggly little boy in appearance, I dressed myself in the same azure-colored pants and black pullover shirt I always wore for classes. And while those buses rattled near our street, ancient Russian somnolence, possibly grounded in fatalism, kept all our parents believing the irreversible hadn't taken place.

That day, my mother said I went to school, and then, because the teachers were gone, returned home right away. But, for whatever reason, I retained a clear memory of my classmates and me assembled in the school gymnasium, where the faculty stood before us, explaining that everyone would be sent home early. Then we were told to stay indoors, wash our hair, and change clothes.

"Your parents must do the same," said one teacher, a rather stern man with wire glasses and a bald head. "Tell your mothers to shut the windows, to wipe all shoes with a wet rag."

"We're putting you in charge of your parents," said another teacher, smiling. "They must clean the furniture and floors with a damp duster, okay?"

The word radioactivity was never spoken.

When I came through the front door, my mother was in the entryway donning a rose-patterned scarf. She wore bright, dusky stockings on her fleshy legs. Her purse hung from a shoulder.

"What are you doing here?" she said to me, incredulous. "Why aren't you at school?"

"I'm supposed to wash my hair."

Then I explained, as best I could, what the teachers had said about not leaving the house. "And you must clean everything," I added. "And wash your hair too, and put on new clothes. I'm in charge!"

"Nonsense," my mother said, and she took my wrist, pulling me outside with her.

It was a short walk to my school, less than a block, made

quicker by my mother's rapid gait. But when we arrived, the playground was deserted, the school gate locked. She released her hold on my wrist, saying, "Where'd they go, Valentin?"

I shrugged. "I don't know. They wanted us to leave."

"Then you'll go to the market with me," she said.

But she didn't move for a while. Instead, she remained in front of the school gate, peering beyond the metal bars at the empty white-brick building, which was dark and ominous inside.

She reached under her scarf, touching her auburn hair, half whispering, "No, it isn't a good day for shopping." Then she examined her fingertips.

Later, we stopped at a small park near our house. My mother moved around the green fir trees, checking the smooth circular leaf scars for clues of devastation. She knelt to scrutinize wild mushrooms; a few, she thought, seemed dusted with a chalky film.

"Keep your mouth shut until we get home," she told me.

Then she removed her scarf, clutching it to her lips and nose. As we went from the park, she walked alongside me with a hand clamped over my mouth—a strange apparition indeed, but one lacking witness. My mother and I passed no one. Our street already felt dead.

When we entered the house, the TV blared from the living room. My mother yelled for my father. "Fedor," she said, throwing the scarf down in the entryway, "is that you?"

"Yes," he replied, his voice sounding alarmed. "Where were you? I was afraid you'd gone! They closed the factory and sent us home!"

"Come here," my mother said, unbuttoning her shirt. Then to me she went, "Undress."

My father strode into the entryway wearing just his underwear.

"It's much worse than I imagined," he said, unsurprised at the sight of us removing our clothes. "The power station blew up! Block number 4 exploded! Misha at work heard. There's not a damn word on TV. Nothing! But last night Misha heard a foreign radio broadcast. Can you believe it? The radiation level has gone straight out the roof!" An evacuation of Chernobyl was imminent, he explained, and all the workers at his factory were instructed to get their families ready. "But I thought you'd left," he said, an expression of sadness filling his ruddy face. "The Ozhegovs have gone to Kiev. People are beginning to leave."

"Don't be stupid," my mother said, dropping her blouse. "I wouldn't go without you."

My mother's story usually ended here: she had my father remove his underwear. Then she pushed our clothing into one big pile by the front door. It was then that my parents looked at each other, terrified, and embraced. Only at that moment, my mother said, did she and my father sense catastrophe. But standing naked beside them, I was blissfully unaware. School had ended early, and I was in charge.

"Now we wash our hair," I said.

And that's what we did.

# 2.

In the long, shaky shadow of glasnost and perestroika, I turned sixteen on a collective farm near Staroye Sharnye, a village nestled in the Ukrainian forest region. My parents had come there to live with my mother's mother, Olya, who, because of her status as a Soviet district member's widow, helped manage the collective. Of the twenty white houses built on the farm—most being traditional wooden cottages—the home we shared with Olya was the largest (made from kiln-fired bricks, surrounded by apple and cherry trees). From my bedroom window, I viewed cattle grazing across lush pastures, and mist often drifted among the backwoods, which stretched as far as the eye could see.

But past the forest was the village Novoye Sharnye, which stretched along the banks of the river Uzh. "That lifeless place," Grandmother called it. And even though it was forbidden, I once hiked the road to Novoye Sharnye, picking blackberries en route, eventually finding myself stopped before a high barbed-wire fence. The village existed a hundred meters away; its main artery, a narrow asphalt thoroughfare, severed by metal coils. A placard nailed on the fence proclaimed: STOP! NO ENTRY! DANGER OF DEATH!

In the distance, cottage rooftops poked above apple trees. An autumn fragrance, sweet and earthy, carried from a meadow beyond the barricade. Golden leaves littered the road. But natural beauty can be deceptive.

My father explained it this way: "Two wells. One right by the other. Except one is deeper, much deeper. The water in that well is safer to drink. But how could you tell by looking?"

At the collective, all the children were taught to avoid the woods, to always stay on the roads. We were told that Novoye Sharnye was off limits. Since the power station in Chernobyl exploded, the village no longer thrived. It was deserted. The river, it was said, had contaminated everything; a fate shared by three other villages in the area—

Dolgiy Less, Motyli, and Omelniki.

Turning about-face on the road, I dipped into my paper bag of blackberries and brought a handful to my mouth. The dark juice dribbled past my lips, dripped to my shoes, the asphalt. Drinking from a deeper well, I thought. Sunlight cascaded out of a blue sky, somehow sharpening the calmness encompassing me.

That night, as we ate dinner, I asked Grandmother, "Where'd everyone in Novoye Sharnye go?"

"Why do you care?" my mother said.

"Scattered in the wind, I suspect," my father said, "like us."

Grandmother looked up from her plate of potatoes, chewing. Her gaze lingered on my face, then she put her fork aside.

"No," she replied, "most evacuated to Mirni, at the edge of the district. It's still no better there than where they were. Mirni had a pesticide depot for crop spraying airplanes. The air is unbreathable. Pesticide covers the ground. I heard this woman there tore up her floorboards–ridiculous–just so she could throw the poisoned dirt underneath out the window."

"Valentin, they don't have flies in Mirni," my father said, "because everything smells like ammonia."

"That's not true," my mother said. "Your father is lying."

"It's true," Grandmother said. "I've heard this."

"Poor Novoye Sharnye," I said, imagining displaced villagers packed in buses, lorries following behind with pigs, cattle, poultry, and farm machinery. Ten years earlier, my parents and I had traveled in such a caravan when fleeing Chernobyl. But because the drivers were unfamiliar with the district, we reached the collective two days late. The buses got lost on back roads, and spring floods delayed the caravan further; at several places, pontoon bridges were constructed in order to move the buses over bloated rivers.

The night we arrived at Grandmother's home, she told my parents, "It's all prophecy." And she had proof. Revelations, Chapter 8, Verses 10, 11: "And the third angel sounded, and there fell a great star from heaven, burning as it were a lamp, and it fell upon the third part of the rivers, and upon the fountains of waters.

"And the name of the star is called Wormwood: and the third part of the waters became wormwood; and many men died of the waters, because they were made bitter."

It was hard to dispute such prophecy, made tougher by the fact that the Chernobyl power station stood beside the Prypiat River's confluence with the rivers Dnieper and Uzh.

There was also *The Dictionary of the Russian Language*, which, in order to illustrate her belief, Grandmother showed my father, an atheist and skeptic.

"See there," she said, pushing the dictionary at him, "I circled it in ink." Then, reciting from memory, she spoke the definition. "Chernobylnik: a variety of absinthe—wormwood—with a red-brown or deep purple stem."

"I know what it means," my father told her.

"The end is close, Fedor," she said, "but at least we're here as a family."

"The end might be near," my father retorted, "but not because of God."

So our village was fated. Perfectly good homes were boarded shut. The cemetery, like the village pathways, was overgrown with weeds. In an effort to revitalize areas once deemed "without a future," the State sent eight builders to construct a nursery school in Staroye Sharnye. But, as construction dragged on and on, the locals began questioning the builders.

"What's this school for?" I remember Grandmother asking. "How many small children live in the village? Almost none! There are not enough girls, but enough young men. Perhaps someday they can use it as an old folks' home!"

Soon the builders suffered from headaches and fatigue, blaming their conditions on high radiation levels. In time, they left. The nursery school, finally completed, remained abandoned.

Yet on the collective we felt safe. A monthly allowance, thirty lousy roubles, was allocated for every farm family.

"That's one extra rouble a day," my father complained. "A coffin allowance," he called it.

Still, the added income helped some. After several months of saving, we made the long drive to Kiev, buying clothes, matches, and books from the black marketers who operated at the shopper's square. Twice a week we ate chicken.

With the coffin allowance, my mother purchased a pair of American 501 jeans for my fifteenth birthday. And on my sixteenth birthday, I received two gifts, one from my parents, and one from Grandmother. The presents, both wrapped in brocaded gold lamé, were brought to me as I dressed that morning. My parents and Grandmother crowded into my room. Grandmother placed a bowl of cherries, mushrooms, and edible roots on the dresser. "Just for you," she said, smiling. My parents each carried a gift.

"This is from Olya," my father said, handing me Grandmother's small, rectangular present, which almost fit in my open palm.

Standing shirtless beside my bed, I carefully untied the lamé, letting the fabric fall around my hand, and examined the contents—a cassette tape with Grandmother's handwriting on the label: *Shostakovich's Eighth & Thirteenth Symphonies.*

"It was a chore getting it copied for you," Grandmother said, "but I thought you'd enjoy it. So somber though. Like you, Valentin."

"Thank you," I said, nonplused by the fact that there wasn't a tape player in the house.

"Guess what we got you," my father suggested.

Setting Grandmother's gift on the bed, I gazed at my mother in anticipation. "I think I already know."

"It's ruined if you already know," my mother said. Then she gave me the slightly larger second present. Being less careful, I removed the lamé with wild fingers, finding a Kino 3000 portable cassette player and headphones underneath.

"What was the cost?" I asked, knowing that black-market models from China were sold at a high price in Kiev. "This is too much."

My parents and Grandmother laughed.

"Too much?" my father said. "Should we return it?"

"No," I replied, elated. "No way."

In two days, I went through three packs of batteries, and rarely did the headphones leave my ears. With a hand deep in my American jeans, the other grasping the cassette player, I wandered the district roads alone while Shostakovich's music transformed my thoughts, like the way I perceived the countryside. The forests, moss covered fir trees and rocks, the blue cupolas on the village church in Staroye Sharnye—all of it became laced with extended minor thirds, brass rumbling, grim oboes, violins struggling in a maelstrom. Tranquillity and chaos merged, nothing was as it seemed.

The week following my birthday, I feigned illness so I wouldn't have to attend school, or help my father draw milk from the cows. Instead, I stayed in my bedroom, headphones in place, sketching on a notepad. The thirteenth symphony was brutal history, and I reported the events with colored pens. Marksmen pointing their rifles. Naked Jews in Kiev. Blood spurting from screaming mouths. "My symphonies are tombstones," Shostakovich had once said.

When my mother saw my drawings, she felt my forehead, saying, "We'll visit Doctor Kavun tomorrow."

"I'm feeling better," I said.

"I don't think you are."

Playing sick had its consequences. At the collective school, there were four pre-schoolers, twenty-two children aged six to fourteen, two aged fifteen and sixteen. I was the oldest. The primary school in Staroye Sharnye closed when the radiation level registered 1.5 milliroentgens. A new school was set up on the farm, where the radiation in the earth was 1.1 milliroentgens and 0.6 in the water. When the collective school opened, the government specialists who made the measurements told our parents, "It won't kill them, but if the children show any signs of bad health, Doctor Kavun in Kiev will see them. He's assigned to your village."

It was a long way to go for medical attention. "You need rest," my mother said. "We're leaving early."

That evening, my cassette player wavered, slowed, then began eating. I listened, horrified, as the Thirteenth Symphony was mangled, irrevocably twisted in the gears of the machine. In frustration, I freed Shostakovich with scissors, cutting the magnetic ribbon in three places, but it was like saving a bird without wings. So I hurled the tape at the wall, yelling, "There's no hope!" And settling into bed, my thoughts suddenly seemed arid–my room a solitary, colorless place.

In a fluorescent-lit room at the Ukrainian Child Health Clinic, I sat naked on an examining table–long legs dangling off one end, thin hands folded across my crotch–while Dr. Kavun pressed his fingertips on my throat. Keeping his head erect and stooping over me with a very pale face, he was a squat, middle-aged man, much shorter than my mother, who stood behind him in her russet-colored dress.

"Does that hurt? Is it tender?" he said in a forced, somewhat militaristic tone.

"No," I replied.

His fingertips went to my abdomen.

"Any nausea? Vomiting and diarrhea?"

"No."

"Fatigue? Chills alternating with fever?"

"No, I don't think so."

He leaned in, putting a palm on my slender rib cage, the other between my shoulder blades.

"Shortness of breath?"

"No."

"Good," Dr. Kavun said, removing his palms. "Look down, please."

I glanced at my hands, which were cupped among curly pubes. He massaged my scalp for a moment, feeling within the coarse dark muss.

"There's no hair loss that I can see." Then he turned toward my mother. "He's fine," he told her. "Perhaps a bug of some sort, but it's gone. He's ready for school again, I think."

"He said he was better," my mother said, "but you never know."

"Yes, well, the boy's healthy." Dr. Kavun patted my knee, and I looked up. "Get dressed," he said. "You're not going to the Youth Guard Hospital today."

"I shouldn't think so!" my mother said, not amused by the doctor's remark. "What a terrible thing to say!"

"I'm sorry," Dr. Kavun said, at once ashamed and flustered. "It came out wrong. I didn't mean it that way."

Later, as I walked with my mother from the health clinic, she said, "That man should watch his mouth. Just because we live in the country, he doesn't think we understand anything."

Perhaps it was true. Still, everyone on the collective was aware of the Youth Guard Hospital in Odessa, a place where children with severe radiation sickness were sent. At school we were taught that radioactive substances, until they were expelled or decayed, irradiated internal organs. Our teacher explained that some particles attached to specific body parts— ruthenium joined the lungs, iodine-131 appeared in the thyroid gland, strontium and plutonium wedded the bones, and barium and moledium mated with the lower large intestines. In the case of Mikhail Ivanovna Kovalyeva, a classmate who was always in trouble for falling asleep during lectures, his lymphatic glands became swollen. By the time Mikhail arrived at the Youth Guard Hospital, he was almost blind. In a month he was dead. With him in mind, there was a joke we older students shared with the younger ones, "If you don't behave, they'll send you to Odessa. Pay attention."

After we left the health clinic, my mother and I strolled on Kiev's busy sidewalks. It was springtime, renewal floated in the air. We found ourselves at the shopper's square, a shaded marketplace, calm and spacious, where my mother explored the stands for corned beef and condensed milk. A young woman pushing a freeze-box was hawking ice cream, but there was little bustle or crowding. Even the ice cream peddler's shouts were kept at a minimum. I wandered off on my own, passing stalls that sold sandwiches and pastries, hoping to find a vendor offering cassettes, or, in the very least, a head-cleaner for my Kino 3000. Either way it didn't matter much. I had no money.

But that afternoon I got lucky. I met a vendor with long gray sideburns, and was surprised by the greasy mane piled back on his head. And though Andrei Yurovsky was about as old as my father, his black jeans and leather jacket made him seem younger. Happening upon his music stand, where a framed black-and-white poster of a gyrating Elvis Presley hung, I searched in vain for Shostakovich. Andrei watched stoically, arms crossed, as I scanned the homemade cassettes lining the countertop: *Radio Free Ukraine, R 'n' B Rave-up, Sock-Hop Shakeout, Rock-a-billy All-night!* I lifted a cassette, but the artists—with names like Little Jimmy Dickens, Sleepy Labeef, Sid King & The Five Strings—were all incomprehensible.

"It's good stuff," he finally said. "What are you looking for?"

"I'm not sure," I said. "I don't know any of this."

"Best kept secret in Kiev, all hard-to-find recordings from America. You can't go wrong. Pick one."

"I wanted a head-cleaner, actually. I can't afford anything now."

"Sure," Andrei said, "no problem. It's been a good day, so just take one. If you like it, pay me if you can. If you don't, return it. I trust you. Believe me, I'm doing you a favor."

"That's okay, really."

"Don't be shy. Go ahead, kid."

So after much consideration, my choice was *Rockabilly Stars & Bars,* featuring The King, Carl Perkins, & Mr. Scotty Moore. And Andrei gave me an issue of *Memphis, Russia,* a flimsy photocopied fanzine which he wrote and edited himself.

"It'll fill you in on everything," he told me. "I'm usually here on Thursdays, but if you got questions, the last page has my address."

That evening, the roadway from Kiev to Staroye Sharnye was shrouded by flowering forests. Along the way, we pulled over and got out of Grandmother's Volga. A bright moon shone clearly. Stars glittered overhead, and we spotted the Great Bear, a transparent ladle sparkling in the sky. My mother and I were in great spirits.

"You're well," she said, "and there was corned beef at the market."

Of course, I didn't mention the cassette in my pocket—accepting gifts from strangers was discouraged, especially in the shopper's square. But, inhaling the spring air, I could hardly wait to get home and put the headphones on.

It's difficult to imagine myself then, sixteen and alone in my bedroom. The same moon that followed us to the collective now filled my window. And there I was in my underwear, cradling my knees, as "Blue Moon" warbled on the Kino 3000; Elvis' solitary voice, almost a whisper, touched everything, and fell like stardust. It was impossible to understand the words, but that didn't matter. I understood his mournful howl, the slow fading of his cry. I was all by myself, not wanting to be, and nothing in the world felt as good as that longing. Shostakovich was suddenly just a cold promise.

A month later—while milking beside my father in the barn—I wore the headphones, lamenting with Scotty Moore's guitar about the "Milk Cow Blues," vaguely conscious of a tingling in my nostrils. Staring at the hay-strewn ground, methodically pumping the cow's teats, I was somewhere else. My father's concerned expression escaped me. It wasn't until he removed the headphones that I realized something was wrong.

"Valentin," he said, "your nose is bleeding!"

Then I noticed the blood on my shirt, licked my lips and tasted it. I tried to speak, but couldn't. Instead I gagged, forcing a gurgled cough. A red bubble grew at my mouth, then popped.

"Put your head between your legs," he told me. So I did. But the bleeding continued.

My father and two milkmaids then helped me from the barn before I fainted, but I only remember crouching near the cow's underbelly, mesmerized by how the blood dripped into the milk pail, drop after drop, swirling among the white froth. "I'm tired," I said. "I'm making a mess."

# 3.

She had blond hair, blue eyes, a purple birthmark on her left cheek. Her name was Tatiana Mokhoyid. She was fourteen, and we met at the Ukrainian Child Health Clinic. I was there with my mother and Grandmother, waiting for the results of a blood test. She was waiting too, sitting outside Dr. Kavun's office with her mother Nadia and younger brother Leonid, a mongoloid boy, no more than twelve, whose mouth hung half-open. And I was struck by the provincial likeness of the three older women, one being a stranger, yet all wearing patterned scarves and matching gray overcoats, clutching their purses with turbid hands.

My mother shook a thumb in my direction. "His nose keeps bleeding," she said to Nadia, in lieu of introduction. "He sleeps all day."

Nadia sighed, nodding. She pointed at Tatiana, who sat quietly beside her, head straight, fingers gripping either side of the chair. "Tatiana has headaches, maybe a tumor, I don't know. She has a microcurie of cesium in her body. Leonid has half that in his. But my husband and I have none. I think it's the children who are most sensitive."

"It's true," my mother said, patting my back. "It's horrible."

"Yes," Grandmother said, facing Nadia. "Let me tell you something. We're from the Staroye Sharnye collective, but all of us made a pact not to drink the milk we produce, forget that it gets sent here to Kiev. Each head of family signed the agreement twice. And still the children get sick."

"From Staroye Sharnye," Nadia said. "You're nearby then. We're from Khristinovka, right up the road. My husband and I run the village shop."

"Of course, I know your husband," Grandmother said, delighted. "He's a fine man, spent a summer on the farm, many years ago. Alexander Mokhoyid, a strong worker."

Upon hearing his father's name, Leonid hugged himself,

sputtering, "Daddy's Alexander. Mother's Nadia. Sister's Tatiana. I'm Leo-nid. Leo-nid!"

Tatiana, showing the hint of a smile, put an arm around her brother's shoulders. She snuggled him, saying, "Very good, Leonid." The boy's big droopy features lit up. Then she glanced down the row of chairs to me; her expression was frail and pale, narrow from ear to ear and ponderous as she enveloped her brother, squeezing him like he was a puppy. While I watched, oblivious to what the others were now saying, her blond hair glowed under the fluorescent lights–her reticent eyes returned to her brother once more. She shook her head twice, nimbly, and her hair fell across her forehead like a gauzy baldachin, silken and lustrous.

Then it was as if I emerged from some wonderful dream. Names were exchanged. And Grandmother was telling Nadia, "Forget the train, that's silly. You can ride back with us. There's room enough in the car." Suddenly I imagined the drive to Khristinovka, where I'd discover Tatiana's home. And, maybe, she would be seated next to me on the trip. It was all too much.

When I was taken into Dr. Kavun's office with my mother and Grandmother, Tatiana occupied my thoughts, even as the doctor said, "It's nothing serious, really. His blood work registers some negligible deviations from the norm–not unusual considering where you live, or dangerous to his health. It's possible this isn't tied to the radiation background. As for the nosebleeds, it's hard to say. These things happen from time to time. What I've prescribed will certainly lessen the inflammation, and I suspect it'll go away altogether, okay?"

"That's it?" my mother asked, sounding somewhat disappointed.

"That's it," Dr. Kavun replied.

Soon we were in Grandmother's Volga. I was scrunched in the backseat between Leonid and Nadia. Tatiana was in the frontseat. Neither of us spoke, but I was overtaken by her then–though her skull was somehow too large, her jaw a little too compressed. Still, I was consumed, not so much by delicacy or ardor, but by my longing and fear: that realization of conceivable loss–of sickness, perhaps. Even at sixteen, I knew desire in our region was often encased with suffering. But I couldn't avoid it. I didn't want to.

In Andrei Yurovsky's *Memphis, Russia* there were three black-and-white pictures from the 1950s, all grainy photocopies–James Dean going down a New York sidewalk, a cigarette dangling from his lips; Marlon Brando on a motorcycle, his cap slightly askew; Gene Vincent in tight leather pants, seizing a microphone with a gloved hand.

*From Kiev's alley clubs to Moscow's back room bars,* Andrei wrote, *you'll find that this isn't just a 'look' but an entire way of life. This is how WE look everyday!*

Soon I was tucking my T-shirt into my American jeans, and turning the cuffs up past my ankles. Then I tried combing my hair back, but it was pointless. So I sent Andrei a letter apologizing for not yet paying for the tape, and wondering if he could help me with my look. His reply came in less than a week, along with a new homemade cassette (*Gene Vincent & The Blue Caps' Greatest Hits*) and several older issues of *Memphis, Russia: Valentin, well babe, I'll try to help you out here. This is a tough one though, geographics make a difference as well as personal preference. I can give you the guy's end of it (mine anyway). First, gel is a big no-no. Grease is the key to a good 'pile'. My pop back in the '60s used petrolatum, but this plays hell with the shower drain. My grease o' choice is Apple State Pomade or Kamianka's Pomade. As far as how to get the cut right, I leave that to the barber. Okay, maybe this helps. The tapes are on me.*

Unfortunately, I found no pomade in the house. But there was petrolatum. And the afternoon I went to visit Tatiana, my fingers worked the unctuous jelly across my scalp, coating the entire crown. Then, with my hair slicked and parted on the side, I styled a prominent quiff.

Later, when passing my father in the living room, he went, "Oh my, it's Elvis!"

"Hardly," I replied, stepping toward the front door, hoping for a clean getaway.

"Stay put," said my father, beside himself. "Nina, Olya, you have to see!"

My mother and Grandmother sauntered from the kitchen, both appearing perplexed by the sight of me.

"What's this?" Grandmother said.

My mother scowled.

"I don't like it. Where you going like that?"

I showed her the Kino 3000, holding it with a greasy hand.

"Walking," I told her.

"What if your nose starts—?"

"Don't worry," I said, putting the headphones on. "I'll be back in a bit."

"Let him go, Nina," Grandmother said. "It'll do him good."

Before my mother could protest any further, I slipped out of the house with Gene Vincent singing, "Be-Bop-a-Lula, she's my baby." Visible in the distance, jutting from the emerald landscape like a stone, was the village of Khristinovka—and as I strode forward, crossing pastures, navigating greenwoods, my hair glinted in the afternoon sun, immovable and perfect.

Once in Khristinovka, I located the village shop, peered through the window, and spied Nadia and her husband Alexander stocking shelves. Aside from them, the shop was empty. So I stepped to the cobbled street, proceeding toward the Mokhoyid's wooden cottage, where Tatiana would surely be waiting. And ambling along, I brought the headphones around my neck and clicked the Kino 3000 off. The silence of Khristinovka was eerie. No birds chattered in the trees. There was no wind. Or cars. Or people, at least that I saw. Just me and my shoes clomping on the road.

When I reached the gate of the Mokhoyid's home, it seemed as if the place was deserted. Weeds grew tall in the yard. A tricycle missing a wheel rested in the pathway. The front door was ajar. But before I could knock, Tatiana, immersed in a paperback of Yevtushenko's poetry, came from the house and rambled into me. The book pressed against my chest, crumpling, and she withdrew it with an odd frown. "You scared me," she said. "What are you doing?" "I'm sorry," I replied, feeling at a loss. "I didn't mean to." My consternation in her presence was paralyzing, but I managed a grin, pointing at the paperback she kept between us. "We read Yevtushenko in school."

"Me too." The frown softened, giving way to her natural shyness and allure. "Why'd you come here?"

"I was only walking," I explained, saying what was furthest from my heart. "I take walks sometimes. It's not that far."

The corners of her mouth drew in. She shut the book, then leaned against the doorway, studying me with a curiousness so benign I could have easily missed it; but I was studying her too. That bruised birthmark. The sobriety, the paper-thin skin on her white arms. I observed the dark circles under her eyes.

"Do you want me to come?"

"Yes," I said, "I was hoping you would."

"All right. Hold on."

Tatiana bent, setting the book on the porch. Then she went inside, calling her brother's name. In a moment she returned with Leonid, who wore a raincoat over his chubby body.

"I'm keeping him today," she said. "Usually he stays at work with my parents, but he has a cold."

"Hello," Leonid said to me, staccato, showing pink gums and dry lips.

"Hi," I replied.

"Hello," he said again, lowering his eyes.

"We can't be long," said Tatiana. "I'm not supposed to go out. Mostly I sit on the steps and read." She smiled, somewhat solemn, and then she took her brother's hand.

Soon Tatiana led the way, and we found ourselves strolling in a meadow on the other side of Khristinovka, saying almost nothing as our shoes crunched into the footpath. I walked alongside her. Leonid strayed behind, stooping every now and then to gaze at something in the tall grass. When we reached a clearing at the end of the footpath, Tatiana showed me the stump of a fir tree, which Leonid proceeded to climb upon.

Then she touched my greased forelock, saying, "Your hair is funny," and rubbed the petrolatum on her fingertips.

"It's my new look," I said.

"Why?"

"Because I'm a hepcat," I replied.

"What's that?"

I shrugged.

"I'm not really sure."

Then I mentioned Andrei and the tapes he gave me. I let her listen to Gene Vincent, watching her bemused expression as "Be-Bop-a-Lula" played.

When she handed me the headphones, her voice faintly said, "I don't understand him. Is he American?"

"I think so," I said. "I'm pretty sure."

After that, words escaped us. Tatiana took a long breath, sucking in the honeysuckle fragrance of the meadow. She gazed at Leonid, who now had his stomach flat on the stump, arms extended, plump legs kicking in the air, pretending to be an airplane. But I couldn't keep my eyes from her. Dots of sweat had formed on her hairline. The hair on her neck was glossy and wet. And those things made me want her.

"We should get back," she finally said, glancing at me. "I don't want to get in trouble."

"Okay," I said. "I don't want that either."

That afternoon, I was both elated and restless, running fleet-footed from Khristinovka and envisioning days spent with Tatiana. Fueled by those stirrings, I raced along the roadway, passing a procession of field hands, the inhabitants of Khristinovka returning to their village–grubby men and women, the weary children they had brought to work–who regarded me with impassive faces, deceived by lives that no longer afforded passion.

For almost a month, my daydreams of Tatiana were fulfilled–I found her after school, in the meadow, where we

reclined against the fir stump. I would give her my head-
phones, and she listened as The Dan Wul Band performed
"Spooky Baby," a surf guitar instrumental with twangy reverb.
"That's my favorite," she said. "Rewind it."

And once, while lying together in the tall grass, I told her
about the American sock-hop dances in the 50s, about the
girls in poodle skirts and peddle pushers. On the following
afternoon I gave her my copies of *Memphis, Russia,* showing
her pictures of girls in tight sweaters and blue jeans and
rolled cuffs.

Eventually we stood facing one another in the clearing,
where I then pulled her close, nuzzled my chin near her neck
and placed my hands on her waist. Silence overcame her. She
was suddenly contemplative, unsure; her palms carefully bore
down on my shoulder blades, expectant and pensive and
rigid as we began dancing. But in time I sensed that she had
lost her discretion, and when pulling her close, I felt her body
loosen against mine, her palms now eager to touch me. They
were the brightest memories of my sixteenth year: the tall
grass encircled the clearing, swaying, as Tatiana and I
embraced in our awkward, tuneless waltz; the sharp, vague,
sweaty smell of her skin, the petrolatum shining in my hair
and on my forehead, the rich honeysuckle aroma floating
from the greenwoods, such sweet air, making it seem as if we
existed somewhere far away.

But at the center of my happiness there was dread. On
sleepless nights, as I recalled Tatiana's eyes, Yevtushenko's
words haunted me in bed: *Her motionless eyes had no expression;
yet there was something there, sorrow or agony, inexpressible, but
something terrible.* My heart quickened, fired by anxiety, and in
my imagination everything I encountered was poisoned,
withered, and somehow dying.

Now there's little in way of hope, other than the fact that
I'm alive. So are my parents and Grandmother. The collective remains in operation. But Tatiana is gone, having left me
one afternoon in the meadow, receding on the footpath as she

headed home—and then, where the trail curved into the tall grass, she vanished wholly. It was the last time we were together, and her hair was in a ponytail, fastened by a length of tightly wound pink elastic. There was rouge on her cheeks, her eyebrows were darkened. Looking somewhat like the American girls in *Memphis, Russia*, she had arrived in the clearing that day wearing her father's brown slacks and white undershirt, all of it being several sizes too large.

"I'm a hepcat," she said, making us laugh.

But her makeup and clothing covered the truth. In the few weeks I had known her, Tatiana's birthmark changed color, from purple to sallow. Her pallid skin took on a yellowish veneer. Her parched breath hinted at what I feared most. So I said nothing. It was better not knowing for sure.

Sitting at the fir stump, she sagged her body against mine, saying, "I can't dance today, I'm worn-out."

"That's fine," I told her. "We don't have to."

Then, while brushing grass from her pants, she said, "Valentin, I might be going soon."

"Where?" I asked. "When?"

"To Odessa, to the Youth Guard Hospital. I don't know when, maybe this week. They'll send someone for me. There's this lump in my brain."

"What lump?"

She lifted her shoulders and let them drop.

"A lump. It just grew there, I don't know."

I moved in front of her, folding my legs underneath me, and began curling my fingers through her hair, searching for a protuberance on her scalp. But Tatiana gripped my wrists.

"Don't," she said.

"I want to feel it."

"You can't. It's inside." She brought my hands to her knees, then let go. "We shouldn't discuss it."

"It's probably nothing," I said, exasperated. "Strange things grow here everyday." Since Chernobyl, I mentioned, many trees in our region had produced enormous leaves or needles. Giant cucumbers often packed vegetable plots.

Sometimes pumpkins blossomed with three stems. "They all
survive," I told her, reassuring both of us, "so stop worrying."

"I'm not worried," she said, flatly. And I suppose my eyes
were watery and frightened, because she cupped my face in
her hands, saying, "It's okay, please don't be sad." Then, as if
we'd been discussing little more than the weather, she asked
to kiss my back.

"Yes," I heard myself say, "of course."

Tatiana helped me tug off my T-shirt, exposing my boney
chest, hairless and fallow.

"Don't move," she said, crawling behind me.

I inhaled self-consciously, aware of the baby fat under my
skin, and stared straight ahead at the stump. She pressed her
lips to my spine. Then her tongue, like wet sandpaper,
squirmed between vertebras.

"You're salty," she finally said, sticking her chin over my
shoulder. "It doesn't taste bad."

"It tickles," I told her.

She scooted beside me, dug in a pocket, and found her
eyebrow pencil.

"I'll give you a tattoo," she said.

"Of what?"

"Just wait," she told me. "You shouldn't look."

So I focused again on the stump, marveling at the jagged
rings widening from the medial, as if time itself was becoming
more expansive. Each ring reflected the uneven circle of history; each seemed less precise than its predecessor, diffused
with increasing imperfections. As Tatiana sketched on my
forearm, I felt that we were beyond time, somehow safe in a
vacuum, and capable now of making anything possible. Later
that day, when she disappeared along the footpath, I conjured
the future in my mind, willing it so: there was no such place
as Odessa, or the Youth Guard Hospital. She would always
be here.

Then I headed for the collective with the headphones on,
confident, stopping every so often in the twilight to examine
my forearm—the words *Spooky Baby* written above a black

heart. And as I neared Grandmother's farmhouse, Tatiana's lump seemed trivial, a minor disruption, like a nosebleed. Tomorrow, I was certain, she would kiss my back once more. She would let me draw a tattoo on her stomach, and we would dance among the honeysuckle and tall grass.

But when tomorrow materialized, Tatiana failed to be waiting in the clearing. So I sat for a while on the stump, gazing hopefully in the direction of the footpath, until an overwhelming dismay filled my gut. Then I sprang to my feet and ran from the meadow toward Khristinovka. When I got to the Mokhoyid's home, rounding the front gate, my legs slowed.

It was Tatiana's father who answered the door, and the sight of me—a stranger with American jeans and slick hair and a portable cassette player—made him frown. He was a towering, slightly crouching, bearded man, wearing what I suspected were the same brown slacks and white undershirt his daughter had worn.

"Yes," Alexander Mokhoyid said, with a bothered, humorless tone, "what is it?"

I had expected him to be at the village shop, so I was taken aback, still panting from the run. Leonid stood behind his father in the entry, watching with his heavy face, his slackened eyes.

"Is Tatiana home?"

"No," Alexander said, "she's with her mother, in Odessa."

"For how long?" I asked. "When will she return?"

"I don't know," said Alexander, his misery apparent. "I'm sorry."

Then, without another word, he shut the door.

I remained on the porch for some time, finding a seat on the steps, imagining Tatiana next to me with a book of poetry. I surveyed the weeds in the yard, the tricycle lacking a wheel, wondering what connection these things had to her—but nothing presented itself. Eventually I heaved myself up, quietly devastated, and went forward.

As I approached the gate, Leonid's burdened voice called out, "Boy!"

I turned to see him trudging down the porch steps. In a hand he clutched the copies of *Memphis, Russia* I had given Tatiana, proffering them as he came closer. His clumsy arm shook the magazines at me.

"Hello," he said. "Hello."

"They're not mine," I told him, appreciative but sounding curt. "They're Tatiana's. They're your sister's. I don't want them." But Leonid continued fluttering the magazines, uncomprehending with an expression as forlorn as my own, so I simply said goodbye and crossed through the gate. And I kept going, suddenly feeling lonelier than ever, forsaken, encumbered by my own being. Everything else in Khristinovka was as it should be, but I didn't belong there anymore.

Traversing the fields and fences, I bypassed the collective—forgetting my parents and Grandmother—and journeyed to Novoye Sharnye, that lifeless place, where only someone as disheartened as myself might find escape. In a green pasture rusted by dusk, I discovered a hole in the high barbed-wire barricade encircling the village and squeezed into the forbidden zone, tearing a shirt-sleeve on the twisted wire. Then I walked hurriedly in the fading light, adjusting the headphones on my ears, increasing the cassette player volume, letting Elvis drown out the solitude of Novoye Sharnye.

In the gardens of boarded-up cottages, red-gold chrysanthemums bloomed.

Flower-beds cradled flagging plants. An orange tablecloth hung in a courtyard. On the rocky banks of the Uzh river, which rushed parallel with the village, I scrutinized the murky water. Somewhere upstream were the remains of the power plant, and bright stars were glowing over Chernobyl like the dimming catherine wheels of fire in my mother's catastrophe story. And as night began shaping Novoye Sharnye, two things happened—blood began trickling from my nostrils, the batteries died in my Kino 3000.

Then I felt lost, in a way that made me adhere to fantasy and imagination, invoking a morning in which I stirred and the sun shone, and, at last freed from a lingering nightmare, my mother's story could never be told. But when considering that wish with the absence of Tatiana, I was crushed. It's a stupid world, I thought, licking the blood off my upper lip. What a stupid world. Then I turned from the river, pinching my nostrils between a thumb and forefinger, and wondered how I would make it home in the dark.

II.

# Five Women in No Particular Order

## 1.

Shirley gets the card table ready anyway. She had been making the queso dip when Connie called to say she wasn't feeling well enough to come. "My stomach's cramping something terrible, Shirl. If it don't ease by tomorrow, I'll go on to Childress and see Doc Pipken."

Then Janie rang almost as soon as Shirley had hung up with Connie, explaining, "Burgess has gone wandering. Probably messing with that silly tree of his, but I'd best find him before the weather does. He's been at my photo albums again."

So Shirley phoned Lucretia and said, "Con's still cramping, so she's staying put. And that fool boy of Janie's ran off for the billionth time. Why on earth does she let him get out of her sights? Looks like it's me, you, and Win again."

That was when Lucretia mentioned the tornado watch. "Just came over the TV, Shirl. Skellytown, Roaring Springs, Claude, and all of King County is under watch until ten tonight. So is Cottle County. So is Dickens County. Tim called from work and told me I should keep home this afternoon.

But I told him not a chance. I said if some tornado decides to drop on Claude, we'll just move the game on down into Shirl's cellar. I swear to god that man searches for any rotten excuse to prevent me from having fun."

And now Shirley unfolds the card table in the living room, but as soon she stands it upright and locks the legs in place the phone rings again. "I'll be a little late," says Winnifred, exasperated by the weight of her own voice. "Thought my hair appointment was at three, but it's three-thirty. Shouldn't be later than four. We're under the weather again, you know."

"Win, Con can't make it. And Janie's boy disappeared to wherever. Probably swept by tornado. And I'm just thinking maybe today ain't the day for Spoil Five. TV says we're in this watch, and you've got your hair to deal with too."

"Well, Shirl, I already got the potato salad done. And I know Cretia's counting on us all getting together. Don't need but three for Spoil Five."

"I suppose so," says Shirley, dipping a finger into the pan of queso warming on the stove.

"We'll get a round or two in before your Bert comes home. I got to run, hon'. See you in a bit."

Shirley licks her finger, listens as the dial tone clicks in with a hum. She returns the phone to its cradle, then pulls the folded red and white checkered tablecloth from a kitchen drawer. In the living room, she dusts the card table surface. Then she spreads the tablecloth across the top, evens the sides, smoothing the creases with her hands. From the garage she brings out three matching olive-colored chairs, pushes them in around the table, while whistling a song she can't quite place in her memory.

The box of poker chips she sets at the center of the table was a gift from her mother. She bought the deck of Bicycle Poker 808 cards herself, but sometimes her husband Bert uses them on those nights when his insomnia takes over. In the past week, on separate mornings, she found him asleep on a bar stool in the kitchen, arms folded on the counter as a pillow for his head, with his house of cards, complicated and precarious, towering above him. And before she shook him on the shoulders, Shirley made a point of thumping a single card so the house would collapse.

Shirley goes to check the clock on the microwave: 2:26. There is still a cup's worth of decaf in the pot, so she fills her mug. She brings an elbow to the counter, and lets the mug linger in front of her mouth. Steam consumes her glasses. She sips. Then inhales.

When she turns her face to the window above the sink, the light coming in appears only as a smudge of gray to her. Then for a moment she senses movement outside. Someone has just walked past the window. Shirley removes her glasses and wipes away the haze. She puts them back on. Going forward, she parts the yellow curtains and looks one way then another, catching sight of no one. But she sees that the sky has grown heavy, a murky ocean moving overhead. The willow in the yard whips at the dry grass. Mrs. Christian's house across the way seems dim and empty. She is whistling to herself again.

Shirley holds the mug under her nose, allowing her lenses to get steamed once more. It's a game she likes to play. She pretends she is almost blind, and, guiding herself with one hand, walks toward the living room so she can fumble with the remote control. She knows if she really had something like glaucoma or cataract, Bert might leave her. She figures she would end up alone in front of the TV, drinking decaf, unable to make out the tornado watch design, a white cyclone at the bottom right of the screen. She wouldn't know the difference between a tornado watch or a tornado warning, and this makes her smile. A little natural disaster, she thinks, could finally drop some excitement smack-dab in the lap of boring ol' Claude, Texas.

## 2.

Lucretia drives her husband's Chevrolet Deluxe fifteen miles west of Claude to The County Line. She browses the shelves of vodka, Bourbon, Scotch, and Irish whiskey. The racks of wine hold her attention for a time, but she just isn't sure. Something harder than Miller Lite or wine coolers seems to be in order. The others had tired of Blue Ritas and mint liqueurs, but Lucretia can't resist the exotic. Her husband drinks beer, and he's about as interesting, she figures, as shit on a horse's tail. Connie is partial to beer too. Janie prefers to nurse white wine. Shirley and Winnifred simply don't care, so, as long as Connie and Janie won't be around to complain, today will be an experiment. The Mexican man behind the counter suggests lemon gin with granita, but Lucretia settles on Shirayuki-Saki, imported from Japan. "Needs to be served warm," the Mexican man tells her.

She accepts her change, saying, "How about in coffee?"

"Don't know why you can't. As long as it's warm, I guess."

She takes the small paper sack from the counter, "I'll let you know," and finds herself clutching her purse against the wind as she leaves the store.

Lucretia deliberately speeds along 287 toward Claude, not because she's in a hurry, or because, as she enjoys imagining, a tornado is eating asphalt in the rearview, but because her desire to blow the engine apart is fervent. Her hatred for her husband's car has been complete since the afternoon he bought himself a new Bronco without consulting her, sticking her with this relic from their high school days. But the car won't die, and her husband is diligent about its survival. He spends at least one evening a week under its hood, or stretched on his back below the hull. "My mistress," he sometimes calls the Deluxe, which makes Lucretia want to shove her fist down her throat to retch twenty-one years of marriage past her lips.

Claude sneaks up on her like a cannibal, suddenly. The water tower lifts from the ground, stabbing at the sky. Then the town pushes over the horizon, cutting between the highway, the flatlands, and grim clouds. She slows to the speed limit after passing the city marker, and cruises Main Street with the tape player warbling Waylon Jennings. She turns into the A&P parking lot wishing she had bought herself some vodka for later in the evening. Inside the grocery store she buys a platter of packaged broccoli and cauliflower with a Styrofoam cup of Ranch dressing. To add a bit of exhilaration to her day, she shoplifts a pack of Swisher Sweet Cigars–because sometimes she likes to smoke when she goes to Shirley's, but only when she plays Spoil Five. The other women enjoy smoking too. Still, none of them really keep the cigars lit for long, they just enjoy having the things in their mouths. Plus, there's nothing better than reaping the benefits of petty theft. In a town like Claude, she thinks, afternoon misdemeanors stop people like me from blowing holes through their brains.

The wind tugs on Lucretia's purse again, smacks on the plastic bag she carries from the A&P, and pausing to fetch her keys, she thinks she spots Janie's son across the street. She is almost certain it is him. The boy has his baseball cap bill pulled low. He leans into the breeze, his T-shirt fluttering against his slender chest. "Burgess!" she shouts, just as he limps around the corner from view, but her voice gets lost in the weather.

She puts her groceries into the Deluxe, then goes to the pay phone in front of the store to call Janie. But Janie isn't home, so she calls Shirley. "Shirl, you might try reaching Janie 'cause I thought I just saw Burgess walking along Main."

"Good lord, which way is he heading?"

"If it's him, he's on 9th now. Hard to tell for sure, but I'd bet on it. He was dragging that leg behind him."

"Okay, Cretia, I'll try Janie but I don't think she's there. She's looking for him."

"What am I thinking? She ain't there. I just tried. I'm at the A&P, Shirl, with a dime and a quarter to my name."

"Mercy. Well, go see if you can catch him. I'll phone Sheriff Branches and tell him what you told me."

"Better call Con too," Lucretia says uneasily. "If that boy's in town, she best know." She stands at the pay phone and waits for Shirley to say something else, but Shirley has already hung up. She finds another quarter, drops it in the slot, and realizes she doesn't remember Connie's number.

# 3.

Janie walks into the arroyo knowing what Burgess will do, how he'll respond to her when she swats him for stealing her pictures and missing lunch. She expects to catch him fiddling among the branches of his mesquite tree fort, perhaps adding the photos to his shrine, or using Scotch tape to repair the torn yearbook pages and purple 4-H ribbons that have fallen from the tree during the night; she expects to see him scowling and hunching as she says his name. "Not me," she expects to hear, in the sluggish voice that tires her. "Not me. No, not me." But he isn't at his tree. So she hikes down the arroyo toward the trailer home of her nearest neighbor—Willy.

Janie knows Willy is home because his Ford pickup is parked out front. She knocks until he opens the door wearing only his briefs, scratching his slept-on hair with a hand, rubbing his pale beer belly with the other. His erection is bent to the left inside his underwear. It's hard for her to remember him as a muscular, clean-cut, handsome boy who once led the Claude Tigers to district play-offs. There'd been talk of an amazing, unparalleled athletic career; he was recruited to play college football. But within weeks, for reasons he never discusses, Willy returned to Claude without participating in a single college game. Now he works part-time for the highway department, purchasing his beer and food with weekly checks from the Texas Rehabilitation Commission.

His chubbiness and growing beard seem so far removed from the boy he was that Janie feels little attraction to him, even though she found herself in his bed on four separate afternoons following her son's accident, while her husband consulted with the neurologist at Memorial Hospital in Amarillo. Yet Willy is solitary and happy. The evenings he spends tossing the football with Burgess ease whatever guilt Janie holds.

"Willy, has Burgess been by?" Janie says in a harsh, irritated tone.

Willy squints his eyes. "No. I was sleeping. He might've come by. I heard knocking. Might've heard you knocking. I dreamt this woodpecker got to pecking on my roof. Did you look under the trailer?"

"Already checked. He's got a mess of grief coming from me." Then she explains about the photo albums. She mentions he wasn't at the tree, how he skipped the lunch she made for him. She planned to do Spoil Five at Shirley's place, but had to cancel. Janie says when she finds Burgess she's going to march him right to that mesquite and make him take down every single picture he robbed. "And if he's in town, and Sheriff Branches gets hold of him, no telling what in hell will happen."

"He'll be fine," Willy says. "Want a drink? I don't got no ice."

"No time for that. We're in a watch, and Burgess is on my last nerve."

"I'll help you look. We can take my truck on into town. I've got a bottle of Jack in the kitchen."

"He's probably back at that tree as we speak," Janie says. "He's probably got some idiot cat by the tail and hammering it on the skull. Best if you stay put in case he shows up, Willy. You'll keep him here, won't you?"

"Of course," Willy says. "Hold on a sec'." He steps away from the door, then comes back with a cigarette and a book of matches. "Take this. You're all excited. This'll calm you. If you don't find him, come on back and we'll take my truck. I got a full tank."

So Janie returns to Burgess' tree, but he's nowhere in sight. "Dammit, you best come out from wherever you are!" she shouts, kicking at the dirt. The many gray arms of the mesquite shudder with the gusts pushing through the arroyo. She tries lighting the cigarette three times, but the matches keep dying almost as soon as they ignite. She has one match left now. She reluctantly unties the pictures stolen out of her photo albums from the branches, and then sits under the tree with her knees drawn to her chest.

Burgess had poked holes in the tops of the pictures with a pencil, threaded yarn through them so they could flutter around and dangle with the rest of his mementos. But her photographs are off limits. She has warned him too often about pulling pictures from the albums, about what will happen if he hides from her, and now he is in serious trouble. And even though Burgess often strays from the arroyo, he knows he'll be punished if he walks to town again. He won't be allowed to wander on his own anymore. The rules are simple. Claude is off limits. Connie's house is off limits. If Willy's not busy and wants to throw the football, then that's okay. Crawling under Willy's trailer home is off limits.

The cow bones hanging from the limbs clank together above Janie's head. Burgess' letter jacket, nailed into the frail trunk through the collar, flaps its sleeves. The clouds have sunk lower, a cauldron swirling and burbling over the plains. Janie goes through the pictures and removes the strings of yarn. She has no idea why her son took these particular snapshots, five in all, each picture in black and white; jungle landscapes photographed by her husband in Vietnam, steep mountains and wet rice fields. The strands of yarn go sailing, one at a time, carried away by the wind.

She sticks the pictures in her pocket. Then she stands and attempts to light the cigarette again. She turns from the wind, strikes the last match, but the breeze sneaks past her cupped hand. In frustration, her fingers crush the cigarette, sprinkling tobacco and paper. The dead match gets flicked. The afternoon has grown dank and chilly, so Janie considers Burgess' letter jacket. She jumps once, grabbing at one of the waving sleeves, and yanks it from the mesquite. The jacket is too big for her, but she enjoys how it presses on her shoulders, heavy and safe. She trudges from under the tree, ducking a mobile made of wire hangers and ribbons cut from a black graduation gown. Her husband shouldn't be bothered at the Court House, she decides. Willy's got a full tank of gas.

## 4.

Connie answers the front door in her robe. "Hon'," Sheriff Branches says, "are you okay?" He is on the porch with a palm resting on the butt of a holstered Colt. A dust devil whirls along the street, brushing alongside the sheriff's patrol car.

Connie blows her bangs off her face. She holds a wad of Kleenex. "Under the weather is all." Then a frightening image flashes in her mind—her husband struggling or pinned beneath the metal of a toppled oil derrick spire. "Is Chad dead?"

"Not as far as I know," Sheriff Branches says. "Unless you know something I don't."

"I don't understand," Connie says.

Sheriff Branches grins. "Got a call from Shirley Monroe. Seems Lucretia Estes might've spotted Janie's boy in town."

"Might've, or did?" Connie says ominously.

"She wasn't so certain, so I'm making sure you're all right. Thought you'd better be aware. The windows locked?"

"Think they'd be unlocked? Jesus Christ, last thing I want is that boy surprising me again."

"Truth is, I think he's harmless enough. A little anxious is all. Hasn't hurt no one, right? I'm more worried about that husband of yours."

Connie knows Sheriff Branches is right. When her husband first caught Burgess crawling through the bathroom window, he was visibly angered but patient. Like almost everyone else in Claude, he had admired the boy's talent as a high school athlete, both in football and basketball. And also like almost everyone else in Claude, for a while at least, he was willing to overlook Burgess' eccentric behavior after the accident, after falling from a motorcycle without a helmet. But the second time Burgess tried coming through the very same window—his legs dangling above the yard, his fingers curled around the towel rack bar—her husband pelted him with a roll of toilet paper, then forced him back outside by slamming his fists against Burgess' sternum.

Connie remembers the morning a bleached rabbit skull with two Scholastic League medals, one silver, the other gold, Super-glued over vacant sockets, appeared on the doorstep. It was the morning in which her husband dumped the skull into the trash, saying, "If I catch him, Con, I'll kill him." And a week later, when the pair of gym cleats were found on the doorstep, laced, with a barrel cactus planted in each shoe, her husband nearly tore the phone from the wall as he dialed Sheriff Branches' office.

"If I see him," Connie says, "I'll let you know."

"Do that. And lock the door. If someone comes knocking, don't just open it like you just did," Sheriff Branches says.

"Okay."

"I'll be cruising the blocks, but Till's working dispatch. She'll find me." He tips the brim of his Stetson. "Bye now. Double-check them windows for me." He makes a clicking noise with his teeth, gives Connie a wink, then turns around on the porch.

Connie shuts the door and throws the bolt. While speaking with the sheriff, she had heard Burgess clanking the fork against his plate, so she goes on into the kitchen with a frown. He twists his baseball cap around on his forehead, avoids her stare, and wipes pound cake crumbs from his chin. "Lord, Burgess, think you could've made a quieter racket?" The fork rests on the plate in front of him.

"More," Burgess says, seated at the table. His voice is so blunted and so aimless that she isn't sure if it's more of her body he wants, or more pound cake. He is undressed, bringing a hand to his jockey shorts. He is filthy with sweat and dirt; he is slender, no longer the weight-lifting teenager, but still toned in the right places. Even so, he is scarred somewhere else beyond the jagged ten-inch line snaking up his neck into oily brown hair. He scoots the chair away from the table, stretches his long legs out, slipping the underwear to his knees. "More, please."

Some afternoon, Connie thinks, Chad will come home early and find me like this, with my lips sucking on the dick of my best friend's son. Then she'll confess how lucky she felt to finally get Burgess in her bed, how she had wanted him since he was in eighth grade–that prankish, funny kid who made substitute teaching interesting by asking the difference between an orgasm and an organism. The accident delivered him to her, and she'd explain that to her husband. She'd tell about Burgess fumbling with his erection while she put a towel under herself on the bed. He ejaculated before getting inside of her, missing the towel and staining the sheets. The second try, three days later, was a complete success.

His body is a gift. Connie doesn't mind the come in her throat; a small, not wholly unenjoyable price to pay. And if Janie's suspicion could be avoided, she might bath him, wash his hair, scrub between his shoulders, between his legs. She might pour honey into the deep, torn cave at the base of his neck, where a rock lodged when he went backwards off the seat of that motorcycle, and lick his wound.

The pound cake is for Burgess. So are her lips. And when he dresses but can't tie his shoes, she'll gladly bend to do it for him. And if he is ever carted away, Connie figures she'll roll herself into a ball and never move again.

## 5.

Winnifred arrives with the potato salad, saying, "I kept you all waiting, sorry, but Ruth took her own sweet time on my hair."

Shirley relieves her of the potato salad and carries it into the kitchen. "The tint is so coppery, Win."

"I know. Ruth's idea. I wanted red. Just red."

"Looks fine to me, dear."

Lucretia sips saki, and then says, "It's supposed to be warm, Win. But we decided not to bother. It's Japanese. Shirl hates it. You'll probably hate it too. Want a cigar?"

"Not yet. Are we still playing?"

Lucretia shrugs indifference and goes into the living room to sit at the card table. Winnifred follows, touching her fingers to her hair, expecting Lucretia to say something nice about what Ruth-the-artiste has done. How can she miss it? The perm is gone. Her hair hangs again, covering the scar between the right ear and cheekbone if she lets it. And she does.

"Janie called to say she found Burgess at the Community Center. Trying to get over that fence as if he ain't ever had a notion of barb wire coils. Suppose he wanted in the pool pretty bad. Suppose he was having fishy thoughts." Lucretia pours some more saki into her glass.

"Is she coming?" Winnifred says, fiddling with the hair on her shoulder.

"No," Shirley says from the kitchen. "She's punishing Burgess. Who's in for potato salad? Win?"

"I'll pass for now. Thanks. I made it for you two anyway, you know I'm not a big potato salad eater."

"Cretia?"

"Just a bit. I'm about stuffed on chips."

Winnifred lifts a stalk of broccoli from the gourmet platter, dips it into the Ranch dressing. "I saw Janie this afternoon in town. Must've been looking for Burgess. She was with Willy Keeler in his truck."

"Good god," Lucretia puffs. "What's that about?"

"What's what about?" Shirley says in the kitchen.

"Win said she saw Janie in town today with Willy Keeler."

"Not meaning to cast aspersions," Winnifred says, talking around the broccoli.

"You don't need to," Lucretia grumbles, barely moving her lips.

"Old news," Shirley says.

"New news to me." Winnifred frowns. She is always the last to hear these things. It's something the others do now. Since the shooting, she suspects, the circle has grown tighter. They share secrets without her, she's sure of it. Her phone rings a lot less these days.

"Potato salad on the way," Shirley says. Winnifred grins, but the right side of her face remains crooked and unchanging behind her hair.

"Ruth did a nice job on you," Lucretia says. "Want some saki?"

"No."

Shirley brings two bowls of potato salad to the card table. She gives one to Lucretia, and sits down with the other. "Win, you couldn't tell what you've been through. You're looking great. Connie was saying the same yesterday."

"She sure was," Lucretia concurs.

Winnifred has had reconstructive surgery. Skin that once bore the traces of buckshot is almost unblemished now. The scars have thinned some, appearing as fine white creases beneath her makeup. Her husband has spared nothing. Twice he flew her to Houston so that the operations could be performed by the best men in Texas. And he is suing the manufacturers of the Connor Double-Barrel, claiming both safety locks were on when the shotgun fell from the gun rack in the den, discharging a single blast through the couch and into the side of his wife's head. The right side of her mouth still has trouble; it's unmovable, partially paralyzed with nerve damage. A surgeon's scalpel lifted the rigid portion of labium three centimeters in an attempt to ease the discomfort, so she can chew more freely now.

"I prefer my hair like this," Winnifred says, and Lucretia nods with a mouthful of potato salad.

"Superb," Shirley says, turning to Lucretia. "Superb potato salad," and Lucretia nods again, but a little differently than before, Winnifred thinks.

Shirley and Lucretia smile with spoons in their perfect, symmetrical faces. Winnifred detects a flash of eye contact between them, an in-joke no doubt, something brief, unsaid, and private. And Winnifred smiles too, as best she can. It is superb potato salad, a secret recipe, seasoned with one string of spit and a splash of urine from a Dixie cup. "Perhaps I'll take a little saki, Cretia. In honor of my hair. I do wish the tint was redder though."

## 6.

The call comes to Sheriff Branches as he cruises Main Street in his patrol car. A storm spotter at the Grow Gin Co-op reported two spindly funnels touching ground about twenty miles from Claude. "They're moving south toward town," dispatcher Till says. "Another confirmation too, Sheriff. Lee Haywood said he's watching them tornadoes from his porch. Said they ain't big, but between the pair they're making a hell of a mess in his fields."

"Till," Branches says, cranking the sirens, "ring the court house. Tell'em to fire the warning horns. I'll be working the streets."

It's Janie's husband who takes the message from dispatcher Till. He wastes not a moment in flipping the switch that sets the horns blaring through four loudspeakers atop the court house gables. Then he phones Janie because he knows she can't hear the horns at their house. "You and Burgess move downstairs to the game room. I'm going with everybody else into the shelter. I'll get home as soon as this passes." Then, with a melodramatic touch that makes Janie wince, he adds, "Be careful. I love you, hon'."

"You too," she says, and hangs up. Tornadoes don't scare her like they did when Burgess was a child. Nothing really scares her anymore, least of all her husband's worried voice.

Janie leaves the kitchen and goes to where she told Burgess to stay put. In his silent, darkened bedroom, Burgess sits alone on the floor. His lips move as if he is speaking to someone, as if the inaudible sounds hold some vast importance–but whether he is actually talking actual words or uttering complete nonsense, she has never managed to catch any of it.

"Go downstairs now," Janie says. "A tornado is coming."

Burgess uncrosses his legs and stares at his mother. "Good," he says defiantly. "How's that, stupid? Good."

Janie sighs. "Don't care what you do," she says. "Go downstairs or not." Then she firmly shuts the door on him and returns to the telephone in the kitchen. She wants to call Willy, but decides better. He won't be there anyway–not when a tornado is in the neighborhood. He'll be in his truck with the camcorder on the seat next to him. The scanner on the dashboard telling him where to go. He'll be driving right toward the storm in hopes of filming a few minutes of disaster. What sort of loneliness, she wonders, makes a man do something like that? What kind of fella chases disaster with a video camera?

Janie dials Connie's number instead. From her bathroom, Connie hears the phone in the living room, but can't bring herself to answer it. The sirens from Sheriff Branches' patrol car had rattled her minutes earlier. Something's happened to Chad on the oil derrick, she thought. Or Burgess muttered something incriminating. But when the patrol car passed her house without stopping, the sheriff announcing from a bullhorn that a tornado approaches, Connie sank into the couch and breathed relief. The court house warning horns sent her into the bathroom with a pan of Rice Crispy treats.

So now Connie waits in the bathtub. She tightens the belt on her robe, and listens to the phone. Ten rings in all. Then nothing. She understands what it's about. Her husband has been whisked and snatched and taken away by this twister. It's not the same as wanting him dead, she thinks, not the same at all; at this moment the assumed tragedy of her husband's disappearance is at its most wretched and enjoyable. Outside, the weather appears calm, still. No wind, only the court house horns screaming over empty streets.

The phone begins ringing again. "Dammit," Connie says. She removes herself from the bathtub, hurries into the hallway, and rounds the corner to the living room. There she grabs the receiver, and, betraying vexation, says, "Hello, what is it?"

"Good god, Con," Shirley says on the other end of the line, "you been runnin' with the horses? You sound beat. I'm in the cellar with Cretia and Win. Wasn't sure if the cordless would work down here or not. Guess it does."

"I was in the tub," Connie says lugubriously. "They say to pull a mattress over yourself. Should I?"

"I wanted to make sure you're okay. We've had a lot to drink I'm afraid. Were you taking a bath?"

"No. I was taking cover. Should I get myself a mattress?"

"Don't see how it matters now, Con. By the time you got a mattress in the tub it'd be over. Best get on back in that tub without it, dear."

"Did you just call?" Connie asks anxiously.

"Just now."

"Several minutes ago?"

"No. Someone rang here too, but Cretia doesn't want me answering in case it's Tim. We wanted to make sure you're all right. Being there alone and all, I was worried."

"Everything's fine," Connie says. "Tell everyone hi. I'd better go."

"Climb into your tub, Con. We'll be down here. I'll call when it passes."

Shirley had carried the card table into the cellar. Lucretia followed with the olive-colored chairs. Winnifred put herself in charge of the cards and poker chips. A final trip was made upstairs for essentials—the broccoli and cauliflower platter, glasses, saki, cordless telephone, and cigars. Now the three sit around the table under a single dim light bulb, smoking, and finishing off the last of the saki. Lucretia reaches out and fans the cards across the table. Winnifred puffs while neatly stacking the chips. The cellar is suddenly comfortable, cool and humid, overcast in gray fumes. In their present inebriation, winning three tricks of Spoil Five seems trivial, boorish even. "We're in the cellar," Lucretia says, dancing her fingers on the cards, "where we belong."

Shirley dials Janie's number, and Janie answers after the second ring. "We're in the cellar," she says, "where we belong," which makes Janie laugh.

"Too bad I'm not there," Janie says. "Burgess won't go downstairs and I don't give a critter's crap. That boy has me whipped and I don't care. I really don't."

"Tornado been by yet?"

"Don't think so," Janie says. Then she tells Shirley she's going outside. "Gonna take two Coors from the fridge, put my ass in the porch swing, and watch that sucker blow on through."

"Good luck," Shirley says.

"Thanks, but don't need it," Janie replies. "I figure I'm a bigger mother than Mother Nature," and that makes Shirley laugh.

"If we're still here," Shirley says, "I'll call when it's over."

"Maybe we'll get lucky," Janie says faintly. "If Claude gets swept away, maybe it'll be rebuilt with a less dumb name. Sort of hope that happens, Shirl. Is that terrible?"

Shirley taps ash from her cigar. She imagines Claude flattened and scattered like her husband's house of cards on the kitchen counter. "No," she says, "I don't think that's so terrible at all."

Lucretia pours the last remnants of saki in her glass as Shirley clicks the OFF button on the cordless. "Here's a hoot," she says. "That tornado kills Tim's Bronco. That's something to hope for. Better yet, that tornado also murders that heap I've got to drive my poor self in. Double vehicular homicide."

The overhead light bulb flickers and dies, and Winnifred gasps in the dark. "It's the electricity," Shirley says.

"Or is it the bulb?" Lucretia says.

"Don't know."

The three sit in darkness, their cigars glowing. "Do you hear anything?" Winnifred asks, but the others are silent. She leans forward at the table, toppling the poker chip stacks with an elbow. "Can't hear a thing."

Then thunder bellows in the distance. "This is it, I think."

"Thank god."

And Winnifred can't help it. She wants everything up above torn apart and bent and made crooked. She wants to leave the cellar and walk among the wreckage; her hair hanging around her face, immaculate, glinting red in the evening.

She wants to stand alive and intact before the splintered creations of men. In the quiet of the cellar, her only deep fear is that nothing will happen–and, truth be known, she is not alone in this regard.

# Viv's Biding

## 1.

Viv rolled into her room after breakfast, working her wheel-chair toward the dresser by the window. Her roommate Simone was already there, having breezed by Viv in the hall-way moments ago, going forward on legs that would soon turn one hundred and one years old—and now she rested upon her bed, kicking those legs in the air as if riding an upside-down bicycle, doing her morning exercises: "One two three, one two three—"

And if Simone weren't so deaf, if she weren't half blind, Viv would have waved a hand at her, commenting about how good their breakfast of buttered toast and scrambled eggs was, much better than yesterday's soft-boiled eggs and waffles. But conversation with her roommate was usually pointless, Viv understood, and she just didn't feel like putting her breakfast thoughts on a note for Simone to read. Anyway, she had more urgent business to take care of; mainly, writing her friend Alice before the mail was delivered and picked up that after-noon, then finishing up a rather troublesome word Jumble that had been stumping her since the previous evening.

"One two three," Simone continued counting aloud, legs cycling. "One two three," she said, her voice punctuated with huffing.

Viv glanced at the wall clock near her small oak dresser. It was almost nine; by ten the noisemakers would begin lurching along the hallways, creating their usual ruckus, often messing their britches and stinking up the place, sometimes running their wheelchairs or walkers into one another. "The crazies," Viv called them. "The worst of the worst." Still, she had almost an hour in which to write in relative peace, perhaps enough time for composing the most important part of her letter—unless, of course, Simone suddenly decided to watch TV (how that woman loved her talk shows, how bothersome that she could only enjoy them with the volume maximized).

"Simone, you need headphones, " she once complained. "You're ruining my ears."

"It's *The View*," Simone replied, pointing at the TV. "*The View*," she repeated, saying it loudly, enunciating slowly, as if it was Viv who had poor hearing.

You're pointless, thought Viv. Can't get a thing I say.

That was before her daughter Debra bought her earmuffs, a nice fuzzy red pair which Viv found necessary to use more frequently these days—when the woman in the next room started her daily moaning ("Oh god—! Oh god—! Bring me the phone! Oh god—!"), when summer thunderstorms raged at night, when the crazies were roaming the halls. So today she would take the earmuffs from a drawer, leaving them on her lap while she wrote, just in case.

"One two three, one two three—"

Straightening the wheelchair, Viv stopped in front of the dresser, blowing dust off its polished surface as she retrieved her earmuffs. And because the dresser had been a high school graduation present given to her by her parents some eighty years earlier, she was careful when opening and closing the drawers, never yanking abruptly or pushing in too quickly. Over the decades, the dresser had traveled with her to college, then to the brick house her husband built, then to the tiny apartment she rented after becoming a widow—ultimately making the long trip from West Texas to this Baptist Retirement Village in Arizona, where the antique now occupied a place beneath her window and, like it had done for her at college, doubled as a writing desk (the top always kept clean and uncluttered; her pens, envelopes, stamps, and notepad all arranged neatly).

Viv put the earmuffs in her lap. She pulled the notepad closer, and then sat there gazing out the window into the courtyard. "All right," she finally said, taking a deep breath, absently reaching for a pen. For it was to be a long letter, though not a particularly happy one. In fact, she had some bad news to send Alice: last Tuesday evening their good friend Sharon had passed away. Perhaps Alice already heard; it wouldn't be that surprising since the two had remained in West Texas (Alice in Lubbock, Sharon in Amarillo), living a few hundred miles from each other. But Sharon's death came as quite a shock, so Viv wished to share her feelings with Alice, to communicate with someone who might also carry the same amount of grief.

Darling Sharon, she thought. *I have felt sad about her severe illness,* she wrote Alice, *and have missed her much since moving from Texas. She was a sweet, dedicated person, and a lot of fun.*

Darling Sharon, with her long brown hair in a topknot, her slender neck, skin so soft and tan, seventeen and dancing with her best friends, Viv and Alice and Lucy—spinning in her flowered sundress during a picnic at the Caprock Canyon, holding hands and twirling as the sky grew dim at dusk and bullbats sailed overhead. Viv had once tried telling Simone about the beautiful devotionals Sharon gave in their church when they were young and unmarried and living in Claude. "She was a very pretty girl," she told Simone. "Then her hair turned pure white, and she became a very handsome woman." Except the words didn't register with Simone; she squinted her eyes, trying hard to understand. "You're as deaf as they come," Viv said, frustrated. "You can't hear me, right?"

"I'm sorry," Simone said. "What's that again?"

Viv shook her head. "Nothing," she said. "It's nothing." One hundred and one in December, she thought. "Next January you'll have dipped your toes into three centuries, but you still won't grasp a thing I utter."

"Sorry, Viv. I didn't catch that, say again."

Why even bother, Viv wanted to tell her. It had been tough enough asking Simone to stop pushing her wheelchair to the dining room, a real chore getting her to understand that she navigated recklessly, that her terrible eyesight and dwindling hearing had nearly caused several collisions with the crazies. Furthermore, on the afternoon that the news of Sharon's death arrived, she tried explaining her loss to Simone without any success. And how curious it was, Viv mentioned, that she had just finished writing Sharon, had sealed the envelope and affixed a stamp, when Nurse Montoya–*Alice, she's such a fat woman, you think a nurse would take better care of herself*–walked into her room for mail delivery and pick up. So Viv handed the nurse a letter for Sharon, and the nurse handed Viv a letter from Sharon's daughter. "It's strange," she said to Simone. "You know, my friend Sharon was on my mind the entire week, then her daughter's letter came." But the odd smile on Simone's face, the confused blinking of her watery blue eyes, made Viv realize she wasn't reaching her. Would have an easier time conversing with a mute, she imagined. Would be better off going to the dresser and writing dear Alice–because Alice would recall those picnics in the Caprock *(Do you remember those trips? I think we were years ahead of our times, inventing ladies night out and all that, don't you think?)*.

And Alice too could envision Sharon as a teenager, talking a mile-a-minute, doing her funny impressions of their school teacher Miss Hicks, pinching her nostrils and speaking in that grating, nasally tone: "You girls there, right now, settle down! Sharon, Vivien, Lucy, Alice–you four settle yourselves this moment and shut your mouths and be quiet!" What a hoot Sharon was, such a clown, never a pill. And while it had

been years since Viv last saw her, she still couldn't believe
Sharon was gone. But the letter from Sharon's daughter
reported the death in detail, letting Viv know that her childhood friend had gotten worse on Friday, pulmonary functions
began failing. Without a ventilator, the family was warned,
Sharon wouldn't live through Friday night. *Unfortunately
Mother didn't have pneumonia,* Sharon's daughter wrote, *or anything they could cure, so we decided against the ventilator.*

Yet Sharon did live on for a time, was even a little conscious on Sunday (though not at all on Monday). On
Tuesday, her family put her in hospice—a short stay as it
turned out. Still, after four weeks in the ICU, Sharon's daughter sensed that her mother was more at peace in hospice, that
near the end she appeared more comfortable. As death
approached, the hospice people showed the family what to
watch for in the final moments, impressing upon them the
importance of loved ones being present when Sharon ceased
to be.

To Alice, Viv wrote: *Most of her kids and grandkids and great
grandkids were there to see her go. How many kids did Sharon end
up with anyway? She had several boys, I recall. Wasn't there a John
and a Michael? There is a Karen, of course. A Joan too, right? The
letter said one of the son's didn't make any effort to come see her go.
He didn't even call. They'd called him three times when Sharon
started going downhill and he never returned the calls. Can you
imagine that? Sounds like there was some bad blood. Know anything
about it?*

Viv glanced up from her notepad, checking the wall clock.
It was almost ten, almost time for her morning cup of
Cappuccino—then her Daily Bible reading before lunch. So
Alice's letter would have to wait a bit longer to get completed. At least the worst of it was finished—when she
resumed she could write about less depressing matters, such
as the midsummer weather there in Arizona; Simone called it
the monsoon season, those humid weeks which brought
downpours every afternoon. Alice would enjoy hearing about
the heavy rainfalls, she'd like knowing that the monsoons

reminded Viv of the blustery springs in West Texas, albeit without tornadoes and mighty dust storms.

Now gazing at the window, Viv spotted Simone's reflection behind her, watching as her roommate returned from the bathroom with a bottle of lotion, or was it baby oil? Then her attention went past the reflection, going out into the courtyard–where already the ocotillos and lemon trees were shadowed by dark clouds. Just last week she was doing the same thing–sitting at the dresser and studying the courtyard, waiting for the rain to begin falling–when she noticed a woman coming across the gravel with a beautiful flower arrangement, daffodils and zinnias and tulips. "Someone's getting some pretty flowers," she told Simone, not ever expecting that someone to be her. But how delighted she was to receive such a beautiful arrangement, sent from her granddaughter in San Diego, a welcome surprise filling the room with a sweet and earthy fragrance.

A week later the flowers continued to look pretty and fresh, not like the pot plant Chaplain Swift had given her a month ago. What a nice pot plant it was, with little purple blooms–except it died within days. Bad dirt, Viv concluded, mostly sand, must've watered it too much. Unfortunately she never had her mother's gift, that wondrous ability to seemingly touch a plant and make it grow. Wasn't in her blood. She was harder, like her father. So the chaplain's plant fell into the trash unceremoniously. But as for the flower arrangement, she planned on leaving it alone for a while (it was from family, after all). Didn't matter if the flowers eventually wilted and turned brown–at least the green vase was elegant and appeared quite attractive on her nightstand.

## 2.

While sipping her Cappuccino, Viv's oldest daughter Debra and her husband Tom stopped by for a visit. Usually Debra came alone in the afternoons, but she and Tom were on their way to a couples Bible study and luncheon in Mesa. And because they were in a hurry, Debra and Tom didn't stay very long, perhaps thirty minutes, leaving once they'd pushed Viv down to the dining room for lunch.

"Love you, Mom," Debra said, kissing her mother while the other women at Viv's table smiled. "See you tomorrow."

Viv patted Debra's hand. "Okay," she said.

Then it was Tom's turn to kiss her, planting a quick one on Viv's crown, his lips sinking into a swirl of curly silver hair ("Cotton candy," he sometimes joked. "Looks good enough to eat"). "You take care now," he said.

"You're A-one," she told Tom.

How the other women talked about Tom after he left. "He's so handsome," Mrs. Kino said. "You're very lucky," said Mrs. Turner. And even though she had already explained it to them several times before, someone invariably asked again, "What does he do for a living?" So Viv would repeat it once more, bringing nods of approval from the others as she spoke: Tom was a retired accountant, he shared a new home with Debra in Sun City West, he had always been kind to Debra and their children—and it was he, not Debra, who insisted Viv move from Texas to Arizona; he paid all her bills at the retirement village.

"That's wonderful."

"Very fortunate."

But they never asked about Debra, only Tom. They had no interest whatsoever in the daily visits from her own daughter (Tom came every Sunday evening to play Skip-Bo, rarely staying longer than an hour). Of course, Tom was a handsome man (tall and trim, his graying hair kept immaculate, reminding Viv of an older Gary Cooper). Furthermore, he made a point of acknowledging the women at Viv's dining table, smiling at each of them. Debra, however, rarely spoke to the others, doting on her mother instead, fussing over this and that—a bent fork tooth ("Careful, Mom, might poke your gums"), the air-conditioner setting in the room ("Perhaps you shouldn't keep it on low, it's rather cold in here"), and gently trying to prod Viv into meeting a hearing aid salesman ("Not saying you really need one, but it couldn't hurt").

Hearing aid?

"Get one for Simone," Viv had urged her. "Do me a real favor." Because, she knew well enough, a person who wore earmuffs in the summer wasn't going deaf. And if at times she didn't reply to a question or comment from Debra, it probably had little to do with hearing loss. Anyway, hearing aids were unsightly, something her daughter—with her freckled face hidden beneath makeup, her graying hair dyed blond—should have realized.

Still, Debra was a loyal daughter, and Viv missed her terribly when she and Tom went traveling (touring the California wine country last month, setting off in a week for the mountains of Colorado). Also, she brought Viv a steady supply of peanut butter crackers ("Lil' dudes," Viv liked calling them.), which made an excellent afternoon snack, especially if lunch wasn't particularly good. But today's lunch was tasty enough, offering lean chicken strips, steamed carrots, and individual butterscotch pies for dessert; the perfect meal to have—not too heavy, not too light—before beginning the slow journey back toward her room.

"Well, I could have that everyday," she told the others once her plate had been cleaned, after she folded her napkin and placed it beside her fork and knife. "I'll see you gals at dinner," she then said, moving her wheelchair away from the table.

"All right, dear."

"Be careful."

As she rolled from the dining room, heading into the hall-way, Viv heard thunder, a single boom that flickered the fluorescent overheads and made her smile–for soon, she felt certain, the letter to Alice would get finished while the court-yard plants glistened with raindrops. I love the rain, she planned on writing in the letter. I love how the earth smells, how everything looks dull and shiny at the same time. There was so much to tell and ask Alice, and continuing onward–rotating the wheels, deftly steering clear of a woman who stood motionless in her walker–Viv found herself hoping that Alice and Lucy might someday come for a visit; they were, after Sharon's passing, her only surviving friends from childhood.

But she had lost touch with Lucy, having last heard from Alice that Lucy's heart was giving her trouble: *She's been in and out of the hospital, Alice wrote. I pray she gets better so she can stay put at home. Her daughter writes me often and says Lucy enjoys living with her. Awfully nice of Eden to take care of her. Just don't like the idea of our Lucy in a care center.* This coming from Alice–who worked for years as a nurse in a care center, who now lived in one. And how long since Alice had written her? Viv couldn't recall for sure. Maybe two months, three? It was hard to say.

"You could at least call me, you know! At my house! You know, my house–!"

There was Mister Malley, that wretched man in his wheel-chair, hands folded limply on his lap, coming down the hall, using his right foot to push himself forward. Crazy old fool, Viv thought. Always carrying on about his house, creating traffic jams in the hall. Furthermore, he had twice come into her room, blocking the doorway, and wouldn't leave. And once, when Viv was in the bathroom doing her business (*It's horrible, Alice. They won't let us close the toilet door unless a nurse is nearby or some of the family is here*), Mister Malley suddenly appeared, talking to her as she sat on the commode, saying, "Where's my house? My house, you know."

"You get out!" Viv had yelled at him. "Go on, you!"

Luckily Nurse Montoya was in the next room and heard her–otherwise, Viv figured, she might have been trapped on the commode for a while. And even though the nurse explained that Mister Malley was almost blind, even though she said he was harmless enough, Viv avoided the man whenever possible, sometimes waiting until he had passed her doorway before leaving for the dining room.

"I miss my house!" Mister Malley rolled past her, his right foot dragging across the carpet. "Where is it—?"

Viv sighed relief, happy he was now behind her. Stop whining, she wanted to tell him. I miss my house too. We all do.

Still, as far as the crazies went, Mister Malley had nothing on Little Tiger, another terror on wheels. Viv didn't know the woman's true name, neither did Simone—so, because of the way she gritted her teeth and growled, they called her Little Tiger. What a mean woman she was, slapping at anyone who got close, shouting gibberish in the hallways. "Poor thing," Viv used to say when seeing her. Poor thing—no older than sixty, with such dark eyes and black hair, face half paralyzed, apparently put into the retirement village by a stroke.

But now she detested the woman, couldn't stand the sight of her. "Totally gaga," she told Debra. "A regular little thief, that Little Tiger." Just yesterday, while writing at the dresser, Viv glimpsed Little Tiger's reflection in the window, watching in shock as she tried stealing the black pants Simone had left hanging on the closet doorknob. Before Viv knew it, she was turning her wheelchair and rolling as fast as she could toward the woman, saying, "Those aren't yours! Give them here!"

"No you don't," Little Tiger said sluggishly. "Oh no no!"

"You best stop right there!"

She was almost out the door, going backwards in her wheelchair—one hand working the left wheel, the other clutching the pants—when Viv caught up to her. Then a tug of war ensued, with Viv seizing a pants leg while Little Tiger struggled to keep her hold. "No no no NO!" And if Nurse Montoya hadn't once again been nearby, Viv felt certain that Little Tiger would have likely won—or, in the very least, Simone's pants would have been torn. But fortunately the pants weren't damaged, and Nurse Montoya quickly disappeared with the woman, pushing her along the hallway as Little Tiger slapped at the air and yelled, "No no no—!"

Thief, thought Viv. Crook. For surely she was the culprit who stole Simone's ballerina music box last week, Mrs. Kino's egg-shaped broach a week before that. Wasn't it obvious? And same as Mister Malley, Little Tiger had snuck into their room in the past, doing so after lunch and while they napped. Viv had seen her, had opened her eyes and spotted the woman exiting their room, mumbling something underneath her breath. So Viv no longer napped consciously during the day; it was too risky with all the crazies roaming freely. "Guess I'll keep an eye on things," she told Chaplain Swift yesterday. "Simone is hopeless. Care centers shouldn't have these problems."

No, a care center shouldn't have thieves—or be called a retirement village, especially if the village was contained within a one-story brown stucco building (a place where the occupants were confined, forbidden to walk freely past the reception desk and outside through the sliding glass doors).

"I suspect it's worse at others, Viv."

"That's probably true."

And now approaching the doorway to her room, Viv wondered if the crazies bothered Alice much at her care center. She wondered if Sharon had ever run into the likes of Little Tiger or Mister Malley.

"Darling Sharon," she said to herself. At peace with the Lord, safe from all the crazies. But had she mentioned the funeral to Alice yet, had she written about the service at First Baptist in Amarillo? Because that was something Alice would want to know, that was something she would appreciate hearing about. And no doubt Sharon looked good in her casket—lots of flowers and people, Viv imagined. Lots of family and friends.

"Coming through," Simonè said, brushing past Viv's wheelchair, practically jogging into their room, beating her again. Just then thunder rumbled, flickering the overheads. A real downpour, thought Viv as she reached the doorway.

"Cats and dogs," she said, making her way toward the dresser–to where the letter for Alice awaited her and, beyond the window, she could see the courtyard plants trembling in the fast falling rain.

## 3.

A week passed without a reply from Alice: *P.S. You owe me two letters,* Viv had written her, *except I do understand how easy it is to fall behind—please don't feel obligated, just a postcard would be nice.* So when the mail arrived, she always checked the postmarks first, hoping for a letter stamped in Lubbock. But nothing was sent by Alice, not even a postcard.

Still, Viv did receive something from her granddaughter in Dallas, a box of goodies—chocolates and cookies—with a heart-shaped balloon attached (the balloon soon escaping, floating to the ceiling where it popped). Then she heard from her grandson Chad—a brief note letting her know that he and his wife Connie were doing fine in Claude. Connie had had a cold recently, though it didn't last very long. She also heard from Sam, her nephew in Amarillo; he said his by-pass operation went well (*Not quite back to my old self yet, can't go fishing for a while*), and went on to mention that his brother Ken was recovering from surgery on both hands (*Carpal tunnel syndrome. Kept him off work two months and couldn't drive*). Like all correspondence sent to her, Viv placed the letters at the center of the dresser top, leaving her writing pen on them until she could eventually reply.

Now—suffering with a little indigestion after dinner, waiting for a nurse to come give her an early evening shower—she sat facing the window and worked on the daily word Jumble. Before dinner she had managed to unscramble three of the four puzzles—tysoo was sooty, noake was oaken, harter was rather—but she couldn't figure the last: murtes.

Sterum? Strume? Rumset?

Viv glanced at the window, finding Simone's reflection and asking, "Is termus a word?" Simone was sitting beside her bed, upright in a chair, motionless, perhaps napping. "Guess not," said Viv, when it became apparent no answer was forthcoming. Just then the Jumble felt pointless, a silly diversion. Anyway, she didn't really enjoy puzzles much, never had; she preferred playing cards: Skip-Bo, Bridge, Kings on the Corner, Hearts, Spades, even Bullshit. Of course, Viv quit calling the game Bullshit years ago, renaming it No You Don't once her children were old enough to play with her. But these days Debra showed little interest in cards, and Tom only played for about an hour on Sundays. Then Chaplain Swift–promising, always promising, to stop by for a round or two of Skip-Bo soon. "Anytime is good for me," Viv told him repeatedly. "I won't be going anywhere."

"I'll take you up on that sometime, Viv, I promise."

"Yes, I'd like that. Anytime is good."

But his promises were false ones. Pure talk, Viv finally concluded. Bunch of lip service. So, more often than not, she found herself stuck with Solitaire, turning the cards over on the dresser, bored and recalling those summer evenings in Claude–those nights when she and Alice and Sharon and Lucy would sit around a kitchen table, playing cards until nearly midnight, sipping iced tea and eating saltines.

"Let's try Casino," Alice might say, dealing out the cards– because Alice enjoyed being the dealer; she liked teaching them new games she had learned at nursing school. "Or let's try Auction Pitch." Or Canasta. Or Napoleon. Or Whist.

But ultimately they settled upon Bridge as the game of choice. By then they had all married–except Lucy, who seemed content living with her mother, sorting mail in the post office, and creating charcoal sketches of the birds and whitetail dear and pronghorn antelope she studied in the Caprock. How they kidded her about men, joking that she would become an old maid. "No flies on Lucy," she would proudly tell them, as if suggesting men were filthy creatures.

"No flies with zippers for Lucy," Sharon once said unex-pectedly, a remark which flushed Lucy's cheeks and brought giggles from the others. Even now Viv could imagine Lucy– shy and soft spoken (unable to talk above Sharon's volumi-nous tenor), frizzy red hair (not long and straight like Viv's brown hair), and so mousy (dwarfed when standing beside Alice's stout body). A wisp of a girl at twenty-one, a shadow with three attractive and married friends. Twenty-one becomes ninety-seven, Viv thought—then the differences aren't so obvious: *Widowed, each of us has shrunk,* Alice had written months ago, *and gone silver with brittle bones, a million years from what we were; my face looks like a crumpled paper sack, I suppose everyone's does at this age.*

Not everyone, Viv knew for certain. Not her roommate, not Simone; her face was strangely unwrinkled, amazingly youthful for someone pushing one hundred and one—a fact she communicated when replying to Alice's letter. It was the same letter in which she asked for Lucy's present address. But Alice hadn't written back, and, since Sharon's death, Viv had grown increasingly anxious to drop Lucy a note—to get in touch and say hi, to inquire about her heart condition. And if Alice was an unreliable pen pal, perhaps Lucy wouldn't be—perhaps she needed the comfort of an old friend, someone she hadn't heard from in years. So Viv began making a list in her notepad, jotting reminders of what to put in Lucy's letter: Sharon, Claude, Arizona, Baptist Retirement Village, monsoons, crazies.

Then there was the crane to report, something Lucy, an avid bird watcher, would no doubt love knowing. Viv wasn't sure if he was a whooping crane or a sandhill crane, but she had spotted him in the courtyard one afternoon following a cloudburst, shaking moisture from his snowy white feathers while his slender legs paced back and forth along the wet grass—until, at last, he came to stand near her window, red and black head gazing skyward. What a tall bird he was, maybe five feet, such a long neck too. Before Viv could get Simone's attention, before she could tap on the window, he extended his wings—six feet in length, seven?—and flapped into the air with a tremendous leap, emitting a goose-like honk as he sailed from view.

The next day, Viv mentioned the crane to Simone's daughter Jane, telling her how close he stood, how wide his wings appeared. "You're fortunate," Jane said. "I've lived in Phoenix twenty years, but the most I see are quail. Can't say if I've ever seen a crane in my life, actually. Mother, have we seen cranes?"

Simone shrugged in her chair, smiling disdainfully, hardly concealing her irritation that Jane usually spent her visitation time chatting with Viv. And Viv—aware of Simone's jealousy, slightly amused by it—couldn't help herself; she liked their conversations, was grateful for Jane's company. Indeed, the woman brought to mind a younger Alice—both were nurses, both were large, big boned, with short white hair, somewhat gruff and humorless—but Jane, at seventy-six, had avoided marriage; Alice, however, had married twice in her ninety-seven years, losing the first husband to lung cancer, the second to another woman.

But if Simone harbored any resentment toward her daughter's friendship with her roommate, Viv too carried a degree of envy—for Jane did her mother's laundry, something Debra would never consider doing (not as long as the retirement village offered the service, not while Tom paid the bills). Furthermore, Jane massaged Simone's feet and legs weekly, and sometimes she took her mother out for dinner, buying her meals at Luby's or Red Lobster. But Viv endeavored to hold her envy in check; after all, she spent hours chatting with Jane while Simone—unable to hear them very well, incapable of adding to their conversation—sat nearby, tapping a foot on the floor and occasionally sighing. "You're a blessing for me and your mother," Viv often told Jane. "Dear, your face brightens my day."

Of course, Jane wasn't the only one; a few other faces brightened Viv's days, each being as welcome as a distant friend's letter—Yuki, the Asian woman who did Viv's hair every month, who always gave her a sampler bottle of scented Baby Oil with vitamin E and aloe; also Ling Ling, the little Pekinese that visited the retirement village twice a month (such a sweet dog, happy to be led into the dining room, grateful for scratches and pets from blotched hands); and Chaplain Swift, delivering his sermons on Sunday mornings and evenings, making the rounds each Wednesday with

*Praise His Name* pamphlets, good for a kiss on the cheek and a pun or two: "Know what the problem at immigration proved to be? A borderline case"; "Know what an oldster sometimes prefers? A siesta to a fiesta."

"Pretty funny," Viv would always say. "You're a hoot."

And even though the chaplain spoke promises he had no intention of keeping, Viv tried overlooking his faults. Anyway, he was a clean man, pale with graying black hair, broad shoulders, and an infectious laugh; his sermons were mostly positive, full of forgiveness and acceptance. "When you stand praying then forgive," he was fond of saying. "Forgive so that your Father may forgive you." How contrary the gregarious chaplain was to the bombastic Brother Groves, that youngish preacher who appeared in Claude one fall, selling fresh eggs and delivering brief sermons for free.

It was in 1929–maybe 1930–when Brother Groves first wandered into town sporting a new Stetson and spotless dungarees, talking fire and brimstone, relating the horrors he had witnessed in the First World War to an Armageddon, he believed, which was surely nigh. "Blessed are God's soldiers that do his commandments," he preached in living rooms, the corners of his mouth wet with spittle, "that they may have the right to the tree of life, and may enter in through the gates. For without are dogs of war, and sorcerers, and whoremongers, and murderers, and idolaters, and whosoever loveth and maketh a lie–so they shall be as polluted rivers and cannot flow into the sea of God."

Lucy was quite taken with him, as were Viv and Sharon. But not Alice; she wasn't impressed by his charm, his lean body, his dark good looks. "A snake," she warned the others. "A scoundrel in disguise. If he's so righteous, why does he smoke?" Why travel from Quitaque to sell eggs? Or loiter in the kitchens of married women? Or insist a spinster such as Lucy go bird watching with him at dusk?

Still, he seemed decent, humble in a way, showing dismay for the slightest of human transgressions–like the time Viv's oldest son Andy and Sharon's son Jim had finished picking cotton (a part-time job that kept them busy on the weekends, giving them some extra pocket change); both boys were resting on Viv's porch steps, tired and dirty, amusing themselves by cupping hands beneath their armpits, pumping their arms and creating fart sounds. But no sooner had they started, when Viv opened the screen door and Brother Groves stepped from inside the house. "'Preciate your business," he was telling Viv, just as Andy brought his arm down—then what noise emerged, terrible and sonorous and potentially foul. Viv could remember the man's face— awash in confusion, registering disgust—as he turned and removed his pipe, saying, "For goodness sakes, boy!" Such shock coming from someone who had seen men blown apart, who had watched friends die abruptly as they scrambled toward trenches.

A few days afterwards Viv learned the truth concerning Brother Groves. "Selling stolen eggs," Alice mentioned, "and planting his seed where it don't belong." An egg stealer for sure—a reality Lucy found hard to conceal, her belly swelling amid rumors and investigations. Alice gathered little comfort in being right about the man, was not smug when Brother Groves' crimes became known—for he was a snake, a scoundrel in disguise, roving from town to town, stealing from farms at night and selling his gain by day (somewhere he had a wife and two children, somewhere else he had stolen a car). Then he was gone for good, a thief on the run, leaving scandal in his wake.

But Lucy would have his child. She would continue to sort mail and attend church, ignoring the stares and whispers and quiet condemnation of Claude. When the child came, born into Alice's hands while Viv and Sharon took turns wiping sweat off Lucy's face, she would be named Eden ("After a place of peace," Lucy said). A fortunate child too, doted on by her mother's friends (Christmas with Alice, Thanksgiving with Viv, Easter with Sharon)—eventually growing into a fine woman who tended Lucy in her old age, knowing only that her father was a handsome soldier, a victim of the battlefield.

As for the war, no one could say if Brother Groves had actually served. So perhaps, Viv imagined, he really had glimpsed hell overseas, perhaps he had seen awful things there. War can damage a soul, she knew; it was enough to make men seek God through a darker faith, discovering scorn where His forgiveness and love should be. And maybe Brother Groves–that liar and crook, that polluted river–was at last resting in the healing light of the Lord, because, as Chaplain Swift pointed out, the sea of God refused no river; everyone was forgiven.

Umtres? Tresum? Setmur?

"Muster, I think."

Simone's voice startled Viv; she hadn't noticed her crossing the room, hadn't spotted her reflection stepping up behind the wheelchair. "What?" she said, glancing at the wall clock. 6:36. The nurse was late; Viv hated waiting for her, especially since she hadn't showered since Tuesday (doctor's orders: showers on Tuesdays and Fridays for skin that was too dry, that over the years had had most of the oil washed from it).

Simone leaned over the wheelchair, aiming a finger at the final Jumble puzzle: murtes. "Looks like muster," she said.

Muster?

"You're right," said Viv, unscrambling the word. "Thank you."

Then Simone–gazing at the window, looking into the courtyard–placed a hand on Viv's shoulder. But it was already dark outside, and Viv wondered what Simone could possibly see there.

"It isn't raining, is it?" asked Simone.

"No," Viv replied, checking the wall clock again. "Not yet."

## 4.

On the morning Tom and Debra departed for Colorado, the sky went from blue during breakfast to overcast by lunchtime. That night it stormed wildly, and the ceaseless thunder–along with rain thumping the roof, lightning continually illuming the window–prevented Viv from sleeping well. At some point an ambulance arrived outside with its sirens sounding: Someone's passed on, thought Viv as she turned in the sheets. And even after summoning a nurse to fetch her earmuffs, she continued shifting restlessly in bed. Then at dawn the clouds cleared off, but Viv woke uneasily, sensing the beginnings of another storm–a twisting inside her bowels, something worse than indigestion. The bug, she thought, punching the call button beside her bed. Simone's bug.

The previous day Simone had fallen ill, throwing up twice–once while eating lunch, again when watching *60 Minutes* with her daughter. "A bug," said Jane, pressing a palm against her mother's forehead; the same bug that was going around the retirement village, that lately made the dining room a less crowded place (yesterday evening only Viv and Mrs. Turner occupied their usual spots, eating chicken strips and peach cobbler at a table normally set for six). Then how heartbreaking it was seeing Simone enfeebled and bedridden. To worsen matters, she had been among those nominated by the staff for queen of the Baptist Retirement Village–and tonight at dinner both king and queen would be announced, the crowns put upon their heads, a photograph taken. Except Simone was far too sick to attend, making her chances of winning nonexistent.

So most likely it was Mrs. Niello who would become queen. A great shame, Viv believed, for the reason that Mrs. Niello was haughty and rude, never friendly, often bragging about the weekend she spent with William Randolph Hearst ("Willy," she called him, "My dear friend Willy"); the last thing the woman needed was a crown. "Isn't right," Viv said last night, holding Simone's hand while Jane rubbed her mother's shoulders. "This one gets the bug, and someone like Mrs. Niello can hardly keep from smiling—gloating over another's sickness, gives me half a mind to cause a ruckus if she wins."

But today it was Viv's turn to suffer: with Nurse Montoya's assistance, she got herself onto the commode seconds before diarrhea flowed. Following breakfast, a meal which she hardly touched, she vomited on the pretty black blouse Debra had given her as a Christmas present. And now—her wheelchair near the foot of her bed, a towel across her lap just in case— Viv watched as Jane helped her mother walk toward the bathroom (Simone's feet shuffling along, the backside of her blue cotton gown stained brown). Then she wished Debra was there, doing for her as Jane did for Simone. She wished Debra could somehow know how awful she felt and would return posthaste from Colorado. It wasn't right, Viv thought, that she should face illness without family—even if nurses and doctors were at hand, even if Chaplain Swift stopped by briefly to check on her, as he had done earlier.

"You want a glass of water, Viv?"

"No, I'm fine. Thank you."

"Well, you pull through this, okay? I'm praying for you."

"Thanks."

He bent, kissing her forehead. He gently squeezed her wrist. Standing upright, he said, "Know why barefoot kids remind me of arctic explorers?"

"Why?"

"They wear no-shoes," he answered, grinning.

"They wear snowshoes," she said, miserably. "I like that."

And maybe his little joke had an effect or his prayers were hastened, because Viv felt somewhat better after he left. Certainly she wasn't as bad off as Simone, who was slowly entering the bathroom, fingers gripping Jane's sleeve. So she breathed deeply, smoothing the towel, straightening it, and realized just then that her diamond ring wasn't where it should be: on the third finger of her right hand.

She shifted the wheelchair toward the dresser—coffee cup, tin of orange-flavored Cappuccino mix, writing pen, stamps, notepad, envelopes, unanswered mail, scissors, but no ring. She shifted to the opposite direction, scanning the top of her nightstand—the wilting flower arrangement in the green vase, framed photographs of grandchildren and great-grandchildren, her Daily Bible and box of Skip-Bo cards, but no ring. "Where are you?" she asked herself, glancing about the floor; her eyes searched the gray industrial carpeting, traveling past Simone's dresser and nightstand, around their beds, finally stopping at the closed bathroom door. Suddenly she remembered: that morning on the commode she had messed her right hand when wiping, so Nurse Montoya removed the ring and set it beside the sink, intending to wash it once Viv was cleaned up.

What a relief. No doubt the ring remained by the sink, and the minute Simone was finished in the bathroom Viv would ask Jane to retrieve it. Then perhaps she might mention the diamond ring being a gift, a surprise from her husband Carl on the occasion of her fortieth birthday. He had purchased it at the pawn shop in Claude, gladly paying five hundred dollars; that was fifty-seven years ago, when five hundred dollars was a substantial nest egg. But Carl's law practice had had a good year, so he didn't mind the extravagance, telling Viv, "You're worth this and more," as he slipped the ring onto her finger.

Such a kind husband, very easygoing, placid. A wonderful father too, filling his pipe in the living room, listening intently to whatever the children were saying, always laughing. And if their forty-one years together seemed uneventful (for rarely did they fight or raise their voices), then at least it was a comfortable marriage, safe and loving. Because Carl did little to infuriate Viv, little to excite her—he was, even when dying of a heart attack, accommodating: "No—please—don't trouble yourself—I'll sit for a while—it's okay—"

"A saint of a man," Alice said at his wake. "You got the best of the lot, Viv."

A saint of a man, Viv agreed. Much different from Sharon's husband, from that Jeff–a hard drinking and abusive man until he found the Lord, a roughneck who, in time, became a respected deacon. Outgoing fellow when sober, mean as hell when he drank. Carl couldn't stand him in their younger days, hated his proximity during picnics or social gatherings. "Can't figure what exactly Sharon sees in him," he said. "Dumber than dirt." A sentiment Alice shared: "Bad weather if you ask me, a born loser." But Viv understood the attraction. Unlike Carl, Jeff had wild eyes and a rangy gait and a coarse manner; he would rather pinch an ass than say hello.

"And the things he does in bed," Sharon confided. "The way he takes ahold and don't stop till we're both plumb tuckered out–never known anything so perfect, Viv, you can't imagine it."

"Really?"

No, Viv couldn't imagine it, although she tried (ornery Jeff stretched upon sweet Sharon, their bodies moving together like the well-oiled parts of a machine). Heaven and hell wrapped together, Sharon said. Everything that's good and wicked. "Don't tell a soul," she made Viv promise. "Our secret to the grave."

"Of course."

There were other secrets as well, things Sharon told no one about–the bruises dotting her back, the welts on her thighs, all glimpsed by Alice: "Seen them for myself, Viv. Plain as day. Went over to Sharon's for my stewpan–and don't know why I did it, I don't–'cept I looked inside 'fore knocking–and there she was, dress hiked to her pits, standing in the living room, rubbing salve on her thighs–I swear, I'll break every bone in that man's body."

But it wasn't Alice who dealt with Jeff, who broke two of his ribs and bruised his chin–it was Viv's husband, gentle and agreeable Carl. "Stays between me and you," he said to Viv, returning home one evening with scuff marks on his Oxfords. Then he sat her down, explaining he had seen Jeff stumble into the alley behind Campbell's Ready-To-Wear. "Drunk as a dog, went there to relieve himself I suppose and passed out." And Carl wasn't looking for trouble; he only wanted a private conversation, to tell Jeff it was wrong hitting a woman. Except Jeff was unconscious, flat on his stomach and snoring beside his own urine. "Made me sick, the sight of him, made me angry—him behaving reckless and wronging Sharon." So Carl kicked him. He kicked his face, then he kicked his side. He kicked hard enough for an agonized grunt to escape between Jeff's snores. "No one can hear of this," Carl told Viv. "Not Alice, not anyone."

"Don't worry," she said. "I'll take it to my grave."

"How you feeling?"

Nurse Montoya brought Viv her mail, two letters and a postcard.

"Better, I think," said Viv, checking the postmarks—Dallas, Amarillo, San Diego (nothing from Lubbock, nothing from Alice, nothing important).

The nurse stooped, asking in her shrill and overbearing way: "You have anything you want sent, any letters?"

I'm not deaf, Viv wanted to tell her. "Not today," she replied. But then as the nurse began leaving, Viv said, "Hold a sec', I nearly forgot." She shifted toward the dresser, reaching for her coffee cup as Nurse Montoya turned on her heels.

"You need something?"

"Don't you know?" Viv asked, holding the cup out.

It was time for her afternoon Cappuccino, time for the nurse to microwave water. "Cappuccino break," said the nurse, accepting the cup. "I'll be right back."

"Thank you," Viv said.

And no sooner had Nurse Montoya strode into the hallway, when Jane opened the bathroom door for Simone. The two moved gingerly forward—Simone supported by her daughter—and Viv inhaled flatulence, a potent smell wafting from the bathroom. Poor dear, she thought. Poor thing. Jane brought her mother to the bed, then assisted her in climbing

into the sheets. "Get some rest, Mom," she said. "I'll bring
you some water."

"All right," Simone said, faintly.

Jane took a glass off Simone's nightstand, and Viv waited
until she had started for the bathroom before asking: "While
you're in there, could you fetch my ring for me? It's on the
sink."

"Sure thing."

Viv smiled to herself, anticipating the ring's arrival on
Jane's palm; for without it she felt naked, incomplete. But the
ring wouldn't be near the sink, or anywhere in the bathroom.
Indeed, it would seem to have vanished completely. "I don't
understand," she said, rolling about the room, searching the
floors. "I don't understand," she said again, after Nurse
Montoya returned and looked underneath the beds.

"It's gotta be here somewhere," Jane said, scrutinizing the
baseboards.

"Yes," Viv said, feeling a sharp pain swirl in her intestines.
"It's here somewhere, it has to be—Carl gave it to me, my husband did." For fifty-seven years she had worn that ring—fifty-
seven years—and, until today, had never misplaced it.

## 5.

Three days passed; each bringing rain, gradual improvement in Simone's health, mail but no letter from Alice, and more fruitless searches for the ring (Chaplain Swift reached inside Viv's slippers, Jane shined a flashlight into the sink's drain, Nurse Montoya went through the laundry hamper). It'll show up, Viv thought. It'll get found. But when the room was vacuumed, once the contents of the sweeper bag had been examined by Nurse Montoya ("Sorry, dear, dust and fuzz is all there is."), Viv began fearing the worst. Then how restless she became, sleeping poorly, absently massaging the ring finger on her right hand. "Least I have my wedding band," she told Jane. "Debra has it for safekeeping–think I'll have her bring it to me, won't feel so bare then."

"How long will she and Tom be in Colorado?"

"Another week, I believe."

Eight days, actually. Eight days without anything on her finger; the very idea nauseated Viv. And even though she had bounced back from the bug, her stomach often rumbled dismally, as if reminding her that something was amiss within the retirement village: first Simone's music box disappeared, then Mrs. Kino's brooch, then Mrs. Garvey's silver-inlaid watch, now her diamond ring.

"We've got us a crook, Jane." Viv leaned forward in the wheelchair. "Suspected it might be Little Tiger," she whispered, "'cept I'm not sure anymore–likely it's someone else, someone on the staff, I think. That Little Tiger just isn't sharp enough to snatch my ring."

Jane also believed a thief roamed the hallways, sneaking into rooms, taking advantage of the elderly and disabled. "You can't trust anyone these days," she said, shaking her head. "I read the newspaper, and the most horrible things don't surprise me anymore."

Viv agreed, telling Jane she quit reading the paper months ago. She had had enough of child-killer moms. She didn't want to learn about Catholic priests infected by HIV, or white supremacists forming student organizations on university campuses. "I clip my Jumble and throw the rest away," she said. "Frankly, I'd rather stay ignorant—don't see the point in knowing how terrible our world has become."

"I really think the end is near, Viv—I really do."

"It is for me," Viv said, grinning.

"Don't say that. You'll outlive us all, I'm sure. Anyway, don't fret about your ring, okay? We'll leave no turn unstoned."

No turn unstoned.

"Pretty funny," Viv said. "I like that."

"My father used to say it to us kids. He liked his jokes—enjoyed riddles, crosswords, all kinds of games."

"Too bad he's not around. Could get his help on the Jumble."

"He'd have liked that," Jane said, patting Viv's knee. "He loved puzzles."

"I prefer cards myself."

And after Jane had gone home, Viv went to the dresser and glanced over the daily word Jumble (hortt, yernt, ajurag, krubee). But the puzzle didn't interest her today. Nothing did. So instead she rubbed at her finger while looking through the window, faintly aware of Simone snoring behind her. Outside, the late afternoon rain was falling, thumping everything in the courtyard. Tonight it'll thunder, Viv imagined. Tonight the earmuffs would be needed.

"Take me home! Where is it—?" Mister Malley yelled somewhere down the hallway.

Viv shook her head, murmuring, "Fool."

Then she noticed her reflection's frowning face—ghostly and transparent, illuminated by an overhead fluorescent—and saw how the fingers of her left hand stroked the third finger of her right hand. Jane, you're correct, she thought. Can't trust anyone these days. For surely someone now possessed her diamond ring, possibly intending to make a nice profit from it at a pawn shop—a circle of sorts which, in Viv's mind, her husband Carl would have found curiously appropriate ("The road might be a new one," he was fond of saying, "but the wheel keeps going round in the same old manner"). At least there's my wedding band, she thought. At least I have that.

Viv closed her eyes, envisioning Carl as a handsome groom, quite dapper in his tuxedo, black hair parted along the middle, nervously putting the wedding band on her finger while Alice, Sharon, and Lucy stood nearby smiling. "You bet I do," he had said on the altar, moving forward for the kiss that sealed their marriage. Being four years her senior, he was already practicing law when they became engaged (Viv had only recently returned from West Texas State, where she earned a degree in Household Administration). Soon three children were born in quick succession—Andy, Debra, Lem—and after a fourth arrived stillborn, the young couple stopped trying for more. In fact, they quit having relations altogether, ultimately taking separate beds. Yet there was no affection lost, no tenderness lacking; anyway, Viv reasoned, both were too busy—she with the children and the house, he with his work—so, in a way, their partnership and family was an ideal one, hardworking and attentive and warm and nurturing, devoid of ephemeral passion, big on love.

But the day they married, that evening, he undressed her beside the bed—then lowered himself to his knees and pressed his lips against her belly, kissing her with such fervor, such craving. All throughout the night their mouths and tongues and bodies were at play, tasting each other, licking here and there, gyrating about. Except it wasn't like love or romance—it was something stronger and wilder, something base which dissolved by morning, leaving their lips chapped and their stomachs growling for breakfast. It was the only time Viv recalled feeling Carl's intense desire for her, and, aside from a single indiscretion later on, she never again indulged in a man's rapacious needs.

"For what it's worth, Viv, he was always a gentleman," Alice said, some ten years following Carl's death. "Your husband was kind to me, never crass. I envied your life with him, I did—he really loved you."

They were sitting inside Alice's Buick, parked off a Caprock cattle trail and near the watering hole where they swam as girls. The two had planned a farewell picnic, a final meal together before Alice—her nursing uniform retired, her red-brick house sold—left Claude for a bookeeping job at a Lubbock rest home. But while driving into the canyon the sky grew overcast, then the wind started picking up, billowing red sand across the road. So they picnicked on the front seat, talking between bites of ham sandwiches, occasionally staring through the windshield at the watering hole (over half a century since Sharon, Lucy, Viv, and Alice first dived beneath the brown water, swimming alongside snapping turtles, kicking their unblemished legs). And if Sharon and Lucy hadn't already moved from Claude—Sharon to Amarillo with Jeff, Lucy to Wichita Falls with Eden—then they too would have attended that last outing, enjoying Alice's sandwiches and recollecting the good ol' days, paying no attention as a vagrant breeze lifted dust devils toward grim clouds.

"Probably best it's just you and me today," said Alice, because she had something important to say. "See, I've wanted to come clean with you for ages. It's been eating at me forever, bothering my head, and even if you hate me I think you should know—not right me keeping secrets like this."

"I couldn't hate you," said Viv, lifting a potato chip from a paper plate on the dashboard.

"Well, you say that now—but hear me out first." That's when Alice revealed her terrible secret—though, in hindsight, it wasn't much: during the summer of 1937, she and Carl had a brief affair. "There's no excuse for it, I don't aim to make any—it happened at my house—in the afternoon—shortly after Louis died. I was grieving for him, Viv, I was—and Carl was so helpful and supportive. But God I felt guilty, he did too—we both did. And almost as soon as it got going we stopped it—for your sake—" Then Alice suddenly began weeping, saying as she sobbed, "I'm sorry, I'm sorry—"

Viv handed her a napkin. "It's okay," she said. "I mean, I guess I should be angry—can't really see the point in it, actually. He's dead, Alice, and we're old. Doesn't mean squat from my end of things." Besides, Viv explained, she wasn't faultless either. Many years earlier, she had secretly desired that snake Brother Groves—"carried lust in my heart for him, longed for him badly"—and she resented his pursuit of Lucy. Then there was Jeff, Sharon's husband: "I let him kiss me behind the church," she told Alice. "I let him put his hand underneath my dress and kiss my neck—"

Alice sat quietly behind the steering wheel, no longer crying, listening as Viv related the details of her lurid afternoon with Jeff—how they removed their clothing in broad daylight, touching one another while Carl was at home and Sharon was in her kitchen. Afterwards, they agreed to pretend it never happened. Still, Viv regretted the experience, and for a week she washed her hands and wedding band continually, muttering prayers at the sink, hating herself.

"But if I can forgive myself," Viv concluded, "I can forgive you and most anyone else. People do stupid things—it's allowed."

"I suppose so," said Alice, her eyes welling again.

So Viv scooted close to her, taking hold of Alice's arm. And for a while they sat like that, watching a growing whirlwind eddy beyond the car—a reddish haze swirling carelessly, obscuring the watering hole and, eventually, everything around them.

Viv had dozed off at the dresser, had slumped her head and drooled onto her paisley neckerchief. But a thunderclap suddenly opened her eyes, jolting her awake as the window vibrated and lightning flashed. Another boom erupted, causing her to jerk upright in the wheelchair. And there near her feet—crouched before the dresser, slowly pulling the bottom right drawer out and peering inside—was Chaplain Swift. "Shame on you," she told him, because his presence startled her.

Taken unaware, he glanced up, forcing a smile, and immediately shut the drawer. "Isn't what you think," he said in a hushed tone. "I was looking for the cards, your Skip-Bo cards–figured I'd better teach myself how to play–didn't want to disturb you is all. Honestly, Viv, it isn't what you think–"

Except she hadn't thought anything, really–not until he spoke so lowly, mentioning the cards; for the Skip-Bo box remained upon her nightstand in plain view, sitting exactly where he had seen it last ("Whenever you're ready for a round or two, chaplain, they'll be waiting right there"). Then studying his expression–those wholesome blinking eyes, that uneasy grin–she recognized the failed deceptions of her own children: Andy calmly proclaiming his innocence after a neighbor's stolen BB gun was found beneath his bed; Debra insisting the purplish marks dotting her neck were bruises and not hickeys; tiny incredulous Lem standing naked beside his mattress, outraged by the urine someone poured on his sheets and discarded underwear.

"Viv–?" Chaplain Swift said, his voice wavering as he brought a hand to her knee.

Ninety-seven years, she wanted to tell him. Ninety-seven– almost an entire century of living, witnessing all the pointless messes people create, the foolish things we do to each other– and you suspect I can't see through men such as yourself? "Shame on you, chaplain," she said again, this time meaning it. "Shame–"

"Now hold on–"

He began chuckling nervously, gripping her knee while casting his eyes about the room–his roving stare pausing here and there (the doorway framing the bright hallway, Simone snoring in bed, Viv's liver-spotted hands folded across her lap). Viv sensed a lie was forming, a pitiful excuse, something she wouldn't believe for a second. The chaplain met her eyes with an imploring gaze, but before he had a chance to speak, before his untruth could get uttered, she said, "You'll find my ring, I'm sure. You'll go and find it, okay? You're a good man–I have faith in you. We're friends."

His hand slid from her knee, then his agitated expression softened. "Tomorrow," he whispered, nodding. "In the morning–I promise."

It was a promise she felt, for once, he would be unwilling to break. "Tomorrow," she said. "In the morning–perhaps it'll appear in my left slipper, where you already looked."

Chaplain Swift continued nodding: "Yes," he said, still whispering, his voice sounding resigned and compassionate. "Yes, of course." Then, rising to his feet, he stooped and kissed Viv on the forehead.

"Take care of yourself," she told him, touching his cheek. "I'll see you tomorrow. You'll enjoy learning Skip-Bo–it's a lot of fun."

"Yes."

And when he went from the room, Viv turned her wheelchair and watched him go, gratified with the knowledge that her diamond ring would soon show up. Furthermore, in the following days, a few other things would certainly materialize–a music box, a broach, a silver-inlaid watch. By then Chaplain Swift could no doubt call himself a Skip-Bo pro; it wasn't a very difficult game, after all, and Viv knew he was now eager to learn.

"Listen, life deals us a whole deck of sins," she recalled the chaplain preaching, "but making amends for our wrongdoings need not entail a costly sacrifice. We can correct our errors in simple ways–by becoming attentive, caring, accepting of the failings of others and ourselves–that, my friends, is how we come closest to our Lord and Savior during our stints on this earth." So true, she thought, turning the wheelchair around, bringing herself to the dresser, where she reached for her pen and notepad. "So true," she said, looking into the courtyard, taking a deep breath while considering how to begin a letter to Alice.

It had almost grown dark outside, but Viv could see the raindrops striking the window. And there in the twilight, she perceived the shapes of the lemon trees, the outlines of thorny ocotillo branches jutting upward. Then she saw something else—the crane's slender silhouette crossing the gravel, escaping the downpour, finding shelter beside a lemon tree and shaking moisture from his wings. Of all the places he could fly to, she found herself wondering, why on earth would he visit a place like this? What might possibly interest him here? Still, she welcomed his company, was delighted he had picked a spot near her window for refuge—because now she had something pleasant to share with Alice, now she could start her letter.

# Sifting Through

## 1.

Earlier, the guy behind the counter at Mac's Pretzels in the mall recognized Takashi from a picture in the newspaper, and now the woman who works at Full Circle Compact Discs mentions she saw him last night on *Action 7* news. "You're all over the place," she says, in the smiley, obvious, I've got you pegged, too familiar way that bugs him. "You're a hero."

"I guess," he says with a shrug. He had been minding his own business, checking song titles on the new Elastic Surf CD—"Brain Damage Breakfast," "Tomorrow Means Nothing Else," "Sit & Spin"—when she brushed against him at the display. He thought she looked like an enchantress, all white skin and black lipstick, with a silver pentagram trinket around her slender neck. "Are you a real witch?"

"Sometimes," she says. "When I need to be." So Takashi asks her if the Elastic Surf CD is any good, but she says it isn't. "It's even worse than the last one." Then she mentions how mournful his brown, slightly mismatched eyes appear. "You're fifteen, right?"

"Sixteen in March," he says.

"Hero, you're too young to have such sad eyes."

His sullen expression, Takashi supposes, is the result of nerves and muscles strung too loose. Three days ago, a newspaper article described him as a soft-spoken teenager with a reserved demeanor. Close enough. After all, he saved six children between the ages of four and thirteen and their two adult babysitters, both in their seventies, from a burning mobile home. One nine-year-old boy died in the house. Now, as the part-time witch reminded him, he is everywhere. Another reporter phoned the apartment yesterday to discuss a human interest story. On Monday, Principal Richardson put an arm around his shoulders and said, "We're proud of you, son. All of us." But the attention is unwanted, forced, altogether disquieting. There was a recent time when he was no one; a slouched, hands-in-pocket boy, ambling around without much bother or notice. He was not a hero then, just a stoner, or a skater punk, depending on the perspective, who most girls didn't talk to in the halls, or even stand behind at the water fountain. Jocks didn't slap his neck in a friendly manner. He could disappear after fourth period without being missed by his peers, and that was only last week. To make matters worse, strangers are suddenly praising him in the mall, as well as noticing his imperfections.

"It's just my face," Takashi explains, then he taps a fingernail against the CD jewel case. "Can I have this?"

The woman's thin, evil eyebrows scoot up her forehead. "Doesn't work that way, sweety," she says, taking the CD from his hand. "God, you're bold." He frowns from one end of his mouth and says nothing as she returns the disc to the display—at least the pretzel guy gave him a free Coke. She begins straightening jewel cases, refiling misplaced CDs, so he leaves her there.

The mall is almost empty, except for a smattering of housewives, delinquents, and energetic geriatrics. School is still in session. At the bookstore, a cardboard goblin and three sinister pumpkins dangle from the ceiling near the magazine rack. Takashi flips through a book on aquarium fish, the same book he always flips through when he comes to the mall (it's too big to steal, but the picture of the Blue-girdled Angelfish is the best he's ever seen), then he finds a paperback for his mother in the True Crime section. It's about the Lobster Boy murder in Florida. There are 16 actual photos, some showing Lobster Boy as an adult with his plotting wife and stepson, who had suffered years of abuse from the huge, fierce, mutated fists of their provider, a famous carnival oddity in his day. Another photo has Lobster Boy slumped over and deceased, the fleshy pincers folded under his chin like a pillow, with three neat bullet holes punched in his head.

Takashi lifts his T-shirt and slips the paperback down into his baggy jeans, securing it behind the waistband of his boxer shorts. The proximity of Lobster Boy's relief picture on the book cover, smiling and brandishing those claw hands, pressing rough against his abdomen, imprinting his skin, makes Takashi uneasy. But there is no other way to smuggle it, really, and he wants to give his mother the kind of book she enjoys reading. Anyway, she has been through a lot lately, what with the reporters and everyone in the world calling or coming by the apartment. She deserves a gift. And the Lobster Boy murder is it.

The lone bookseller watches Takashi exit the store with either mistrust or, as Takashi suspects, uncertainty. "Excuse me." A pair of blue, bloodshot peepers gaze through bifocals at the slack-fitting, frayed denim dragging around the soles of high-top sneakers. "Were you on the news?"

"No," Takashi says, without turning. "Not me." He escapes over a fluorescent lit causeway, and wanders toward the arcade with a sense of some change in himself, a loss of his space and movement, anonymous, separate, and mystifying–the price of celebrity, however meager or fleeting. Takashi figures he must alter his appearance accordingly. Tomorrow, he will return to the mall and drift from shop to shop like a ghost again. A baseball cap will cover his shaved scalp. The nose ring can stay home until all the hoopla passes, and sunglasses are always cool, even on cloudy afternoons like today.

Inside the dim arcade, Takashi pulls the book from his boxers. He moves Lobster Boy to a back pocket, a more agreeable location, where the pages bulge thick, obvious, cumbersome. Advancing toward Samurai Fury, he finds his last two quarters and grits his teeth in anticipation of battle.

# 2.

Lance is busy concealing wedges of chocolate-flavored Exlax in the wrapping of miniature Hershey bars, a time-consuming and meticulous Halloween prank, when Takashi opens the front door while still knocking. "Get your Jap ass in here," he says in a loud, animated drawl, so affected, so Texan, so obnoxious, and so Lance that it pushes a grin from Takashi's lips. "Who are you this week anyway? Aaron? Mike? Travis?"

Since the seventh grade, Takashi has changed his name often, three or four times a month by Lance's estimation. It began as a joke more than anything else. One afternoon he'd go down to the library and get another new library card and show it to his friends the next day. Apple Shimura. Ellen Shimura. King Bee Shimura. Last year he settled on an array of fish names. Thicklipped Gourami Shimura. Sarcastic Fringe Head Shimura. Oily Gudgeon Shimura. Black Phantom Tetra Shimura. The library no longer issues him new cards though, and lately he's been thinking seriously about a permanent and real moniker. Something like Lance. An all-American guy's epithet. Brad. Steve. Perhaps Norman. Norman Shimura. Of course, thanks to the local newspapers and network affiliates, his given name is now well-known all over town, unavoidable and persistent.

"I'm no one," Takashi says, putting himself on the couch beside Lance. "Just me. Just Takashi."

"Sorry to hear that," Lance says, preoccupied. He removes his flimsy, straw cowboy hat, flicks it across the living room, where it almost nails his mother's sleeping orange tabby on the recliner chair. "Damn." He brings a hand through his shoulder-length hair, then dips his fingers into the plastic pumpkin on the coffee table. "I'm about out of Exlax. Think you could give me some help with this?" He retrieves a palm-full of Tootsie Rolls, peanut brittle, and tiny Hershey Bars.

"No," says Takashi, who pays little attention as Lance separates the Hershey Bars from the rest of the candy. There isn't much on the coffee table except the pumpkin, an empty Miller Lite beer can, and the tools of Lance's perverse caper— a roll of aluminum foil, three boxes of laxative, a kitchen knife, and a ruler.

"You skip all day?" Lance asks while dropping the peanut brittle and Tootsie Rolls back into the pumpkin.

"Just after lunch."

Takashi comes to visit Lance when he blows off his afternoon classes. Lance is the wildest person he knows, in the way that a caged bronc can be said to be contained but volatile. He is also funny and stubborn, a high school dropout who lives with his parents and works part-time at High Plains Skate & Cycle.

"Couple of longnecks in the fridge," Lance tells him. "Help yourself. Pop won't miss them. Fucker can't ever remember what he's drunk or not." He spreads the Hershey Bars out in a neat row on the coffee table, takes the kitchen knife, and leans forward to continue his dirty work.

"No thanks, but thanks anyway," Takashi says. "I'm going to the aquarium after Paulo gets home from the assembly." He crosses his legs on the couch, clamps his hands around his ankles, and stares to where a TV broadcasts the ending credits of *General Hospital* with the volume turned low.

"Shit, don't even ask me to go," Lance says. "No offense, the thought of another fish trip gets me all saggy below the belt. Hey, ask someone about a job there, then you'd be around them fish all the time."

"Wouldn't be so bad," Takashi says without ardor.

Even if a person has seen them a million times, Takashi figures, the Red-tailed Black Shark, the Raccoon Butterflyfish, and the elongated Coolie Loach are reasons enough to wander the dark, humid aisles of the aquarium at least once a month. At first he had thought that Lance no longer liked going to the aquarium because Paulo is gay and always tags along. But now he realizes that, so passionate is Lance's feeling for all things visceral—the slam of Monster Truck wheels, the crunch of football helmets, the felled buck with the crossbow arrow deep in its neck—he is unable to appreciate the delicate, ornamental qualities of some marine life, unless, as has been the case, a joint is smoked beforehand.

"You and Paulo come around tonight," Lance says. "Mike's bringing a lid over soon as the folks crash."

"I'll see. Maybe." Takashi follows Lance's fingers as he creases aluminum around a measured and cut portion of chocolate laxative. "You know how Paulo is."

"Ah, screw Paulo. Don't get me wrong, he's okay and all, but he sure puts a strain on a good time."

"Shouldn't call him faggot so much, that's all. It bugs him."

"God, it ain't like he ain't queer or nothing. Haven't called him cocksucker, at least to his face. Jesus Christ, son, there you are again!"

Lance is looking at the muted TV. And Takashi is too. An *Action 7* news break between soap operas shows the charred hull of the mobile home in daylight, desolate and hollow, with the sky visible through a broken window where the ceiling should be. A quick cut goes to the night of the fire, the mobile home consumed and filmed from across the street, a small crowd of passive spectators on the sidewalk. Then Takashi appears, sooty and stunned and nervous, squinting under the halogen glare of a single video camera's lamp attachment; an arm sleeved in crimson polyester reaches into the frame to aim a microphone at his chin. The mug shot of Snoopy Garcia, the mental case who started the blaze, is inserted, followed by the brief image of paramedics carrying a body bag buoyed with the insubstantial remains of a child. The TV screen fades to black, and then a commercial for Conroy A.C. Auto Service begins. Takashi glances at the plastic pumpkin on the coffee table.

"Now that you're a regular superstar," Lance says, "maybe you'll get pussy. Maybe you can get some chicas to come on over and share that lid with us."

"I don't know, Lance," Takashi replies, sounding mopey and glum.

Lance fixes him with a blue gaze. "Not too happy to mention this, Tak, but you're a real drag of late–know it?" His expression is suddenly stern, reminding Takashi of how Lance scowls in the mosh pit, shirtless, glistening, with elbows flailing, so angry at everything and nothing at all. "Here," he says, "give this to Paulo," and flips a phony Hershey Bar like a coin.

# 3.

Takashi stands outside Paulo's bedroom window, watching through parted curtains as Paulo, unaware, drops his backpack to the floor, turns the stereo on and up, then belly flops onto his mattress. Hidden behind bushes on the narrow trail that runs between the hedge row and the house, Takashi smokes his last Camel. Inside, Paulo thumbs through some magazine he has pulled from between the bed and box spring, but Takashi can't see what the magazine shows, nor does he really care. He exhales smoke in a steady, directed stream, which dissipates across the window pane nearest his face.

The Halloween yards Takashi crossed on his way here—yards where jack-o'-lanterns grinned from porch steps at yellowing lawns—made him think that fall has arrived unwelcome and too soon. With the maples shedding their leaves, the quality of light contrasting gold and dark to greater degrees, and the air becoming sharper, carrying the woodsy aroma of fireplaces burning in the evenings, it's as if, he believes, everything he moves past is steeped in despair. Moreover, he fears he is solely to blame. When he walks under trees, leaves plunge in his wake. The grass his sneakers tramp over cracks and withers. Earlier, a black cat hissed at him from the hood of a Pontiac. No doubt, when he goes near that Pontiac again, the cat will be on its side and dead.

Takashi takes a final drag on the cigarette. He flicks the butt to the ground, stomps it flat, then knocks on the window, half-shouting, "Boo!"

Paulo's head comes out of the magazine, startled, abashed, his mouth turned into a gaping, almost circular black hole betraying the metal of a retainer. He spots Takashi smirking at the window above the headboard of the bed, and slowly his lips loosen. "I'm not letting you in," Paulo says. "Not now!"

"Okay," says Takashi, who lifts and drops his shoulders once, then steps backwards into the hedge.

"Stupid, get back here!" Paulo crawls across unmade

sheets to the headboard. When he flips the latch to open the window, he is standing on a pillow with the weight of his slender body, his socked feet, testing the springs of the mattress. Takashi stares up at him as he climbs through the window and tumbles to the bed. "We've got a front door," Paulo says.

"I know that," Takashi says. He stretches out on his side, lets his legs dangle over the edge of the mattress, and pushes off his shoes. Paulo's magazine is crumpled beneath his rib cage, so he extracts it carefully, smoothing a few pages before taking in the contents.

"Be warned," Paulo says, shutting the window. "Not so sure it's your thing. No tits." He pulls the curtains together, then places himself alongside Takashi, the magazine between them and their propped elbows.

"Weird," Takashi says. His fingers keep a careful distance from the men in the magazine, who are posed alone in a locker room shower, naked, or in a state of undress—a T-shirt slung across wide shoulders, a jock strap or boxer shorts pushed around muscular thighs, seductive bodies, youngish, lean, with hard-ons and shaved balls. "Where'd you get this?"

"It's a secret," Paulo says. "I can't tell. My aunt said she'd murder me."

But Takashi knows all about Paulo's aunt in Lubbock, the lesbian who owns a used bookstore near Texas Tech. He knows about Paulo too, because during their freshman year, Paulo finally admitted that he was queer. They were getting drunk at Lance's place, playing poker one night, doing shots of Cuervo, when Lance said, "If you could screw any chic on the planet, any ol' one, who would it be? My pick is Cindy Crawford. Cindy Crawford, or that whacked chic who married that ancient millionaire guy."

"What's-her-name Nicole Smith?"

"Yeah, her too."

"Damn, I'm not sure," Takashi said. "Probably someone like Demi Moore, I guess. Ione Skye's good."

"I just like guys." Paulo paused. "Don't know why. Just do. The dead guy from Joy Division is hot. So is Keanu."

And it never seemed like a big deal to Takashi. Why would it? He wasn't really surprised anyway, especially after how Paulo went on and on about Morrissey, or how he started crying over the phone once when reading the lyrics of "Late Night, Maudlin Street" like it was poetry. Even Lance, for all his dumb jokes about fags farting come in hot tubs and dyke nuns with crucifix-shaped dildos, didn't appear too shocked by the revelation, saying only, "That's different, Paulo. Okay. No problem. Who gives a fuck, right? Deal the cards, Tak."

A few more revelations followed, but not on that night. There was the time Takashi and Paulo passed a joint while sitting in swings behind their old junior high. It was summer, and the afternoon was overcast and unseasonably cool. Takashi blew smoke into Paulo's mouth twice, something Lance called "a Colombian kiss," and afterwards, as they set off across the playground, Paulo said, "Don't freak, but I think I'm in love with you."

"No, you're not," Takashi told him. "You're horny is all. And you're baked."

That August, Paulo shaved Takashi's head with electric clippers he had stolen from Walgreens. Morrissey, pouty and aloof in black and white, scrutinized from four posters—one on each of Paulo's bedroom walls—as Takashi sat in a chair with a towel hung around his neck and bare chest, his coarse, black hair getting mowed away in clumps.

Later in the evening, after Paulo had bleached his own head with a peroxide developer, Takashi found himself staring at the spinning blades of a ceiling fan from Paulo's bed. His smooth scalp felt sensitive, cold against the pillow he shared with Paulo, who still reeked from the vinegar rinse he had used on his new mess of blond hair. They talked about the approaching school year, friends they were looking forward to seeing again, and how great it'd be if they both finally got laid. Then Paulo admitted to having a painful crush on Lance. "It's making me nuts, Tak. I used to think he was pretty gross, really gross, but it's not like that now." This confession sent a tiny surge of jealousy through Takashi, which seemed at once shameful and ridiculous. But Paulo said he couldn't help it, and that lately, when he went around to Lance's house, it was becoming harder and harder to just speak to him like a friend. "I turn into this dork, all stupid and shit, and he knows it too."

"Don't worry about it," Takashi said. "You'll find someone else. This year, ten bucks says so. We'll both find someone good."

They continued to talk into the night—about their high scores on arcade games, the mysterious Planet X that is rumored to lurk behind the sun, and who made a better Dracula, Christopher Lee or Gary Oldman—until Takashi shut his eyes while opening his mouth to yawn.

"Stay over," Paulo said.

"I better not."

"I won't try anything, if that's what you're thinking. I promise."

Takashi sighed. "You don't have to promise. I know you won't."

And soon they were sleeping side by side, Paulo under the sheets, Takashi on top of them. In the morning, when Takashi stirred first, he felt the warmth of Paulo's body radiating through the bedding, intense and strangely comforting, like a wash of laziness on a summer's day.

But now it's October, and anything to do with summer feels like much less than a distant memory. Takashi turns to the cover of Paulo's magazine—*Manmusk, Hot & Young...& FULL of Spunk!!!* "You're right, this doesn't float my boat." He shakes his head some, frowning, then glances to Paulo. "Let's go to the aquarium."

Paulo lets his elbow drop and falls back on the mattress. "I'm not really up to it, Tak. Not today, I think."

"How come?"

"I don't know. Nothing personal. I guess I'm tired is all."

"That's okay," Takashi says miserably. "Doesn't bother me. We don't have to."

Paulo sniffs the air, "Man, your feet stink," and waits for Takashi to deliver an insult in return.

But Takashi says nothing. He sits up in the bed, dumps the magazine on the floor, then folds his legs, bringing the soles of his feet together. He pushes his shoulders to the headboard, and stares down at his lap. Almost imperceptibly, he begins to rock.

Paulo rolls over and looks sidewise at Takashi. "Oh, God, I nearly forgot to tell you," he says, "Principal Richardson mentioned you at the assembly this afternoon, gave this sappy little speech about you, said he wanted to recognize you for your heroic efforts. Sounded pretty retarded to me. Then he asked you to stand, but you didn't because, duh, you weren't there. Everybody was all clapping and stuff too. You should've been there, Tak."

"Don't matter," Takashi says. "Glad I wasn't, to be honest. It's all shitty anyway, and I can't go anywhere any more without someone telling me how awesome I am or what I'm like—and I'm not really happy about anything, Paulo, because it all sucks anyway." He suddenly looks bewildered, frightened. The image of the single body bag comes to mind, somehow too real, moving across a TV screen. He has seen it played over and over again since the night of the fire. His mother even videotaped the news segment for posterity. "Screw it, if someone calls me a hero again they'd better watch it," Takashi murmurs. "Call me a hero again and I'll fuckin' rip the top right off their heads like a psycho. I mean it."

"Sorry," Paulo says warily. "Damn, where'd that come from?"

"I'm bad luck is all and I can't sleep," Takashi says, after thinking it over. "I'm just grumpy."

"Tak, you did a good thing. Everything's fine."

"Nothing's fine with me, Paulo. Nothing at all. So are you going to the aquarium or not?"

"Sure," Paulo says, nodding. "If it'll make you happy, I'll go."

Takashi stops rocking. "Thanks," he says.

# 4.

In the Asian Rain Forest room at the aquarium, Takashi gazes into a murky tank, and Paulo at another. They are the only people in this dank place, with its mossy-colored walls and deep-set marine aquaria filled with decaying vegetation. The tanks are fed by a waterfall (constructed of plaster and chicken-wire), which, Takashi is always quick to mention, helps boost oxygen levels underwater.

As Takashi studies a Chinese Sailfin Sucker, pursing his mouth and cooing quietly at the fish like it's a baby, tapping his fingers against the glass to get its attention, Paulo senses none of the weariness or pessimism that his friend displayed before coming here. It's as if Takashi has made a wonderful, calming shelter for himself at the aquarium. He can go to it, escape among the marine life, and nobody can mess with it. In fact, while buying tickets in the gift shop, Takashi didn't appear at all bothered when the Hispanic girl working at the counter said, "I know who you are. You're that guy, right? You saved those kids."

Takashi just half-smiled, saying, "Yeah," with a solemn expression, and Paulo thought he looked embarrassed, perhaps even a bit flattered.

"We got something in common," the girl said. Her face was coated with too much makeup, which was so different from her natural skin color that it appeared as if she had dabbed pink paint all over a brown, pocked terrain. "You know my cousin."

"Who?"

"Snoopy. Snoopy Garcia."

Takashi nodded. He imagined Snoopy's dirty blue baseball cap, the camouflage pants with holes at the knees, his toothless grin as dry grass burned under the mobile home on that Saturday night. When Takashi happened upon the scene with his skateboard, Snoopy was on the sidewalk, watching the fire and laughing, hoping that the wind-whipped flames would bring Gotam, the chief of a thousand demons. Takashi didn't learn about the Gotam weirdness until he read the story in the Sunday edition: "I saw the spirit in the fire. I just stood there, and he was happy," Snoopy told the *King County Register*. "I didn't want to hurt anyone. I just like looking at fires, to see Gotam and make him happy." The paper said Snoopy had been setting fires since he was twelve.

"He's absolutely whacked," Takashi told the girl.

"For certain," she said. Then, because it was nearly closing time, she let Takashi and Paulo go on into the aquarium without paying for their tickets.

Now Takashi thinks about the Chinese Sailfin Sucker. The basic color of the original species is golden brown; the one in the tank before him is of a pinkish rust hue. Three wide, dark bands cross the body vertically, the last covering the short caudal peduncle and mixing into the spread caudal fin. The head is small, and an eye is milky-white, indicating blindness. "This dude's old," he says to Paulo, who is making faces at the huge, torpedo-shaped Koi several feet away.

"How old do fish get anyway?" Paulo asks.

"Depends on what ones you're talking about."

Paulo moves toward Takashi. He stops in front of a tank full of Anemonefishes, the fish that live among the tentacles of sea anemones. The water in this tank is clear, seemingly cleaner than any of the other tanks in the room. Paulo immediately notices a small, tomato-colored Fire Clownfish floating still above the waving reach of the anemones. He taps the glass, but the Fire Clownfish is unresponsive; its compressed body rolls over like a leaf falling in slow-motion. "Check it out," he says, and Takashi steps up behind him. Paulo points. "What's it doing?"

Takashi rests his chin on Paulo's shoulder. "It's dead."

"Shouldn't it float to the top?"

"Some don't," Takashi says, leaning his head against Paulo's ear.

## 5.

Outside of the aquarium, Takashi and Paulo go in opposite directions after performing their ritual handshake (slap palms together, touch thumbs, curl the fingers in, pull back so the fingers lock together for a moment, separate), and Takashi reluctantly starts home. And even though he walks an extra block to avoid the street where the fire occurred, Takashi can't help but think about how the mobile home melted around him like a marshmallow—or at least that's the way he remembers it. He had called into the house, but no one answered. The front door was unlocked, so he rushed inside to see if anyone was trapped. In the living room, his attention was drawn to the ceiling, to where flames rippled overhead. Waves, he thought later. Upside-down waves on a crazy ocean.

He found the children and their elderly babysitters sleeping on two queen-sized mattresses in a back bedroom—a total of eight, four to a bed. "It was weird, like they were all having the very same dream," he told Paulo and Lance. "Like they'd just finished playing and just zonked out all at once." And despite the violent blaze, he roused them and single-handedly got them to the sidewalk, where Snoopy Garcia danced and hooted nearby in ratty sneakers.

It wasn't until the following morning that Takashi realized what he'd done. "I got scared then," he explained to a reporter. "I didn't sleep that night. I kept thinking about the boy. How'd I miss him. I mean, he was in there somewhere, I know that today. But when they removed the body, that's when I knew I'd missed one. The whole thing was confusing—flames were moving up the walls, across the roof. Stuff was melting. It was like a marshmallow."

When Takashi gets home, his mother shakes her head and sighs from where she works a jigsaw puzzle at the kitchen table. She is a short, compact, plump woman. Her hair is thin and swarthy, combed straight back from a widow's peak. In Japanese she tells him Principal Richardson called. In English she says, "He said your attendance hasn't been consistent, at best." She mentions the assembly, adding that Principal Richardson told her Takashi's truancy shouldn't overshadow his heroism.

"I'll do better," Takashi promises. "I've got all these things in my thoughts. I'll get it together." Then he takes the Lobster Boy paperback from his rear pocket and hands it to her. "Looked like something you'd like. I got it new." The pages are bent in places, the binding split.

His mother holds the book at arm's length, studying Lobster Boy's picture on the cover through her trifocals. "Good grief," she says. "Good Lord." Then she sets the book aside while explaining about what she'd seen on the afternoon newscast. A stray cat in Boston had saved all her kittens from a burning building. "She went right on in and carried each one out. Just like you did. Burnt her all up too. But she's alive and recovering, and the kittens are fine. That's amazing, huh?"

"Wow," Takashi says involuntarily. "I think I'm going to lie down." He kisses her on the forehead. She pats the side of his face.

"Say hi to your father before you do. Are you hungry?"

"No. Maybe later."

In the living room, Takashi shakes a prayer bell five times at his father's funeral altar–a small shrine in an alcove near the TV which consists of fake chrysanthemums, worship candles, a bronze incense holder, two Shinto bells sent as a gift from his uncle, and a gold-plated urn. The centerpiece is a rather stern photograph of his father in a teak frame. He lights a stick of incense with a candle, then bows his chin once at the photograph. His father glares helplessly through wire-framed glasses with an abstracted, expressionless face. The man's receding hairline is graying, but nicely kempt. It is an official portrait, a passport picture, enlarged, grainy in black and white. He has been gone for almost six years, but the ghost of him still lingers in the apartment.

In the study that also doubled as his father's dressing room, some clothes hang on a hook beside a kimono. There is a pocket watch on a dresser. An unfinished, handwritten manuscript (*The Aquarist and Fishkeeping*) sits on his desk. On the walls, high up, are framed citations, one of them reading: *Letter of Commendation. Dr. Kenji Shimura is hereby given recognition for twenty-five years of devoted service. March 23, 1978. Signed: Chairman, Federation of American Aquatic Societies.*

Takashi inhales the pungent smoke drifting off the incense. "Hello," he says to his father, "and goodnight." Then he pads along the hallway to his room, where the door stands ajar and the evening shadows touch everything.

When Takashi clicks on the lamp by his bed, he sees that his mother has been here. A folded stack of laundered jeans and T-shirts are on the floor. She has made his bed. He throws himself across the mattress, and sleep comes quickly, sinking into him without any effort or resistance on his part. It is a heavy, brief slumber, and he stirs three hours later feeling anxious. Then he goes down the hall to the bathroom. The rest of the apartment is pitch-black. He had left his door open, and returning toward his room, he doesn't bother to put on the hall light. The door of his mother's dark room is also open, and as he is passing by her voice comes to him. "Are you up?"

"For a little while," he says.

"There's chicken in the kitchen," she says. "In the oven."

"Okay. Thanks."

He hears her mattress creak as she turns in the sheets. "You need to sleep more. It's not healthy not to sleep like you do."

"I know," he says. "I will."

Takashi goes on into his own room and shuts the door. Alone in the hero's domain, he thinks. It is an amusing thought. At the end of the day, the hero is alone with his careful crayon drawings of marine life littering the walls on construction paper. He thinks he might as well be in someone else's space, because nothing here really seems like it ever belonged to him. The box-kite suspended from the ceiling with fishing wire, the posters of New Order and The Sex

Pistols and Nine Inch Nails, the skateboard leaning against a stereo speaker—none of it suggests a connection to him, and he's not sure why. It's as if layer upon layer of his self has been seared away during the week, leaving him raw and exposed and restless. This isn't altogether a bad thing—the possibilities are just beginning to creep into his mind. His bedroom is all kid's stuff, but he isn't. And no one, he knows, should feel as alone as he does now.

It is almost midnight. Takashi finds a plate of chicken wings in the oven. Then he sits in his mother's chair at the kitchen table, gnawing away, and fiddles with the puzzle pieces before him. She has nearly finished this jigsaw, which appears to be an autumnal scene with aspens on a mountainside. The Lobster Boy book is exactly where she left it—the cover turned facedown on the table—but he could care less.

Right now Lance is getting stoned, Takashi thinks. But the last thing he wants to do is be with Lance, smoking a joint and talking loud. Paulo is by himself in his room with the radio on. And it's quiet outside.

Takashi has decided. In a few minutes, he will leave. He'll go to the sidewalk, losing himself in the anonymity of night, and wander past the glowing, smiling pumpkin faces. This is how his day will conclude—crawling through Paulo's window to where a warm place waits. And Paulo won't mind, after all. But first he must finish eating.

# Totem

## 1.

Like my friend Aubrey, I've been alone in the Alexander Archipelago for almost a month. But Aubrey is on another island, and I'm the only person on what's usually marked as uninhabited territory; a place shaped by glacier-scoured cliffs, topped with rainforest, surrounded by narrow inlets of the sea, accessible mostly to floatplanes or salmon boats. Today, I'm bored and sore, with my back against this dying spruce. When I woke inside my sleeping bag at dawn, I found my neck cricked from the lumpy duffel sack I use as a pillow. So now I keep my head tilted a bit to the left, and that eases the pain at the base of my skull.

The spruce is my totem. If the old carvers in Klawock saw what I'm making, they'd probably laugh their wrinkly asses off because my pole is sort of sloppy and shoulder-high and far from traditional. The carvings don't all swirl together, or really bleed into each other; they're more like frames with pictures in them. But four panels are completed so far, not bad considering I don't have the adzes, knives, and chisels needed for detail stuff. I call my totem Spring and Summer

Story, which is a ton better, I think, than a lot of the other names poles get stuck with (The Frog Tree, or Blackfish Pole, or Raven and Whale, or Bullhead and the Fight with the Land Otters).

I discovered the spruce here, in a clearing of muskeg grass, when I first walked from camp to this peak on the nameless mountain. I was hoping to spot the island where Aubrey might be banished, but I haven't had any luck. Most days, the deep fjords below my outlook are covered in a low-lying mist, so it's as if I'm standing between clouds on an overcast, windless autumn afternoon. Anyway, I figure the spruce got nailed by lightning a zillion times, that's why it's splintered and scorched black at the top but pretty much intact near the ground. I've hiked to the clearing for the past two weeks to make my carvings. There's just one more panel to do, right at the bottom. Then the tree will be finished.

I started the totem with a panel of Aubrey's face, but it doesn't really look like him. It's close enough though, except his head appears swollen twice its natural size, distorted in an ugly way; his eyes are long slits, his nose is about as big as a fist and squashed flat. But I'm proud of the hair; it hangs over an uneven forehead, falls around bumpy cheekbones, curls under a wide chin. Of course, a carving isn't very good company, so it doesn't matter much if it seems like him at all. The truth is, I just wanted someone to stand in front of and talk to on this lousy island; even if that someone's nose, hair, eyes, and mouth were dug out of wood with a dull shiv made by my grandfather.

Maybe I wouldn't bother with this totem if I'd thought to hide some photographs in the duffel bag. Six undeveloped rolls are sitting on my dresser in Klawock, but I didn't ever have enough money to get them processed. Or when I got a few bucks from helping Grandfather sell his raven drums and toy dogsleds to tourists on the Alaska Marine Highway ferries, Aubrey and I would ditch school the next day, take the ferry to Ketchikan, and blow most of my earnings at Saxman's Arcade. Then we would wander the common downtown thoroughfares (boardwalks and wooden staircases built around steep hills and propped on wooden pilings). Before the last evening ferry departed, we often killed time by walking along the rickety boardwalk that runs beside Ketchikan Creek, scanning the water for king and silver salmon. At summer's end, when the creek was full of spawning fish that swam upstream to die, we brought coolers packed with ice and gathered the freshest of the dead salmon from the banks.

Sometimes we prowled through the junk at the town dump in Ketchikan. Once Aubrey dug a pair of welder's goggles out from under a stack of tires. He wore them around his neck that afternoon. "Next solar eclipse happens," he said, staring through those goggles at the sun, "I got myself a front row seat with these babies, Cole." It seems like we were always turning up something interesting at the dump to take home—spent shotgun shells, fishing hooks, a rusted Huffy bicycle with the wheels missing, lots of stuff.

There was this stack of *Penthouse* magazines we found in an old milk crate. "Great fucking luck," Aubrey said. We plopped down in the trash and took forever flipping through the pages. Aubrey kept rubbing the front of his jeans, groaning so much that it was getting on my nerves. But he was all grins, practically drooling on whatever picture he was studying, saying horny crap like, "My dick is hurting. It's really killing me. What about yours?" And I'd nod, eyes bolted to the naked women spread on my lap, with my dick bent hard inside my underwear. Then we divided those magazines, and that evening we sat quietly on the ferry to Klawock with our stashes secured behind our jacket zippers.

Last spring, Aubrey and I came through a grove of cedars to the dump grounds. We'd been in the forest taking pictures, but the trees were too tall, shading everything we shot. So we decided to go to the dump and see if something might be worth photographing among the hills of waste and torn Hefty bags. And even though I've never developed the pictures we took there, I know we got at least two good ones. Actually, it was me making most of the pictures, because Aubrey liked being in front of the camera instead of behind it.

The first good shot I took was of Aubrey having a piss on this gutted deer carcass. It was his idea. The stinking carcass was near a row of discarded cinder blocks, and Aubrey stood over its cavernous stomach as he urinated. "Liquid sunshine," he said, aiming his stream at the blackened snout. Then he peed down the hull of the carcass, dampening patches of fur and gray exposed skin. A stink floated off the deer, sulfurous, like beer farts, so I pulled my shirt past my nose. But Aubrey didn't seem bothered at all by the stink. He shook his dick back and forth, causing the piss to spiral like it'd got thrown from a sprinkler. And that's when the shutter snapped.

In my mind, I imagine the photograph this way: a spray of urine is caught in sunlight, glowing, as Aubrey stares down with black hair covering his face. His jeans are pushed to his thighs, and a gray Seattle Mariners T-shirt almost hides what he's holding in a hand. And his left sneaker is planted by the carcass' rigid legs, turned inward by the hollow gut, a place where flies creep and hover.

The second good shot I took that day would've turned out better if I wasn't such a chicken. I mean, when Aubrey and I saw that big grizzly rummaging at the far end of the dump, we stopped cold in our tracks. And even though we stood at least fifty yards away, that sucker looked bigger than life. It was clawing at this suitcase, huffing and snapping its jaws. So Aubrey whispered, "Let's get closer."

"Stupid," I said. "No way." I repeated what Grandfather told me to do if a bear appeared in the neighborhood. "Don't approach it, don't feed it, and don't run."

"Bullshit," Aubrey said. "Get the camera ready." Then he started walking forward real careful and calm. I was watching with the viewfinder when he got about twenty-five yards from that grizzly. Then he turned his back on the bear, puckered his lips at me, and praised the sky by lifting his long arms above his head. The funny thing is, that grizzly was so preoccupied with getting the suitcase open it didn't ever notice Aubrey. Or maybe it smelled him but figured he wasn't worth its spit. Either way, I think the shot must be fairly unusual: Aubrey's mouth blowing a kiss, low clouds stretched over heaps of trash, a grizzly tearing at a suitcase in the background.

My camera is a Minolta XG-1 (wide-angle lens, self timer, skylight filter). It belonged to this white guy from Vancouver named Ed, a funky balding hippie with a ponytail and sunglasses. He wore this tan vest that had all these pockets on it for carrying film and lenses. We met him in Ketchikan after leaving the arcade one Saturday. Aubrey and I were just minding our own business, sharing a cigarette on the sidewalk by the Tongass Historical Museum, when Ed came right up to us and asked if we'd pose for a picture in front of a totem. "You paying?" Aubrey said.

"Sure," Ed said, giving us this crafty smile. "How much you criminals want?"

"Ten each."

"Robbery, kid. Five total. You can split it."

So Aubrey glanced at me, and I shrugged. Next thing we knew, Ed was telling us to lean against the Chief Johnson pole at the intersection of Mission and Stedman. Then he took a ton of pictures from different angles. He'd be on his knees saying things like, "Fold your arms. Don't smile. Fantastic!" Or he'd be pushing that camera in our faces, pointing a finger, going, "You, look at your feet. And you, stare at him while he's looking down at his feet. That's it!" And afterwards, once we got paid, he offered to buy us dinner if we showed him around town for the remaining afternoon.

Ed told us he was a photographer with some travel magazine, but that he was working on a project of his own. "It's a travel book," he said, "except I want to document the unseen Alaska and Pacific Northwest. I want real things, real people, not that nice shit made cute for the tourist trade." So Aubrey and I took him along Creek Street to Dolly's House, which used to be Dolly Arthur's whorehouse. Dolly died a long time before I was born, so the whorehouse is now a museum.

Anyway, Ed loved being in the old red light district, even though the places there are now trinket shops and cafes.

The sun was setting as the three of us arrived at the Totem Heritage Center, but Ed still had a field day snapping those nineteenth-century poles. With poor available light, he worked quickly to photograph all thirty-three of the totems, pausing twice—once to reload, once to get a few shots of Aubrey and me horseplaying on the grass. Aubrey had me in a headlock, and I was trying to grab his neck. "Keep at it," Ed said, urging us to continue, the shutter clicking. "Pin his ass! Come on! Get on top of him!" When both of us were exhausted, we let go of each other and rested side by side among the weeds. "Nice," Ed said, taking one more picture before he wandered off to finish shooting the totems.

During dinner, Ed wanted to know if our tribe was Tlingit. "What is it? Tinklet?"

"Tlingit," I corrected. "With a t but say it like clink-it."

"That's us," said Aubrey.

We were eating cheeseburgers and curly fries on the boardwalk, sitting at an outside table in front of the Alaska Rainforest Inn. Ed wasn't having dinner, so he asked us questions while we ate. He said it was for his book. I did most of the talking, explaining that we weren't from Ketchikan, that we lived in Klawock on a small island joined to the west shore of Prince of Wales by a slight causeway.

"You boys in high school, or what?"

"Yeah. I'm a junior. We both are."

"Got girlfriends?"

"Sometimes," said Aubrey.

"We do okay," I said, lying.

We lied about other stuff too. When Ed asked our given names, Aubrey frowned. "What do you mean?"

"Seriously. What kind of names are Aubrey and Cole? That's not Tlingit."

"Sure it is," I said. "Only name I got, as far as I know."

"Same here," said Aubrey.

Who knows why we didn't tell the truth. It's not like I'm

ashamed of being As<u>x</u>'aak, or Aubrey hates that he's really
Hinléiych. Maybe we just got tired of his questions. All the
same, Ed didn't push it. "Whatever," he said. "It's cool."
Then he mentioned this joint he was planning to smoke
upstairs in his room at the inn. "You boys light up?"
   "Of course," Aubrey said.
   "Whenever we can," I added.
   The door of Ed's room was unlocked. "Shit, I'm always
doing that," he said, shutting the door behind us. Aubrey and
I fanned out, moving around with quiet interest, taken in by
the TV bolted to the wall, the leather camera bag and various
zoom lenses on the dresser. Ed, his fingers rolling a fat joint,
sat on the edge of his king-sized bed. Then he dug a lighter
from his vest, watching us silently with the Minolta hanging at
his chest from its strap.
   "You got cable?" Aubrey said.
   "Don't know. Haven't watched it." Ed motioned for us to
come closer. He brought the joint to his lips and lit it. Then
he inhaled with his eyes closed, stifling a cough. A faint, harsh
smoke, stinking like burnt rope, blew past Ed's teeth as he
held the joint out to Aubrey. "Jesus, sit down," he said. "Can't
relax with you guys standing over me."
   Pretty soon I was stoned. So was Aubrey. So was Ed, but
it was hard to tell. We were toking, talking all kinds of crap.
Ed said if we got too wasted, we could stay there until morning, which didn't seem like such a bad idea. I mean, we
already missed the final evening ferry to Klawock, so we'd
have to sleep somewhere. And because it was a weekend
night, I knew Grandfather wouldn't be waiting. For all the old
man knew, I was at Aubrey's house watching videos, or playing Joust on the Atari.
   Anyway, the three of us were on the floor getting goofy,
sucking on our third joint. About the last thing I recall before
crashing was that Ed had his arm across Aubrey's shoulders,
and I was trying to stay awake as they yapped on and on
about Atlantis. "Ain't no such place," Aubrey said. "I don't
believe in it."

"It's true, pal. You don't know the facts." Ed glanced at me. "You believe in Atlantis, Cole?"

"Not sure. Could be true."

"Damn right it's true!" Then Ed pinched the joint between his thumb and forefinger, shaking it. "Better take control of the peace pipe. Me and my buddy here been hogging it."

"No, thanks," I said. "I got to piss."

When I stood, my legs felt weightless, unconnected. In the mirror above the bathroom sink, bloodshot eyes returned my gaze, telling me I'd smoked too much. Then I slumped to one side in front of the toilet, resting a shoulder on wallpaper patterned with schooners and steamships. What's weird is that I remember peeing and then splashing water on my cheeks, but not crawling into the bathtub. I guess I figured the bathtub was as good a place as any to sleep. But I don't think I'd been in there very long when Aubrey stirred me. There was this spooked look on his face, like he'd seen the worst thing in the world, and he kept glancing at the bathroom doorway, going, "We got to go. Come on, Cole, get up!"

Maybe I wasn't totally awake yet, or maybe I was still a little screwy from the pot, because all I could think to say was, "What's Ed doing?"

Then Aubrey's voice got kind of low, and at that moment he didn't seem so stoned, just nervous and scared. "We're in trouble, Cole. We can't stay."

As I followed Aubrey from the bathroom, I heard Ed's ragged, congested breathing. "Don't stare at him," Aubrey said, but I couldn't help it. Ed, curled on the floor beside the bed, clutching the Minolta with one hand, was half-conscious with his nose busted flat, his lips split and already swollen. Blood dotted the carpet near his chin. There was a massive red crease on his forehead, welted like some crazy horse had whomped him good.

"What happened?" I said, but Aubrey just glanced at me with this dazed expression. Then he grabbed my T-shirt, dragging me along with him from the room into the hall.

And right as we were about to run, Aubrey suddenly got

flustered, whispering, "Fuck, hold on." Then he went back inside, leaving the door ajar. I was jittery as hell by then. My hands wouldn't stop trembling, so I stuck them in my pockets. I figured any minute a bunch of angry people were going to step from their rooms demanding to know what was going on. When Aubrey returned, he had Ed's camera. "I left him the strap," he said, closing the door.

Ketchikan was slumbering, undisturbed by the lonesome smacks our sneakers made along the sidewalk on Park Avenue, and the only other sleepless things on the street were a couple of horny cats and an otter hound. The spring night was cool, but not freezing. At City Park, we stopped running in a clearing encircled by cedars, found a bench, and sat there catching our breaths under a starry sky.

Aubrey wiped snot on the sleeve of his jacket, then set the Minolta in my lap, saying, "You can have it."

I took the camera, wedging it between my palms. When I brought the viewfinder to my eye, it was too dark to see anything. "Aubrey," I said, "what'd you do?"

"It's all psycho," he said. Then he explained about Ed wanting a couple of photographs of him without his shirt on: "I say no, so Ed says he'll pay. Ten bucks. Don't seem that bad, you know. Two pictures is it. But he keeps bugging me. He'll give me an extra ten to drop my jeans. I say no, no way, except he don't listen. He goes for my pants, starts unzipping them. That's when I push him. Then I stomp his face, Cole. I stomp it really bad."

"Fucker deserves it," I said. "Good thing I was crashed, I'd have smashed him dead."

Aubrey nodded with a frown. "That's why I got the camera. It's got the pictures inside. If he gets the police, we got proof on what he did."

My head had cleared during our run, and it seemed like a whole other lifetime had gone by since I held the joint in Ed's room. "He won't get the police," I said. "There ain't a chance he'll do that."

"I know. I was worried, but not no more. Hold on."

Aubrey reached in a pocket and pulled out a handful of crumpled bills. "This was in Ed's wallet," he said. "Sixty-five dollars. You get thirty, and I got you something else." Then he dug in his jacket, retrieving six rolls of film.

At dawn, we caught the morning ferry to Klawock. Aubrey and I stood outside on the top deck, glad that the night had ended. Sunlight dazzled on the railings, shimmered on the choppy currents below us. A sharp breeze blew across the deck, swirling Aubrey's long hair around his ruddy cheekbones. Flinching against the wind, he bent over the deck, squinting at the thrashing waters below—and I lifted the Minolta, anticipating my first shot.

## 2.

Because there's still carving to do, I don't want to nap yet. But my aching body doesn't feel much like moving. From where I sit on the nameless mountain, my spine pressing into the spruce's jagged bark, I can see steep meadows, all gray-brown, dotted with nagoonberry leaves and deer cabbage. The thin air buzzes with insects, and three dragonflies lounge above me, stock-still on the second totem panel; their wings glitter like glass beaded with raindrops.

If those dragonflies knew any better, they'd understand a basketball game is being played underneath them. For almost four days I scraped on that second panel, trying my damnedest to get the court to look the way it does in Klawock–half-court only, bent hoop rim on the backboard, no net, village homes on a distant hill, a tall forest of cedar, hemlock, and spruce in the background. There's some other stuff on the panel, but none of it turned out so well. Aubrey's boom-box at the edge of the court got all screwed, so now it appears to be nothing more than a weird block or a bench.

I was going to put in the little kids who always watched us play, as well as the older guys who shoot hoops on the weekends, but in the end it seemed Aubrey and I were enough: Aubrey is at the foul line with his hands lifted; the basketball arches toward the basket; I'm under the backboard, jumping with one arm out, reaching, hoping for a rebound. And beyond the court, I added Jack Shotridge's grave house, where Aubrey and I went to smoke our cigarettes during game breaks, where last spring Crazy Koyumi with the cloudy eye stepped naked from her pants.

I don't know anything about Jack Shotridge, but a sign by the grave house says he died in 1889. And even though the place is some sort of historical preservation site, the beam ceiling collapsed years ago. There's this big frog design on an outside wall, and the inside is gutted out, weathered, splintery and gray. Weeds grow all over the house, except for on this bumpy dirt patch where Aubrey and I crossed our legs and blew smoke. Aubrey told me that the patch of dirt is where Jack Shotridge's corpse got nasty with decay. He said, "Nothing grows here, Cole, 'cause what comes from your guts when you die is poisonous," but I'm not so sure he was being truthful.

All the same, it was there on the weedless spot that I put myself on top of Crazy Koyumi. I'm not so sure why she's supposed to be crazy. She's just very quiet, maybe a little strange, I guess. At school, she was always getting in trouble for spitting. Back in junior high, she climbed the slide steps, covered her ears, and sprayed slobber at the kids swinging below her. But she doesn't spit much anymore, so I don't think she's too psycho. Koyumi's mother is Tlingit. Her father is Japanese, or at least that's what she likes to say. She said he owns a restaurant in Juneau, though Aubrey doesn't believe it. "He's probably your uncle," Aubrey told me. "Or my uncle, or anyone in Klawock." I mean, besides her name and her one blind eye, she looks about as Indian as the rest of everyone in Klawock, so Aubrey's probably right. What's no secret is that almost every evening Koyumi's mom drives six miles south to the logging bars in Craig, and sometimes she doesn't get home until after noon the following day.

Anyway, it was Aubrey who got Koyumi to walk with us to the grave house. She'd been by herself on the basketball court, skipping rope while Aubrey and I played 21. It was overcast, and a few grade schoolers were nearby having a stickball game. When we decided to break for a smoke, Aubrey yelled, "Hey, Koyumi, come with us! I want to ask you something!" And he said that right in front of all those little kids, who didn't have no idea what was on Aubrey's mind. Neither did I.

"What you want with her?" I said, but Aubrey just flashed this stupid grin. And next thing I knew, the three of us were standing in the grave house, and Aubrey was feeling under Koyumi's blue sweater. He didn't even ask her if it was okay. He just went ahead and did it. And Koyumi wasn't bothered one bit. In fact, it was like Aubrey had done this to her a million times before. And when he pulled the sweater to her chin, exposing her flabby stomach and droopy breasts, Koyumi stared right past him. It was like she wasn't even there, like she was some bored zombie or something. "You're going to owe me," she said.

"We're broke," Aubrey said, cupping one of her breasts.

"Give me cigarettes." Koyumi said. She sounded glum and worn.

"Sure," Aubrey said, slipping his arms around Koyumi's waist. "No problem. I got half a pack left." He tried kissing her, but she pushed him away.

"I don't like that." Then Koyumi unbuttoned her jeans, pulling them to her ankles. "Better be quick." And suddenly Aubrey seemed distracted. He glanced at me, then to Koyumi, who was stepping from her pants.

I suppose Aubrey didn't take too long with Koyumi; it's hard to say for sure, because in my mind it was forever. I'd gone outside to keep guard, so maybe I waited fifteen minutes, or maybe it was more like ten. I leaned against the grave house, concentrating on the stickball boys. From the empty court, Aubrey's boom-box thumped Mr. Gangsta Bass: *You say I'm a sucker, but fucker you're the only sucker gonna get his ass torn here!* Noisy gulls and cormorants circled overhead, and behind me, coming as almost a whisper, I heard Koyumi go, "Stupid, be careful. You're hurting my legs."

When Aubrey finally appeared from inside the grave house, he pretended to be dizzy, stumbling like a drunk. "She's waiting," he said, grabbing my shoulder for support. He aimed a finger at my nose. "Want a whiff?"

"Man, that's gross," I said. "No thanks."

Aubrey snorted a laugh, then he took one of my hands, saying, "After you're done, give her these." He slapped a Marlboro pack into my palm. "Get on in there," he said, "'fore sloppy seconds gets old."

The grave house smelled of sex, musty like wet clay. Koyumi, absently chewing a fingernail, lay on the dirt mound with her bare legs spread. Her pants rested in a clump among weeds, and the blue sweater had become a pillow under her neck. "See what you're dumbass friend did," she said, pointing at the wiry bush around her pussy, which was lathered with Aubrey's come.

Then Koyumi sat up on her elbows, and we studied each other as I moved forward. Her body was a stranger to me, though hardly surprising. There was a thin scar on her abdomen, small rolls of fat, tawny nipples. But I knew that unrapt face too well—her brown round head, with its flat nose, one good eye and long mane of blackish hair, amazingly straight.

Then there was her bad eye, milky-white at the center and dead, giving me the creeps. The sight of that spooky pupil could keep any dick limp. I suppose Koyumi understood this, because as soon as I knelt between her legs, she reached out. Suddenly two of my fingers were in her mouth. Her pointed tongue, flicking at the cuticles, tasted my fingertips and coated them with a gummy saliva. I was motionless, transfixed by how her cheeks sucked into the hollow of her face, by how her chin moved back and forth near my wrist. A yearning sensation stirred in my belly, then grew and unfurled. I slid my fingers from Koyumi's mouth, and her wet lips twisted a smile. Then she said, "I can't have babies, so it don't matter."

I quickly dropped my pants and underwear. When I thrust myself over Koyumi's body, my hard-on, like a ripe squash gourd, pressed the tough hairs above her pussy and mingled in the mess Aubrey had left there. Then I lifted my thighs reflexively, exposing my asshole to the world. "Here," Koyumi said. She spit in a palm, then lubricated my dick. And for a moment, as her hand brushed my balls, I remembered her on the playground in junior high, spewing thick gobs at those close by. "Put it in," she told me, arching my hard-on down, aiming it at the warm, dry opening of her pussy. And I breathed deeply, doing as she said.

There's not much else worth mentioning. I went into her maybe ten times before coming. That was it. Then I stood, pulled my underwear and pants on, and took the pack of Marlboros from a pocket. "You got matches?" she said.

"Just a lighter."

"Give it to me." So I did. Then I left Koyumi there on the dirt mound.

Outside, the gloomy sky had cleared some to the north, and the stickballers were gone. Sunlight shone on the basketball court, where Aubrey now practiced lay-ups by himself. For some reason, I was still horny and my dick remained slightly hard. But a warm feeling stuffed with satisfaction carried me away from the grave house. As I jogged along the trail leading to the court, the bass on the boom-box grew stronger, pumping my gut and chest, filling me with wildness. I'd never been with a girl before.

And for an hour or so, I ruled the court in 21, exhilarated, making nearly every shot I attempted—behind-the-back lay-ups, hooks, banked-in jumpers. I careened, pivoted, and jumped past Aubrey, who'd shout, "Asshole!" And whenever the ball spun from his fingers, I swatted it hard and mean. Honestly, it was like nothing could stop me. But something finally did, at least for a few seconds: I was taking the ball behind the foul line when Aubrey said, "Check her out." I turned, cradling the ball, and saw Koyumi walking away from the basketball court, an unlit cigarette in her mouth, with the skip rope dragging behind her through the tall grass like a snake.

As we watched her go, the ball slipped from my hold and bounced off. I lifted two fingers to my nose, inhaling, but they reeked only of rubber. Just then I couldn't imagine myself ever having been inside her. And that night, closing my eyes in bed, the clearest thought I had was of me and Aubrey on the court, our arms in the air, the ball flying toward the basket.

## 3.

I spent my last three summers in Anchorage, where Grandma Elvera lives with Uncle William. Or really it's William who lives with Elvera, because the old house on Denali Street is hers. During the oil crisis in the mid-Eighties, when William lost his job on the trans-Alaska oil pipeline, he moved in with Grandma. So now he works from late August to early May as a driver for the Dynair Charter shuttle service at Anchorage International Airport. And from late May to early August, he travels to Naknek, working 12 hour shifts, earning good money in a commercial fishery. That's when I go visit Grandma.

Elvera is my mother's mother, and she is older than dirt. Her braided hair is all gray-yellow. Her face is a brown relief map of long valleys and rough plateaus. And even though Grandfather, my father's father, thinks she's a regular crank, Elvera is pretty nice to me–probably because I reminded her of my mother. She always cleans out William's room for my stays, makes the bed each morning, and keeps my stomach full with fried bread and smoked salmon. "How come you're so skinny?" she's fond of saying. "When you're skinny like that, you get sick easy. You're mother was too skinny her whole life."

Up until the end of my past visit, the weeks at Grandma's were usually uneventful. Most days I woke at dawn. Elvera had breakfast ready by the time I was showered and dressed. And soon as the meal was scarfed down, I left for my paper route. She had lunch waiting when I returned. Then the afternoons were spent either grocery shopping, or watching TV. Or sometimes both. After dinner, we played Banker and Broker on the kitchen table. Then Grandma went to bed, and I stretched out on the living room sofa and stared at the TV until I got tired.

It's kind of boring at Grandma's, but it never drove me nuts when I went there. I mean, the food was great.

Everything was tidy. I didn't have to do much, except fold and deliver newspapers with my uncle's friend Albert. Sometimes I took the ten minute bus ride to The Imaginarium, with its displays of glaciers, the Northern Lights, polar bears, and dumb-looking moose. Afterwards, I usually walked a block to the Alaska Experience Center, got a front-row seat in the Earthquake Theater, and sat in darkness as this movie showed scenes from the 1964 disaster. The coolest part of that film came near the end, when suddenly all the chairs in the theater started shaking like they would in a real 4.6 tremor. So I guess it was good getting away from Klawock, where the most interesting things were the island's best grocery store, twenty-one restored totem poles in the town center, and Aubrey.

Last summer, the boredom seemed worse at night, maybe because there wasn't much to do. So besides watching TV before bed, I played solitaire, or did sketches in this notebook William bought me. He also gave me a pen and stamps so I could write him, but I never got around to it. Anyway, as far as the sketches go, most were copied from the framed pictures hanging on Grandma's walls. The three I'm proudest of feature Grandpa Peck, Elvera's husband, who died when I was six. In one sketch, he's about my age in his Sunday best, the European-style suit Tlingit men used to wear daily, but his face is stern, dark, with thick cheekbones. In another, he's a few years older, holding his cornet in a Klukwan Native Band uniform. Then there's my favorite sketch, which shows Grandpa Peck in his twenties, clowning with this Russian priest from the St. John the Baptist Society. There are clan houses in the background, and Peck is resting his head on the priest's shoulder, after having exchanged hats with the man. That was the drawing Grandma asked to keep, because she said it was better than the photograph.

I also tried doing sketches of several homeless men I saw on my route, but none of them turned out so hot. Maybe as a result of working from memory. Or maybe on account of the men being other Indians, drunk and wasted by noon. It's not easy drawing guys with 40-ounce bottles and thousand-mile stares. "Urban Indians without a pot," Albert called them. "I could've been like them too, Cole. But I more or less knew what to expect when I got here."

In May, before going to Naknek, Uncle William set up my job with Albert, who only took me on as a favor. It's not like Albert needed any help delivering papers. At first he hardly spoke. And when he did, he just sort of pointed, almost grunting, saying stuff like, "No, kid, fold the paper three times, then tighten it with your hands. Then put on the rubber band." But eventually he warmed to me some. And pretty soon he was chatty, even grinning and flipping me the bird in the rearview mirror as I flung newspapers from his truck bed.

I did a drawing of Albert with his Harley-Davidson T-shirt and toothless smile, but it never got finished. "I got relatives who moved here," he told me, "and they came home for holidays and talked about it." We'd finished our route early one July morning, so Albert and I, sitting at a picnic table in Delaney Park, split a six-pack of Miller Lite. He said, "I needed work bad, and the relocation program seemed like a good idea. Sometimes the Bureau of Indian Affairs pissed me off. Seems like they tried fucking with me sometimes. But, shit, I was drinking hard then. Sometimes my skull got as bloodshot, confused, and trashed as those guys we pass on the street. You got no idea what it's like, drinking for months straight like that, everyday. Then I had DT's. Sometimes I saw things that ain't there, crazy crap like that. You wake from a drunk like that, seems like you're cold and hot at the same time. Sweat covers you and it's such an awful feeling. I said to myself so many times, 'Don't want to do this no more. God, please help me, don't let me be like this again.'

"But I was drinking like that before I came to live in Anchorage. See, now it's only beer. I don't drink everyday, don't drink any hard crap, because I find there's more to do, to keep your mind occupied and shit like that. But if I was out in the country I'd be laying around, nothing to do in the winter time, listen to the radio, and it's freezing outside, and so you drink. But here, at least you can go to a movie or something like that. There's always something happening. I guess it's a problem of boredom."

"I know what you mean," I said, popping the top on a second beer. "About being bored and all that."

"Do you?" Albert said. He appeared surprised. Then he lifted his beer and we bumped our cans together in a toast. "Damn straight," he said. "Damn straight."

That day, we didn't finish the six-pack until sometime past lunchtime. And when I came through the front door at Grandma's house, I was somewhere between buzzed and drunk. My cheeks burned, my tongue was dry as cloth. Elvera had cooked lunch in the kitchen, and the smell of ground beef and cabbage carried to the living room, where I stood uneasily by the couch.

As I fell heavy into my seat at the kitchen table, trying my hardest to look sober, Grandma peered at me with a severe frown. "Where you been?"

"Doing papers with Albert."

"You're late."

"Oh."

"How come you're late?"

"I don't know. I'm late?"

"How come today takes longer than others?"

"I don't know."

She lifted the skillet from the stove. And I stared down at my empty plate. Not much else was said during lunch.

That evening, as I shuffled the cards for our nightly game of Banker and Broker, Grandma set two Dixie cups and a vodka bottle on the kitchen table. Taken aback, I stopped shuffling. Elvera smoothed the front of her blue-green bathrobe. Then she put herself in the chair directly across from me, saying, "Promise me you won't drink no more with that Albert. If you want a drink, you can do it here, with me. But I don't want you out somewhere else doing it. Most of your Indians moved to Anchorage from places where they already learned how to drink. That Albert is no different. But here it's more obvious because they get picked up more. That's not going to happen to you. In Klawock, Indians are in a place. They drink there, and stay there, and here they get out on the streets and the police find them. So you promise me, and tonight we'll drink." So I promised her. And then she filled the cups.

Not in a million years did I ever imagine getting drunk with Grandma. But that's what happened. Needless to say, Banker and Broker went out the window once the third round was poured. And soon we were hammering shots like no tomorrow.

There was Grandma, Dixie cup in a hand, swaying her head like she was enjoying music on a jukebox or something. And there I was, elbows on the table, legs tucked under the chair, listening as she went on about having Russian blood. "And you've got it too, Cole. That's why you like the vodka like me." She said almost everybody has white blood in them. "I say there ain't a dozen full-blooded Indians here in Anchorage. Some people believe they are, but trace far enough, you'd find them wrong."

Then Grandma mentioned my mother, and got all weepy. She fixed herself another drink, and the bottle was nearly spent. She said, "I loved her. She was my baby. And she sure loved you. No one should starve to death, Cole. No one should do that to themselves. Why'd she do that?"

I had no good answer. I said, "I don't like to think about it." But what I really wanted to say was, "I don't care. I was little, and she quit eating and died, and I don't remember her much, so it's like some bad dream."

No matter how I try, it's impossible to recall a whole lot more from that night. Only a couple of specific things come to mind, like Grandma asleep at the kitchen table, her face nuzzled in the nook of an arm, and me roaming the house with my camera. At first I was planning to draw Elvera while she slept, but when I held the pen with my drunk fingers, it took on a sloppy life of its own. So I dug the Minolta from my suitcase, put in a fresh roll, and got three or four shots of Grandma.

Then I wandered into the living room, taking weird shots of a fuzzy TV channel and the ceiling lamp. I photographed the ratty couch, as well as Grandma's pictures on the walls. And even though it was all black outside, I aimed my camera at the creaky porch steps. Then I moved forward, and nothing escaped me. Not the small garage, or the row of young cedars the city planted near the sidewalk. Not the moon above, or the streetlight shining over Denali Street. I completed the roll on the lawn, turning the lens toward the old place. From where I stand on this nameless mountain, my Grandma's house, box-like, with peeling paint exposing splintery planks underneath, sits below a huge half-moon on a summer's night. That's what I carved on this spruce. That's what the third totem panel shows.

I suppose my summer in Anchorage would've ended without trouble if Aubrey hadn't visited, if we hadn't got all stupid one night and robbed that pizza delivery guy. It was Aubrey who beat him so badly. I only kicked him once. But Aubrey went ahead and punched him over and over again. The whole thing was psycho. I knew it then. And I've thought a lot about it since. My regrets concerning that night are probably higher than this mountain I'm on, and I hate myself for what we did to that guy. But what really gets me is the thought of Elvera on the front steps, so bewildered, so flustered and sad, unconsciously tightening her bathrobe while the police loaded us into their cruiser.

There are other regrets too. I mean, Aubrey had only been in Anchorage two full days when we were arrested, so I didn't get to show him The Imaginarium or the Alaska Experience Center. We didn't shoot hoops at Delaney Park, or do much of anything, except sleep, watch TV, eat, and play cards with Grandma. And if I'd had enough money, we might have taken in a movie, maybe scouted out an arcade, instead of drinking Crown Royal at Albert's apartment. But like Grandfather said, "You can't unshit, it's done."

Still, things just should've turned out different. The news

of Aubrey's visit couldn't have come at a better time. I had little more than a week left in Anchorage, and my job with Albert was finished. After our final paper route together, Albert added a ten dollar bonus to my weekly check, then shook my hand, saying, "Maybe you'll stop by my place before you leave. We'll rent videos, have a beer or something." And that was it. Suddenly I was free to sleep late. I could sketch and watch TV until dawn. And when I heard Aubrey was coming, my stomach tingled like I'd just stuffed a rebound. It was Grandfather's plan, and he phoned Elvera's from Klawock to say, "I'm sending you your buddy, Asx̲'aak. That way you got company to get you home."

I was worried that Grandma might be put out by an extra guest–especially since Grandfather hadn't asked her if it was okay–but after serious consideration she relented, saying Aubrey's stay would be fine. In the kitchen, her cheeks puffed and deflated as resigned air blew through her teeth. "So I get to know this boy you talk so much about." One side of her mouth curled. Her eyes grew narrow. "But no roughhousing, Cole. Not inside. No loud talking at night." Then she had me carry a musky mattress from the garage to the front lawn, so I could beat dust from it with a broom.

Two months had changed Aubrey some. He stepped off the Gray Line bus with his hair trimmed short, buzzed along the sides, parted neatly along the center, and with his left hand wrapped in gauze; the palm had been sliced by a razor while he was gutting chinook. Then there was his severe, unsmiling face, giving the impression that something miserable had occurred on the trip from Klawock. With a backpack hanging from a shoulder, Aubrey approached Elvera and me in the terminal, nodding at us like we were strangers. To Grandma he offered a quiet, mumbled, "Hi." And to me he said, "Hey, how's it going?" But on the transit ride to Denali Street, he clammed up, preferring instead to stare at passing buildings and homes. And when I asked him something, his replies were, "Yeah," "No, not really," "I guess," "Not bad," "Sure, sounds good."

Initially, I was disappointed. I thought, This isn't my
Aubrey. This isn't the friend I'd daydreamed about all summer, who I'd bragged about to Grandma. "Get him started
and he'll talk you to death," I'd told her. "Man, he's so hys-
terical. You should've seen it when the nurse came from
Ketchikan to give the football team physicals, and Aubrey
put apple juice in the cup instead of pee. Then he gulped it
right there in front of that nurse, and she didn't get disgusted
or nothing. She just handed him another cup and pointed at
the door. He's great." But now seeing this dull, sulky pal of
mine on the transit bus, I could sense that Elvera was unim-
pressed. She sat with her purse in her lap, paying no attention whatsoever to him, or me. And it was like both their
silences created an awful racket in my brain. So I kept yacking and yacking, making stupid comments like, "It's awesome you're here, Aubrey."

The truth is, I was pretty depressed when we arrived at
Grandma's house. But soon as I showed Aubrey our room, he
started to act like his old self again. "You don't know how bad
I wanted out of Klawock," he said, sounding relieved. "Your
grandfather saved me, man. I was losing it." His mattress,
fixed with clean sheets, was on the floor, and he dropped his
backpack beside it. And while Elvera got dinner ready, we
crossed our legs on his bed and talked. He explained the
gauze covering his knuckles and palm, saying he had held the
chinook with one hand while cutting with the other, and as he
dug inside to clean it good, an edge of the razor actually
poked through the fish, sinking deep into his grasp. "So jerk-
ing my dick is a real pain," he said, smiling at last.

"You're lucky it didn't get your wrist," I said.

"I'm so dumb. If I'd used a knife it wouldn't have happened."

We talked about other stuff too. I described my days in
Anchorage, the paper route and Albert, getting drunk with
Elvera. He filled me in on his summer in Klawock, mentioning how he went fishing by himself on the weekends, and
how he'd almost gotten in a fight with a logger during a

basketball game. Then he leaned in close, lowering his voice
to say, "And me and Koyumi slept in the grave house."

"When?"

"I don't know. A lot."

"When was the last?"

"A few weeks ago."

I was jealous. Twice I'd dreamed of Koyumi, her mouth
sucking my tongue in the grave house, her tits moving beneath
my chest, and both times I awoke horny, breathless in wet
underwear. But it was an odd kind of jealousy. I mean, while I
was bothered by Aubrey having screwed Koyumi, it also
bugged me that she had been with him. And I imagined myself
here, many miles away in Elvera's shower, absent from the
equation, spattering the white tiles with come as they fucked.

"You're lucky," I said. "I haven't found no action here."

Aubrey shrugged. "It's not that amazing, I guess. We did
some crazy things though. But she's whacked, man. She let
me do her ass for a laugh."

"Nothing wrong with that."

"Yeah, well–" He shrugged again, frowning.

"You okay?"

"Sure. Just everything got messy, 'cause she's acting all
pregnant and shit."

"But she can't have babies. That's what she said."

"I know. But she ain't saying that no more. She says it's
me. Then she says it's someone else, some guy living with her
mom. I don't know. I think she's lying."

"Don't worry about it then."

"I'm not. Jesus, why should I? Even if she is, it might be
anyone's kid. It could be yours, right?"

"Maybe. I don't think so."

"And if she is, and she wants to insist it's mine, I won't let
it happen, Cole. Don't care what I'll do, she won't have it."

"Same here," I said. "I'll abort it myself."

"Don't sweat it. She never mentioned you anyway. She
says it's either me, or her mom's boyfriend. But I think she's
full of crap. Hey, I got to piss. Where do I go?"

I aimed a finger at the open bedroom door. "Left, down the hall, first door on the right."

Aubrey heaved himself from the mattress. "Back in a sec'." As he slouched into the hallway, I climbed to my bed, putting my spine against the headboard. Koyumi appeared in my mind, not as the strange, unpredictable girl from grade school, but as something more dangerous and fearful. You can't have babies, I thought, so it don't matter. That's what you said. Still, I wasn't too concerned; I had been with her once, and that was months earlier. If she was pregnant, the baby didn't belong to me. All the same, I was suddenly afraid of her.

When Aubrey returned from the bathroom, he stretched out on his bed and sighed tiredly. "I like it here," he said, propping his arms behind his neck. "I'll sleep good tonight."

For dinner, Grandma served chopped mollusks on black-husked rice. "Gooeyduck," she called it, except I don't know why. There wasn't any duck in the meal. The rice and mollusks were far from gooey. "Hope you boys like gooeyduck," she said, "because there's lots of it."

Aubrey and I ate like seals in a hatchery, which pleased Elvera. We had seconds. Then we had thirds. We chatted around mouthfuls, cracking jokes, entertaining Grandma with our Klawock stories. "Last year this big ol' grizzly mauled some tourist outside town," Aubrey said to her. "That bear dragged that man all over the place, scattered his camping gear and everything. A week or so later, this mountain guy named Paul Demmert found some of the gear, took it to town, traded it with my dad for chew and a bunch of stuff. And everyone got upset, but my dad said it was only fair, said he was encouraging the tourist trade. My dad's insane that way." He had come to life since his arrival, and Elvera doted on him. She poured more Dr. Pepper in his glass, scooped more rice onto his plate. And after my third portion, I patted my stomach while Grandma gave Aubrey a fourth helping.

When the tabletop was cleared, I sorted the cards for Banker and Broker, and Elvera asked Aubrey to remove the gauze. The wrap unspooled on the kitchen table, foul smelling and grubby. A jagged fissure, at least three inches in length, was revealed; the slit looked raw, the skin around it fleshy and moist. Grandma held Aubrey's wrist, studying the inflamed wound like a palm reader. "Got yourself a new life line," she said. "It's infected. Go to the sink."

"That's okay," Aubrey said. "I keep it washed."

"What you put on it?"

"Nothing. Soap."

"Get over there," she ordered Aubrey, scooting from her chair. "Run him warm water, Cole." Then she marched out of the kitchen.

I stood beside Aubrey as he stuck his left hand under the spigot. Steam lifted past our dinner plates in the sink. "She shouldn't bother," he said.

"Try telling her that," I said.

Elvera returned with Neosporin, sterile pads, a roll of fresh gauze, and scissors. She set her load on the counter, organizing them like a surgeon preparing for an operation. "You need taking care of," she finally said to Aubrey. "Let me see your cut."

I watched while Grandma cleaned his wound. She patted the slit dry with a sterile pad, then carefully applied the Neosporin. And he didn't say a word. He just bit his bottom lip as she dressed his palm.

Two evenings later, when the police came for Aubrey and me, the three of us were standing in almost the same spots in the kitchen, and Elvera, dabbing with paper towels, was trying to stop blood gushing from the reopened slash. But the police didn't let her finish. They hauled us away in handcuffs, and Aubrey continued bleeding until a paramedic bandaged him at the station house. "Motherfuckers didn't care," Aubrey told the paramedic. "If I'd been shot or something, they'd still brought me here." Sitting nearby in the holding area, I felt helpless and mad at myself. And the night Grandma cooked gooeyduck seemed like some ancient memory.

On the morning following our arrest, Elvera came to the station house. "Why'd you do it?" she asked, her voice flat and unemotional. Eventually, my Grandfather asked the same question. So did the police. So did our appointed public defender. Why'd we do it? I don't know. I'd spent my money on cigarettes, and we were drunk. Aubrey had a couple of bucks, but that was it. We weren't hungry. It's not like we even needed what the pizza guy had on him.

"It's crazy," I told Elvera, "just crazy. I'm sorry."

"They put that boy in the hospital. His skull got busted."

"I'm sorry," I said again.

"Don't say it to me," she said, disgusted. "When you say it it sounds like you don't mean it. I'm upset. You know that?"

"Yes, I guess."

"Why'd you go to Albert's? You were supposed to be at Delaney Park. And I was worried too, Cole. You didn't come home to eat. And then you come home and Aubrey's bloody. Then the police. I didn't sleep. Do you think I could sleep?"

"No. I didn't think about it."

"You say what happened. I'm going to have to tell your grandfather."

I tried to explain as best I could, but it was tough. "We thought Albert might buy us some beer," I said. "But he had Crown Royal, so we drank it there at his place. Then he said we had to go because someone was coming over or something. So then we walked around and stuff, because we didn't want to come home because I knew you'd be pissed at us for drinking. So we went to Delaney Park. We found a bunch of golf balls on the golf course, threw them around some and didn't do much else.

"Then we decided to go back to Albert's apartment, but he wouldn't answer the door. So we were leaving when the pizza guy arrived. He got out with this pizza box, went to do his delivery, I guess, left his truck running and unlocked. And Aubrey thought he might have money in his truck. And that's what we were looking for when he caught us. I swear, the guy tried to slug Aubrey from the start. But Aubrey popped him a couple of times. That's all. I kicked him when he was on the ground. We took the money bag and ran. I swear I didn't think he got hurt so awful. Stupid shouldn't leave his truck like that. That guy wanted a fight."

I lied; when Aubrey swung into the pizza guy's jaw, I heard bones crack. There was no resistance either. The guy crumpled to the asphalt, and Aubrey came down on his rib cage with a knee. Then Aubrey pounded both fists against the guy's head like a madman. "You're fucked!" Aubrey kept yelling. "You're fucked, yeah, you're fucked!" He was making so much noise that people started peeking from their apartment windows. And I shifted my weight to the balls of my feet, took one step forward, and smashed the guy's crotch with a tennis shoe—and Albert, watching from his balcony, observed me do this. But I never realized that he was there, or that he saw us steal the money bag.

"You're in this trouble," Grandma said. "Who you think is going to stick by you when they know what you've done? You think Albert will?"

"I don't know."

"You know he turned you in?"

"No."

"That's your good friend Albert. So besides me, the only other friend you got here is locked in jail with you. And he worries me too. How's his cut?"

"It's fine."

"It didn't look fine last night."

She was right. When we arrived at Anchorage Cemetery near Denali Street, Aubrey noticed blood oozing from under his gauze. It was dark outside, but the grounds were lit by floodlights. I was full of adrenaline, shaky and worn-out from running. We'd gone there to open the money bag, finding exactly forty dollars inside (a twenty, a ten, two fives). We split it even, then Aubrey tossed the bag into a tree. But when he threw it, warm drops hit my face and his. "Shit," he said. We went to a floodlight, and he put his left hand in its glow. It was like someone had splashed his palm with red paint. He peeled off the gauze, saying, "Damn, this isn't good."

Because of the bleeding, it was impossible to see the gash. A mess bubbled thick and continual in the middle of his palm. "It's bad," I said, my insides twisting. "It's not good at all. You shouldn't have hit him that much."

It wasn't until we were officially charged with the robbery that I learned the pizza guy's name was Mike Everett. He worked two jobs, one delivering pizzas, the other tutoring emotionally disturbed kids. A newspaper mentioned he once played guitar in some rock band, and that he'd moved from Los Angeles to escape the violence there. It was like Aubrey and I picked the nicest guy in Anchorage to ruin. If I didn't feel so awful about what we did to him, I might think that was funny.

## 4.

On the fourth totem panel, my grandfather fingers the peppered stubble on his chin, the whiskers unshorn and rough. He gazes forever across this clearing, focusing beyond the sheer drop at my outlook's edge, where the sky, faded by clouds and an ocean haze, exists like a massive movie screen. Sometimes sunlight creeps along the spruce to his face, shifting the wide wooden creases on his brow and around his eyelids into shaded rivulets.

Today, a brisk wind dances through underbrush, bustles the muskeg grass–and for a moment I imagine the breeze in Grandfather's silvery streams of hair, flapping the tan rim of his Stetson hat, patting his outdoor flannel shirt as his callused hands gather cedar for carving. In my memory, I recall him sawing exact lengths from drift logs on a distant spring evening. And I'm there too, hoping he'll let me use his ax to break the lengths. But he doesn't. Then we head home. I carry the split chunks he chopped in my arms. Grandfather walks with the ax handle placed over a husky shoulder, a cedar section still buried in its blade, the wood resting against his back.

In Klawock, Grandfather is known as Jakwteen. But most everybody calls him Jack, or Mr. Betts. A few years ago this husband and wife, both college professors interested in Tlingit culture, spent a week in Klawock. They practically interviewed every elder in town, but ended up staying at our house for days. Grandfather is a great talker, and he knows more about our tribe's history than almost anyone. He also has a lot of pull in local politics–probably because when Grandfather was younger, he was part of an organization that registered ninety-seven percent of all the Native population in Alaska to vote. Anyway, that husband and wife recorded hours and hours of Grandfather yapping. He showed them his Bible translations for Tlingit language, explaining, "I believe our Christian schools in Southeast Alaska have a wonderful motto that this community strives toward: compassionate Christian brotherhood." And eventually those professors published this book which quoted Grandfather as saying, "Tlingit didn't leave Siberia and cross the land bridge into Alaska so they could conquer anyone." So he's kind of famous and respected, at least on Prince of Wales Island.

I mean, only someone like Grandfather could go to Anchorage and convince a state Superior Court judge to release me and Aubrey for a hearing by the Tlingit tribal court. And that's what he did too. He stood before that judge in his best suit, holding his Stetson against his heavy chest. He said, "Sir, my tribe has laws that deal with crimes of this sort. With all due respect, Tlingit laws are based on the rehabilitation of sick spirits, not punishment like yours. Perhaps you'll have the courage to deal with us and our laws."

The prosecutor, a fat woman with wire-framed glasses and red hair, was annoyed by Grandfather's request. To the judge she said, "Of course I'm in favor of alternative sentencing for youth offenders. I'm also more than aware that Native Americans have had less than a fair shake in the past. But how can I agree with any notion that possibly grants Indian tribes superior sovereignty than, let's say, Canada or Great Britain. It's ridiculous, your honor."

Then to Grandfather she said, "Do you understand the brutality of the crime? These boys beat Michael Everett so severely that he has a permanent hearing loss in his left ear. This isn't about oppression of Native Americans by an unfair judicial system. It's a first-degree robbery charge, and they've pled guilty."

"Yes, ma'am, I understand that," Grandfather replied. "Furthermore, I know very well what happens to young boys in the penitentiary. They are taken and made to be like wives. They never learn to be men. I fail to see how that'd help make anything right."

And when the judge asked Grandfather what manner of rehabilitation a tribal court might consider, he answered, "Banishment, as well as complete restitution to Mister Everett."

Honestly, I never thought the judge would go for it, especially after the prosecutor made such a stink. But, following a brief deliberation in his chamber, the judge returned, saying, "Mister Betts, I've decided to release the boys on a thirty thousand property bond. The court will delay sentencing for eighteen months, at which point the case will be reviewed. If, at that time, rehabilitation, proper restitution, and full atonement are not evident, this court will proceed with an appropriate edict." And to my surprise, in a matter of hours, Aubrey and I found ourselves in Grandfather's custody. By evening, we were already on the long journey home to Klawock.

During the bus ride to the town of Skagway, where we'd then catch a ferry for Ketchikan, I slept. So did Aubrey. We slumped against one another, using each other as pillows, while Grandfather, sitting across the aisle from us, studied his Bible. It's hard to explain how tired I was on that Gray Line. In the lockup, my bed was narrow, all saggy and thin too. The metal mesh of the bed-frame nearly pushed through the mattress, jabbing my chest and spine whenever I turned. And the bedding was so doused with disinfectant, it was enough to make a guy vomit. But there on the bus, upright in my seat and beside Aubrey, I was as comfortable as I'd been in weeks. And I was clean.

Before leaving Anchorage, Grandfather took us to Elvera's so we could shower and gather our luggage and tell her goodbye. Without doubt, it was the greatest shower I've had. Standing under the spout with hot water burning my body, I washed myself at least twice, scrubbing the residue of jail off my skin. Then I sat in the tub, covering my face while the warm spray fell over me. I must've started dozing or something, because Aubrey startled me when he came into the bathroom and said, "Hurry. Jack says we got to go soon, and I been waiting my turn."

Once Aubrey and I were dressed and packed, we found Grandma and Grandfather drinking coffee at the kitchen table. It was weird seeing my mother's mother and my father's father in the same room like that. And though they regarded me and Aubrey with faint expressions of disappointment, they were at least polite to one another. But what struck me then was this: after my mother died, my father left Klawock and hasn't returned. "Ungrateful seed," was how Grandfather described him. "No damn good to begin with." Last I heard, Dad was working somewhere in Texas. Truthfully, I don't care if I even meet the guy again. I was a baby when he went, so it's like Grandfather has always been my father anyway. As for Mom, I don't remember her, so it doesn't matter. Elvera is my mother now. So there in the kitchen, the closest I have to parents were sipping coffee, frowning as they glanced at me. But I'd never seen them together before. I wanted to mention that to them, but it didn't feel like the right time. So I let it go, tightened my lips, didn't say a word.

"When all this trouble passes," Grandma told me, "you'll be welcome here next summer." We were on the front steps. Aubrey wore his backpack. I held my suitcase. Grandfather kept checking his watch. "This is your other home, okay?"

"Okay," I said, and she kissed me goodbye.

Then to Aubrey she went, "Not so sure if I want you to visit again. We'll see. Show me that cut." Aubrey gave Elvera his hand. A brownish scab had formed on the slit. "Good," she said. "It's mending."

"Thanks for everything," Aubrey said to her, except it came out mumbled and low. But Grandma didn't mind. She smiled a bit, then pulled him against her and kissed him.

"Need to run," Grandfather said. "We'll miss the bus. It was nice to see you, Elvera."

"You too, Jack. Have a safe trip. Watch after yourself, and these two."

"You know I will."

And that was it. Grandma quickly about-faced and didn't look back. And as we moved down the steps, the screen door slapped behind us.

At dawn, the bus slowed in downtown Skagway. I stirred and stretched my arms. Aubrey yawned while rubbing junk from the corners of his eyes. Grandfather was already in the aisle, reaching into the overhead rack for our luggage. He tossed Aubrey's backpack to him. Then he set my suitcase in the middle of the aisle. And when I said, "Morning," Grandfather pretended not to hear me.

As the bus entered the Gray Line station, Aubrey said, "I'm starving." His stale sleep-breath made me turn away.

"Me too," I said, glancing at Grandfather, who remained standing.

"You'll get something when we get to Ketchikan," Grandfather grumbled, staring toward the front of the bus, and I knew then that his mood was grim.

If Grandfather was in a funk that day, Aubrey, by comparison, was in excellent spirits. In fact, I hadn't seen him so jokey since the night we ate gooeyduck at Elvera's house. On the ferry to Ketchikan, he'd bump against me, whispering dumb stuff like, "That bird shit all over the railings looks like come." Then he'd start laughing. Who knows what got into him. He had no reason to be happy. But maybe he thought we were home free. Or maybe he figured the tribal court in Klawock would slap our wrists and tell us we had to do community service. I don't know.

Anyway, I guess Aubrey's humor was contagious, because I couldn't help but joke around too. We were sharing a bench on the deck, and when someone came walking past, like a tourist or some kid, Aubrey would go, "Excuse me." And when they'd look to see if he was talking to them, I'd go, "Never mind. We thought you dropped something." For some reason that cracked us up.

But Grandfather wasn't amused. He sat there with this rigid scowl, and didn't say a thing for the longest time. Finally, right as Aubrey was going to say "Excuse me" to this woman holding a baby, Grandfather nudged my ribs pretty hard, gouged Aubrey's thigh with a finger, saying, "You smart asses think on this. There ain't no written law showing banishment as tribal punishment. If anything, custom has folks like you get a hand or finger hacked. Hacking ain't funny, so you two should be worrying some."

That did the trick. Aubrey slouched down, bringing a fingertip to his scabbed palm. I shifted on the bench; the thought of an ax shearing my wrist sprang to mind, and I tried to think about other things.

"That's right," Grandfather said to us. "That's better."

In Ketchikan, where we waited for the transfer boat that would take us to Prince of Wales Island, Grandfather treated Aubrey and me to a late lunch. "Get what you want," he said, so we ordered a large pepperoni pizza and bread sticks at Gino's Pizzeria on the boardwalk. Then we ate like monsters. Aubrey dribbled sauce on his T-shirt, and I chomped bites big enough to choke a horse. And when we boarded the ferry for home, I smuggled a bread stick and three pizza crusts in my pocket for a snack.

We arrived in Klawock near dusk. I was exhausted. So was Aubrey. Lugging my suitcase at my side, I wanted nothing more than to undress in my bedroom and then sleep. But, when I saw what welcomed us as we wandered toward town-center, that desire was replaced by worry. A hushed crowd had gathered in front of the grocery store, and I immediately recognized a few faces. Besides four or five elders who always killed time outside the grocery store, Aubrey's mother was there with his little sister. So was the tribal police chief Jessy Cropley, and his only officer Les Millholland (a turd of a man, fat as a sumo wrestler). And soon we were hemmed in, front and back, by more familiar faces; friends from high school, little kids, whole families, all exchanging feverish whispers and sudden laughs, which really bugged me. Aubrey and I slowed in our steps, but Grandfather, following behind, pushed us forward. "Don't say nothing," he said. "Behave and stay quiet."

Then the crowd grew louder; everyone was yapping a mile-a-minute, gazing at us like we were freaks. Aubrey's mother was going, "I hope you know what you done! I hope you're sorry!" And someone else was shouting, "Shame! Both of you! Shame!"

Grandfather spoke above the racket, telling Aubrey and me, "Town jail is full, so you'll be put in the storeroom at Brotherhood Hall. There's cots there and it's been swept. Chief Cropley will make sure you're okay." Then he asked for my suitcase, so I gave it to him. Then he took Aubrey's backpack, and handed it to Aubrey's mother. Next thing I knew, Chief Cropley was putting handcuffs on me, while Officer Millholland cuffed Aubrey. That's when everybody got calm again and watched.

I never felt more like murdering a bunch of folks in my life. I mean, if I'd had a machine gun or bazooka, I'd have let loose on that crowd. I'd have been more than happy to blow some skulls apart. Aubrey must've felt the same, because he was saying, "Fuck this! Fuck this shit!" But it was spooky the way he kept uttering those words. "Fuck this shit! Fuck this!" And he was sort of smiling to himself, scanning that crowd like he was taking names.

"Let's go," Chief Cropley said. Then he and Officer Millholland began escorting us through the crowd. Suddenly something splattered my cheek. "Ha ha ha!" I heard Koyumi chant, singsong-like. "Ha ha ha!" She was in our path, arms folded across her breasts, her one good eye marking Aubrey. Glancing sideways at him, I noticed yellowish gobs of spittle on his forehead and chin. Then Koyumi stepped aside, cackling point blank in Aubrey's ear as he passed. But it was like he refused to notice her. He just bent his head and went on, except he wasn't smiling to himself anymore.

When we were locked inside the storeroom at Brotherhood Hall, our wrists no longer cuffed, I dug the pizza crusts and bread stick from my pocket, offering an equal share to Aubrey. "No thanks," he said, sounding gloomy. Then he stretched out on a cot, closing his eyes under the single overhead bulb, and carefully touched the places were Koyumi's spit had dried.

Gnawing on a pizza crust, I went aimlessly to the other cot and sat. Then I ate while taking in the windowless storeroom, that had been converted into a cozy cell with poor ventilation. But there was plenty of space, so I didn't feel all cramped like in the Anchorage jail. The bare concrete floor looked mopped. The high cinder block walls, once hidden behind stacks of boxes, were clear. Someone had left us toilet paper, a blue wastebasket, and several dated *Sports Illustrated* magazines. A plastic pail containing soapy water sat in a corner, and each morning Millholland replenished the pail and brought us new towels so we could at least wash a bit. There were also four buckets, two beside each cot: "One for piss, one for shit," Chief Cropley had said. "Don't mix them." And because we couldn't hang ourselves from anything, Cropley and Millholland didn't remove our shoelaces or belts. They didn't even check our pockets for knives or razors.

Anyway, after a while Officer Millholland knocked on the storeroom door, saying, "I'm putting the light out. If you want something tonight, better say so now."

"Cigarettes," Aubrey said.

Millholland's deep friendly voice came through the door. "Sorry, man, I'll check with Chief tomorrow. Don't think he'll go for it. What else?"

"How long you keeping us here?"

"Couple of nights, I think. They're holding the hearing here."

"When's breakfast?" I said. "What do we get?"

"Haven't the slightest, Cole. I'll bring it at sun-up, you'll know then. All right, light out." And the overhead bulb clicked off.

I finished eating in the dark, listening as Millholland's big footsteps clomped around Brotherhood Hall. He dragged a chair from somewhere and placed it outside the storeroom door. Then I heard the chair squeaking beneath his huge ass, and knew he was settling in for the night.

"Aubrey," I whispered. But he didn't reply. "Hey," I said, "you asleep?"

"No."

"Man, I can't see. Can you?"

"It don't matter," he said.

"Why?"

"It just don't. I don't want to talk about it."

"You mad at me?"

"No."

"Hey, what if one of us has to piss tonight. How we supposed to hit the bucket without seeing?"

Nothing.

"If I got to shit, I can hold it," I said. "But, damn, when I got to piss, I got to piss. It'd suck if I missed and peed all over, huh?"

Nothing.

Finally, in a huffy way, I went, "Goodnight."

"Goodnight," he said, the word barely seeping from his throat.

Things only got worse. The following day, Aubrey stopped talking. He stayed on his cot, picking at the scab on his palm, sometimes flipping through a *Sports Illustrated*, or napping with his face toward the wall. In fact, he slept more than anything. When Millholland brought us breakfast (toast, scrambled eggs, orange juice, and bacon), Aubrey barely touched it. And when I tried speaking to him, he seemed unable to make a noise. Luckily, Millholland gave me a tennis ball, so I occupied myself with bouncing it off the walls, slamming it against the floor and watching as it zoomed to the ceiling.

"Aubrey sick?" Millholland said. "Not much in his buckets." He was accompanying me on a stroll outside Brotherhood Hall, which we did twice a day. He took me first, fastening the handcuffs loosely, then he took Aubrey afterwards.

"Not sure," I said. "Guess he's depressed or something."

"If it's Koyumi, he shouldn't worry. She's screwy, man. She's been screaming about being pregnant, telling everyone it's him, but it ain't. You know how many people she's said done knocked her up in the last year?"

"Lots?"

"Yep. But where's the baby? How come she ain't showing? She pulled that shit on me, man, and I ain't even been with her. It's attention she wants. And you and Aubrey are in the spotlight, so she's getting a ton of mileage."

"Maybe you'll tell him that. Might help if you do."

"Sure thing," Millholland said. "Jesus, he shouldn't trouble on it. He should put his thoughts elsewhere. You too. What you boys did has landed in this town's lap. No one's paying Koyumi any mind." Then he mentioned that Grandfather and a panel of twelve other judges, drawn from various houses of the Tlingit nation, were fasting together before the hearing. He said a lot of reporters were in town to cover the case. "Figure it'll be a circus," he told me. "You'd think Klawock never had criminals or crimes. Down at the jail we got three loggers who got drunk and set fire to a mobile home. No offense, Cole, but they're a lot meaner than you and Aubrey. Think them reporters give a hoot though? Hell no. Don't ask me why."

What's weird is that I used to think Millholland was sort of an idiot. I mean, he didn't appear very smart, and Aubrey and I sometimes called him "lardass" or "Barney" when we spotted him downtown. It seemed as if Chief Cropley couldn't find anyone else to be his officer, so he hired the biggest, slowest, goofiest Indian in Klawock; a guy who has sweat on his brow even when it's snowing. But while stuck in that storeroom, he kind of grew on me; probably because he didn't treat us as prisoners, and tended to us in a decent man-ner—like bringing me the tennis ball, or giving Aubrey a ciga-rette during their strolls.

As we entered Brotherhood Hall, wandering toward the storeroom door, passing row upon row of perfectly aligned foldout chairs, Millholland said, "Look, I'll talk to Aubrey about Koyumi, but you do me a favor. Soon as the hearing starts tomorrow, don't act proud. Your grandfather is getting flak on account of how he's organizing everything. Some folks say he's humiliating Tlingit people by creating a mock court. They're saying he's making tribal custom as he goes. But he's saving your hide, kid, so you be humble. You avoid him any disgrace."

"All right," I said vaguely. "I'm not proud anyway."

Later that day, once he returned from strolling with Millholland, Aubrey immediately undid his pants, sliding them to his knees, and squatted over a bucket. I was sitting on the floor, leaning against my cot, tossing the tennis ball in the air. "Don't look," he said. "Can't shit with you looking." So I reclined my head some, resting it on the cot, and blinked at the ceiling, where the single bulb burned patterns on my irises. For a moment I heard Aubrey straining, followed by a hollow plop in the bucket. A sharp, unmistakable odor filled the storeroom. "Throw me the toilet paper." I lifted my head from the cot. The toilet paper was beside one of my buckets, so I reached for it and then rolled it across the floor to him. "Thanks," he said, sounding less glum. And when he finished, Aubrey came and sat on the floor next to me.

"Did Millholland tell you about Koyumi?" I said, my curiosity stirring.

"Yeah. But it don't matter. She doesn't mean nothing to me."

"I thought you might be upset or whatever."

"Not really. I mean, sort of, but not really." He was scratching at the scab, unaware, digging a nail into the thick crust. "She's only part of everything, and that's what eats me. Want to know something?"

"Sure."

"A few times, for the hell of it, I'd slap the shit out of her," he said in a low voice. "Sometimes I'd do it while we was fucking. Other times I did it right after we'd screwed. I'd slam her one good. Maybe punch her stomach, or bend her fingers back. And it didn't matter. She didn't cry or yell or nothing. It makes me nuts thinking about it now."

"Why'd you do that?" I said, knitting my brows.

"I don't know," he answered coolly. "Felt like it, I guess. Like I said, she didn't mind. But now it seems creepy, so I wish I hadn't done it. Wish I hadn't done anything with her. She's bad luck."

"That's why you're upset."

"She's just part of it. It's like we're getting punished for everything, like everybody in Klawock is pointing at us for things we didn't do."

"Like what?" I asked, slightly bewildered.

"Beats me. But I'm not sweating it no more. Millholland says we're getting banished no matter what. It's already decided. They're taking us to some islands somewhere and that's it. Fine with me though. The way I see it, I'll be gone in a week. They can't keep me there. I'll escape, so it'll work out. And I ain't ever coming to Klawock again, that's for sure."

"We'll go together," I said in a shrill childish voice that caught in my throat.

"That's the idea," he said, his eyes sparkling. "No looking back, start all over again, all that stuff. Maybe get a job at some logging camp. They can't keep us on those islands. There's no chance. And if we come back here, you and I might become ignorant Indians like the rest of them. Except we're not like them anyway."

Aubrey suddenly snatched the tennis ball from me, then he stood, wound up for a pitch, and sent it flying into the wall. I leapt to my feet, catching the ball as it ricocheted toward us. Then we took turns trying to sink the ball in the wastebasket. And that's how we spent our last evening in Klawock, smashing the wall like two good friends, shooting imaginary hoops in the storeroom.

Our hearing lasted less than an hour. It wasn't much of a hearing, but Grandfather and the other judges of the Kuye di Kuiu Kwaan Tribal Court, five of which were Grandfather's brothers, did their best. Dressed in ceremonial robes, they were seated behind a long table, facing the noisy spectators that packed Brotherhood Hall. It was like everyone on Prince of Wales Island was there, and those who didn't find a chair had to stand at the rear of the hall with the television crews and reporters.

Before being led from the storeroom, Aubrey and I were given traditional Tlingit regalia (black vests, robes bearing our clan crests, red scarves to tie about our heads). Chief Cropley instructed us to wear the regalia inside-out as a sign of shame. And even though Aubrey grumbled some, he went ahead and did it. So did I. Then we were brought into the hall, where two chairs waited in front of the long table. Nearby, someone banged a sacred drum in downtown Klawock, and someone else was outside the hall with a devil stick, beating the old building so demons would flee the area. For a while we sat silent in front of those scornful elders while that clatter went on. And when it ended, the members of the tribal court began.

Honestly, I've never heard so many lame questions in my life. Some of them were so dumb, Aubrey and I couldn't help but smirk. I mean, one of the judges, a Haida elder, said, "Do you know what kind of pizza Michael Everett was delivering when you robbed him?"

"No," Aubrey said. "What does that have to do with anything?"

And then later, another elder asked, "When you stole the money bag, did you take it for the money inside?"

"Of course," I replied.

"We didn't want the bag," Aubrey said, grinning.

As the questioning became less relevant, Aubrey grew more sarcastic.

"Why did you run from the scene of the crime?"

"Why do you think?"

"That's not an answer."

"I thought it was."

"Do you understand what robbery is?"

"Yes. Why are you asking that?"

But I tried to say as little as possible, because I saw Grandfather breathing heavily, his agitation sprouting and mushrooming. And when Aubrey answered an elder with, "That's stupid," Grandfather snapped: "You've no regard for tribal law! What's worse, you've shamed your families and yourselves and you ought to be damned ashamed as well!" There wasn't much after that. A few more questions were asked, and Aubrey and I replied with flushed faces. I'm not sure if it was sudden shame we felt, but I do know that Grandfather's outburst startled us.

Eventually, the tribal judges called a brief recess, returning maybe ten minutes later to render their decisions. The thirteen elders now stood at the long table. "As restitution for Mister Michael Everett," Grandfather announced in a husky, assured voice, "the court has unanimously agreed that the tribe will construct a duplex home for him. If he wishes, he can live in one side and use the other unit as a rental, therefore insuring him income." Then he looked towards me, his dark eyes gleaming like currants, saying, "As punishment for their crimes, the court has agreed eleven to two that Cole Betts and Aubrey Judson Henry will be banished to separate islands for a minimum of twelve months. Those are our judgments." With that said, a mixture of claps and boos came from the spectators, and, in keeping with tribal law, the elders turned their backs on us.

While Chief Cropley and Officer Millholland ushered Aubrey and me through the hall, the television crews stepped forward to film us. Then everything got wild. Flashtubes erupted, almost blinding me. It seemed like a million people were jabbering at once.

"Kangaroo court," yelled some white woman I'd never seen before. She was at the door with a notepad, jabbing a pen in the direction of the judges. "What a travesty!" she said, and I wanted her to just shut up. I would've told her as much, except my attention was taken by a photographer with a Minolta XG-1. He practically jumped in our path, crouching and moving backwards to get his shots. To be honest, I can't say for sure if it was Ed, but I'm pretty certain it was; he had the same ponytail, the same kind of sunglasses pushed high on his bald head. Behind the camera he was going, "Feel like you got what you deserved?" Click. "Can either of you tell me that?" Click. Click. "Was justice served today?"

"Screw off!" Aubrey said.

"Move it!" Millholland told the cameraman. Then more

flashes exploded around me, stunning my sight. When my vision returned, the cameraman was gone, and a clammy anxiety churned inside my belly.

We escaped Brotherhood Hall under a low cloudy sky, which glowed with afternoon light. And as we were taken to where the salmon boat Pronghorn waited, a solitary chant trailed in the distance behind us. "Ha ha ha," it went. "Ha ha ha!"

"Jesus Christ," Aubrey sighed.

"I know," I said, overwhelmed by the urge to cry. I couldn't bear it.

# 5.

If gulls circled overhead right now, this is what they'd see: in
a clearing on the nameless mountain, a skinny, black-haired
Tlingit boy kneels before a dying spruce, chipping away soft
bark with his Grandfather's shiv. That's what the fifth and
final totem panel will display. But it's misting as I work, so I
doubt I'll get anywhere close to being done today.
Furthermore, the shiv has grown blunt with use; its blade,
fashioned from polished black stone, is round at the tip, the
edges are flaky. So just cutting bark takes all my strength.
Also, while stabbing at the wood underneath, I'm careful that
the brittle blade doesn't get in a bind and snap, otherwise I'd
be screwed.

It was aboard the *Pronghorn* that I received the shiv.
Aubrey and I were on the deck with Millholland, who was
left in charge of our exile. As the boat sailed northwest
through a narrow strait, chugging a path through breaking
swells that lifted and sank below us, Millholland reached
inside his jacket, removing two handmade shivs. "Cole, your
grandfather figures you'll both need these," he said, giving
one knife to me, the other to Aubrey. "I was supposed to stick
them in your duffel sacks, but I don't think it'll hurt you getting them here. Don't tell no one though."

"Who we going to tell?" Aubrey said.

"That's true," Millholland replied.

I wasn't much in the mood for conversation, so I crossed
the deck to where my large duffel sack lay, opened the top,
and placed the shiv inside with the rest of its contents (a com-
pass, a rough map of my island, a canteen, one bottle of jungle juice, a pot for cooking, flint, seven flannel shirts, seven
white T-shirts, seven pairs of wool socks, seven changes of
underwear, one role of biodegradable toilet paper, and provi-
sions for almost three weeks: six pounds of venison jerky,
twenty-one cans of baked beans, twenty-one cans of Spam,
fifteen dark chocolate bars). Millholland had packed our duf-

fel sacks himself, and he saw to it that his mother's venison jerky was included. "Once you eat that food," he'd told us, "you'll have to start hunting. Don't worry. There's lots of small game where you're going. Lots of fish too."

The sea was an undulating expanse of bleakness. Evening had begun to saturate the sky. I sat on the duffel sack, hugging a rolled sleeping bag against my chest, and found myself looking across the deck at Aubrey. As if pondering the submerged whir of the Pronghorn's motors, he was smoking thoughtfully with his head cocked at an angle. His unkempt, oily hair, which had become hopelessly matted in places, fluttered some in the wind. Then he turned, exhaling smoke through his nostrils. And when he noticed my gaze, Aubrey stifled a smile. He flicked his cigarette overboard, and crossed the deck.

"Got it memorized," he said.

"What?"

"The route they're taking. If they dumped me in a canoe at this moment, I'd find home. I'm paying attention." Aubrey glanced briefly at Millholland, who was sipping coffee and chatting with the Pronghorn's owner, a burly guy with a beard like an Amish farmer. Then he half-whispered, "You're getting dropped first, so I'll remember where you are. I swear, give me a week or so, I'll get to you."

"How?"

"Not sure yet. I got to plan something. But be looking for me. I'm serious."

"Okay," I said. "Can't imagine I'll have anything else to do."

But as much as I wanted to believe him, I knew it was pure talk. Nothing was that easy. And as I stood on the shore of my island, watching the Pronghorn leave, I understood that I really wasn't going anywhere. Still, I loitered near the beach for over a week, hoping Aubrey might suddenly appear. But he didn't. So one day I knelt down and started to pack my duffel sack with dirty hands. My tribe had banished me, and my best friend was somewhere else. I felt loneliness descend on this island like rain, covering me, spilling on everything, leaving me unable to breath. I stooped, gathering my belongings from the coral-colored scree. Then, tucking the shiv behind my belt, I faced the surrounding hills, sobbing.

The entire island is now shrouded in gray, but glistens all the same. Moisture hangs from spruce needles, collects on my cheeks, and soaks me through. The skin under my clothes is cold, dewy. And the wetness continually dripping around my mouth gets licked away while I carve. But I'm not really bothered. Strange as it seems, my thoughts are lifted by the very drizzle that hampers my work, that makes Aubrey's island impossible to find from the outlook. Truth is, because there's renewal in this chilly haze, I want to pull the mist against my chest and hold it until winter sets in. But then I'd never finish the totem. Plus, there are more pictures to carve, hundreds of other spruces waiting to be scrapbooks—and when I'm finally done here, I'll go deeper into the dark forest, find another tree, and begin again.